July, July

July, July

Tim O'Brien

This large print edition published in 2003 by
RB Large Print
A division of Recorded Books
A Haights Cross Communications Company
270 Skipjack Road
Prince Frederick, MD 20678

First published in America
by Houghton Mifflin Company, 2002

Publisher's Cataloging In Publication Data
(Prepared by Donohue Group, Inc.)

O'Brien, Tim, 1946–
  July, July / Tim O'Brien.

    p. ; cm.

  ISBN: 1–4025–6381–7

1. Baby boom generation—Fiction 2. College graduates—Fiction.
3. Class reunions—Fiction. 4. Large type books. 5. Minnesota—
Fiction. 6. Psychological fiction. 7. Humorous fiction. I. Title.

PS3565.B75 J85 2003
813/ .54

Typeset by Palimpsest Book Production Limited
Polmont, Stirlingshire, Scotland
Printed in the United States of America
by Bang Printing
3323 Oak Street
Brainerd, Minnesota 56401

With thanks to Larry Cooper, Janet Silver, Wendy Strothman, Clay Harper, Meredith O'Brien, Les Ramirez, Nader Darehshori, Adrienne Miller, Bill Buford, Tim Waller, and the Roy F. and Joann Cole Mitte Foundation.

For Meredith

We had fed the heart on fantasies,
The heart's grown brutal from the fare.

—William Butler Yeats

CHAPTER 1

CLASS OF '69

The reunion dance had started only an hour ago, but already a good many of the dancers were tipsy, and most others were well along, and now the gossip was flowing and confessions were under way and old flames were being extinguished and rekindled under cardboard stars in the Darton Hall College gymnasium.

Amy Robinson was telling Jan Huebner, a former roommate, about the murder last year of Karen Burns, another former roommate. "It's such a Karen sort of thing," Amy said. "Getting killed like that. Nobody else. Only Karen."

"Right," Jan said. She waited a moment. "Move your tongue, sugar. Details."

Amy made a weary, dispirited movement with her shoulders. "Nothing new, I'm afraid. Same old Karen story, naive as a valentine. Trust the world. Get squished."

"Poor girl," Jan said.

"Poor woman," said Amy.

Jan winced and said, "Woman, corpse, whatever. Still single, I suppose? Karen?"

"Naturally."

"And some guy—?"

"Naturally."

"God," Jan said.

"Yeah, yeah," said Amy.

Earlier in the evening, they had liberated a bottle of Darton Hall vodka, which was now almost gone, and both of them were feeling the sting of strong spirits and misplaced sentiment. They were fifty-three years old. They were drunk. They were divorced. Time and heartbreak had exacted a toll. Amy Robinson still had her boyish figure, her button nose and freckles, but collegiate perkiness had been replaced by something taut and haggard. Jan Huebner had never been perky. She'd never been pretty, or cute, or even passable, and at the moment her bleached hair and plucked eyebrows and Midnight Plum lipstick offered only the most dubious correctives.

"What I love about men," Jan was saying, "is their basic overall cockiness. That much I adore. Follow me?"

"I do," said Amy.

"Take away that, what the heck have you got?"

"You've got zero."

"Ha!" said Jan.

"Cheers," said Amy.

"Pricks," said Jan.

They fell quiet then, sipping vodka, watching the class of '69 rediscover itself on a polished gymnasium dance floor. Unofficially, this was a thirtieth reunion—one year tardy due to someone's oversight, an irony that had been much discussed over cocktails that evening, and much joked about, though not yet entirely deciphered. Still, it made them feel special. And so, too, did the fact that they were convening on a deserted campus, in the heart of summer, more than a month after the standard graduation-day gatherings. The school had a forlorn, haunted feel to it, many memories, many ghosts, which seemed appropriate.

"Well," Jan Huebner finally said. "Bad news, of course—Karen's dead. But here's some good news. Gal never went through a divorce."

"That's a fact," said Amy.

"I mean, ouch."

"Ouch is accurate," Amy said.

Jan nodded. "Twenty-nine years, almost thirty, and guess what? That slick ex-hubby of mine, Richard the Oily, he grins and waves at me and strolls out the door. Doesn't walk, doesn't run. Strolls. Talk about murder. Am I wrong about that?"

"You are not wrong," said Amy.

"We're discussing the male gender, aren't we?"

"We are."

"Well, there's your moral," Jan said. "One way or the other, they'll kill you dead. Every time, flowers and gravestones. No exceptions."

"Stone dead," Amy said, and leaned back to scan the crowd of aging dancers. Thirty-one years, she thought. A new world. After a time she sighed and

5

freshened their drinks and said, "What say we get laid tonight?"

"Yes, ma'am," said Jan. "By pricks."

"For sure."

"Big, dumb, bald ones."

Amy raised her glass. "To Karen Burns."

"To divorce," said Jan, and then she turned and waved at Marv Bertel, a come-dance-with-us motion, but Marv shook his head, tapped his chest, and leaned back heavily against the bar.

Marv was recovering from a dance with Spook Spinelli, wondering if his heart could take another hit. He doubted it. He doubted, too, that he should risk another bourbon, except the drink was already in his hand, cold as a coffin, and might quiet the jump in his heart. Partly the problem was Spook Spinelli: those daredevil eyes of hers, that candid, little-girl laugh. Over half a lifetime, through two tepid marriages, Marv had been massaging the fantasy that something might develop between them. Pitiful, he thought, yet even now he couldn't stop hoping. All those years, all that wee-hour solitaire, and he was still snagged up in Spook Spinelli. Also, of course, there was the issue of a failing triple bypass, the butter in his arteries, the abundant flab at his waist. All the same, Marv reasoned, this was a goddamn reunion, possibly his last, so he knocked the drink back and asked the bartender for one more, on the rocks, double trouble.

★　　★　　★

6

Across the gym, under a flashing blue spotlight, Spook Spinelli was dancing with Billy McMann. They were hamming it up, making faces, being sexy for each other, but Billy did not once take his eyes off Dorothy Stier, who stood talking near the bandstand with Paulette Haslo. After three decades, Billy still hated Dorothy. He also loved her. The love and the hate had hardened inside him, one reinforcing the other like layers of brick and mortar. In a few minutes, Billy decided, he would treat himself to another drink, or maybe three or four, and then he would amble up to Dorothy and explain the love-hate dynamic to her in all its historic detail.

Dorothy knew Billy was watching. She knew, too, that Billy still loved her. Later, she told herself, there would be time to take him outside and admit to the terrible mistake she had made in 1969. Not that it *was* a mistake, not in the long run, because Dorothy had a sweet husband and two incredible kids and memberships in a couple of smart-set country clubs. Still, if Billy needed a lie, she saw no harm in offering one. Almost certainly she would kiss him. Almost certainly she would cry a little. For now, though, Dorothy was busy telling Paulette Haslo about her breast cancer, which thank God was in remission, and how supportive her sweet husband and two incredible kids had been.

★   ★   ★

7

It was July 7, 2000, a humid Friday evening.

The war was over, passions were moot, and the band played a slow, hollowed-out version of an old Buffalo Springfield tune. For everyone, there was a sense of nostalgia made fluid by present possibility.

"So sad, so bizarre," Amy Robinson was saying, "but so predictable, too. The old Karenness, that's what killed her. She never stopped being Karen."

"Who did it?" said Jan Huebner.

Amy wagged her head. "Nobody knows for sure. Some guy she had a crush on, some creep, which is par for Karen's course. Never any luck."

"Never, ever," Jan said. "And the thing is, she could've been a knockout, all the ingredients. That gorgeous red hair, tons and tons of it. I mean, she *was* a knockout."

"Weight problem, of course," said Amy.

"So true," said Jan.

"Plus her age. Face it, she was piling up the mileage like all of us." Amy sighed. "Total shame, isn't it? The golden generation. Such big dreams—kick ass, never die—but somehow it all went poof. Hard thing to swallow, but biology doesn't have politics. The old bod, you know? Just keeps doing its silly, deadly, boring shit."

"True again," said Jan, and blinked down at her hands. "What happened to us?"

"Got me," said Amy.

"Maybe the Monkees."

"Sorry?"

"Plain as day," Jan said. "A whole generation kicks off with the Monkees, how the heck could we expect things to work out? 'I'm a believer, I couldn't leave her'—I mean, yikes, talk about starting off on the wrong foot. So naive I want to cry. Last train to Clarksville, babe, and we're all aboard."

Amy nodded. "You're right," she said.

"Of course I'm right," said Jan.

"May I ask a question?"

"Ask."

"Where's our vodka?"

Similar conversations were occurring all across the darkened gym. Death, marriage, children, divorce, betrayal, loss, grief, disease: these were among the topics that generated a low, liquid hum beneath the surface of the music. At a table near the bar, three classmates sat discussing Amy Robinson's recent good fortune, how after years of horrid luck she had finally met a decent guy, a math teacher, and how on her honeymoon the two of them had won a sweepstakes or a bingo tournament or a state lottery, something of the sort, no one knew quite what. In any case, Amy was now very well off, thank you, with a fat bank account and a brand-new Mercedes and a swimming pool the size of Arkansas. Her marriage, though, had failed. "Barely two weeks," someone said, and someone else said, "Talk about irony. Poor Amy. Finally gets lucky, lands a guy, and then the *guy* turns unlucky. Back to square one. Even her good luck goes rotten."

Thirty-one years ago, in the brutal spring of 1969, Amy Robinson and many others had lived beyond themselves, elevated by the times. There was good and evil. There was moral heat. But this was the year 2000, a new millennium, congeniality in public places, hope gone stale, morons become millionaires, and the gossip was about Ellie Abbott's depression, Dorothy Stier's breast cancer, Spook Spinelli's successful double marriage and the fact that she seemed to be going for a triple that evening with either Marv Bertel or Billy McMann.

"The terrible thing," Jan Huebner was saying, "is that Karen was obviously the best of us. Huge heart. Full of delusions, I'll grant you, but the girl never once gave up hope."

"Which is what killed her," said Amy.

"Sorry?"

"Hope. Lethal."

Jan thought about it for a while. She also thought about her ex-husband, how he waved and strolled out the door. "Maybe we should just stop hoping," she said. "Maybe that's the trick. Never hope."

"You think so?" said Amy.

"Sort of," said Jan.

After some consideration Amy Robinson shrugged and said, "Boy, let's hope not," and the two of

10

them laughed and moved toward the bar to check on Marv Bertel's heart.

The music now was hard-core Stones translated for the times by clarinets.

Techs were tumbling. Portfolios were in trouble.

Karen Burns was murdered.

"Hard to believe," classmates would say, about this, about that, about belief itself. And as people conversed, shaking their heads, disbelieving, a pair of slide projectors cast fuzzy old photographs against one of the gymnasium walls: Amy Robinson as a pert, freckled, twenty-year-old rabble-rouser; Jan Huebner dressed up as a clown; Karen Burns eyeing a newly hired professor of sociology; David Todd looking trim and sheepish in his blue and gold baseball uniform; Spook Spinelli posing topless for the Darton Hall yearbook; Dorothy Stier in a pink prom gown, ill at ease, glaring at the camera; Billy McMann clutching Dorothy's hand; Marla Dempsey chasing Paulette Haslo with a fire extinguisher; Ellie Abbott and Marv Bertel and Harmon Osterberg playing cantaloupe-soccer in a crowded noontime dining hall. According to a reunion brochure, sixty-two percent of the class had settled in the Twin Cities area—Amy Robinson and Jan Huebner lived seven blocks apart in the nearby suburb of Eden Prairie. Forty-nine percent had paid at least one visit to divorce court. Sixty-seven percent were married. Fifty-eight percent described themselves as "unlucky in love." Almost eighty

11

percent had selected "romance and/or spiritual fulfillment" as the governing principle of their lives. In the gymnasium that evening, under cardboard stars, there were six attorneys, twelve teachers, five physicians, one chemist, three accountants, nineteen entrepreneurs, fourteen full-time mothers, one chief executive officer, one actor, one minister, one Lutheran missionary, one retired librarian, one lieutenant governor. Billy McMann owned a chain of hardware stores in Winnipeg. Amy Robinson practiced criminal law. David Todd, who had lost a leg in 1969, and who was now divorced from Marla Dempsey, ran a successful custom-made furniture business. Paulette Haslo was a Presbyterian minister, although currently without a church, which was still another topic of conversation. "Hard to believe, isn't it?" said a former point guard for the Darton Hall women's basketball team, now a mother of three. "Little Miss Religion, our own Paulette, she got caught breaking into this . . . I shouldn't say. Big scandal. God fired her."

"Wow, that's horrible," said a former teammate, an accountant for Honeywell. "Maybe we should— you know—go say something."

"About what?"

"I don't know what. Try to help."

The former point guard, now a mother of three, shook her head and said, "No way, I'm in heat, I deserve some fun," and then she moved off swiftly toward the bar.

A solid one hundred percent of them, the brochure declared, had come to the reunion "ready to party."

It was a muggy evening, oppressively hot. In an open doorway at the rear of the gymnasium, Ellie Abbott fanned herself with a fallen cardboard star, sharing a cigarette with David Todd and Marla Dempsey. The three of them were cordial enough, even laughing at times, but here too, as with Amy Robinson and Jan Huebner, hope was a problem. Marla was hoping that David would stop staring at her. Ellie was hoping that Marla would stop talking about their classmate Harmon Osterberg, who had drowned last summer in the waters of northern Minnesota. David Todd was hoping that Marla regretted leaving him in favor of a glib young stockbroker with a wallet only slightly fatter than his head.

"He was a dentist," Marla said. She looked at Ellie, then at David, then down at her folded arms. "Harmon, I mean. And a good dentist, too. Super gentle. At least that's what people said." She stopped, looked away. "Maybe you already knew that."

"I did," said Ellie.

Marla sighed. "God, it makes me sick. Such a dear, dear guy, always so happy, and now he's just—no offense—he's this dead dentist. I mean, if Harmon could be here tonight, I bet anything he'd be telling dentist jokes."

"And drowning jokes," said David.

Ellie said nothing. For eleven and a half months she had said nothing.

She made a vague flipping motion with her wrist, took a last drag on David's cigarette, excused herself, slipped inside, sat alone on the bleachers for a time, waited for the loons to leave her head, waited for Harmon to finish drowning, and then went off to find her husband.

In the gymnasium's open doorway, David Todd and Marla Dempsey watched Ellie slide away into the crowd of dancers.

"Take a guess what I'm thinking," David said.

"Ellie and Harmon," said Marla. "They came close a million times. Maybe finally . . ."

"Like us?"

"No. Not like us."

A quiet came between them, which they recognized from their years of marriage: power failure. They'd always wanted different things. It was no one's fault. Even while they were together, Marla had made it clear that she could not wholly commit, that their marriage was an experiment, that David's missing leg sometimes gave her the creeps. She hated touching the wrinkled stump, hated looking at it. And there was also the scary suspicion that this man could sometimes read her mind, like a fortuneteller, as if some spy or peeping tom had been slipping him all her secrets over the years.

Even now, as David smiled at her, Marla wondered what the smile concealed. He was a good man, yes, but even his goodness frightened her.

"So go ahead," David was saying. "I'm ready."

"Go ahead what?"

"Ask where I'm staying."

Marla frowned. "I'll bite. Where are you staying?"

"On campus. Flarety Hall. We can be there in sixty seconds."

"If we run?"

"Gimp," he said, and slapped a hand against his prosthesis. "Take our time, move slow, it'll be like—"

"Stop."

"Right. Sorry. I'm stopped."

Marla studied him with flat, neutral eyes. "Anyway, look at me. Eight extra pounds. Not a clue where it came from."

"You look exquisite," said David.

"Sweet, sweet lie."

"My pleasure." David took the cigarette from her lips and threw it to the ground. "Don't do that to yourself. Makes a girl infertile."

Marla glanced at him, surprised.

"I hadn't noticed that you've stopped."

"No. But I'm me, my love. You're you."

"'My love'?"

"Sorry again. Divorced, right?"

"Light me another one, David."

"No can do. What about those unborn babies?"

"Pity," Marla said, "but they'll have to live with it. Come on, fire me up."

David tapped out a cigarette, slipped it between her lips, struck a match, and watched her lean in toward the flame. Lovely woman, he thought. Steel eyes. Silver-blond hair, cut short. Trim. No hips. No sign of any extra eight pounds. They'd remained friends over the years, sharing lunches, sometimes sharing a bed, and David found it impossible to believe that they would not somehow end up living together and getting old together and finally occupying the same patch of earth. Anything else seemed mad. Worse than mad. Plain evil.

Marla blew smoke into the July night.

"Much better," she said.

"Not for our babies."

"David, please, just lay off the baby bit. I'm low on the estrogen. Empty tanks. I'm old."

"You're not old."

"Oh, I am. Always was." She looked away, looked back at him, went up on her toes to kiss his cheek. "It's this reunion crap, David. Makes people mushy."

"Mushy, mushy me," said David.

"Absolutely. Mushy you."

"I need to ask something."

"Is it mushy?"

"It is," he said.

"No," she said. "Don't ask."

Marla folded her arms and stepped back.

She was fond of David, and wished things could

16

be otherwise, but what he wanted from her had never been a possibility. Ordinary love—what most people thought of as love—meant little to her. All she'd ever wanted was to be alone.

"Let's dance," she said. "I'm not good at this."

"At what?"

"This. Talking."

"Fair enough. But if you don't talk, I don't dance."

"The leg?"

"Not the leg," he said. "I was just hoping . . . Forget it."

"You could watch, couldn't you?"

"Sure," he said.

He followed Marla inside and stood watching as she danced with Dorothy Stier and Spook Spinelli. It was true, he thought, that she'd put on some wear and tear. The sockets of her eyes had yellowed, and her skin had a brittle, crumbly texture that took him by surprise. She looked her age, which was fifty-three. But even so. A stunning fifty-three. In point of fact, he decided, a sublime and heartbreaking and drop-dead magnificent fifty-three. For all the years, there was still the essential Marla glow, a magnetic field, whatever it was that made Marla into Marla, and that made his own life worth the pain of living it.

After a time Marv Bertel cut in and took Spook off into a corner, and a moment later Dorothy Stier went off to make peace with Billy McMann, and then Marla danced alone.

17

Well, David thought.

Dream girl.

He turned away.

The evening had been hard on him, because he wanted Marla so badly, and because she'd lived inside him for so many years, through a whole war, then through a nine-year marriage, and then for the decades afterward. To her great credit, he realized, Marla had never feigned passion, never promised anything. David believed her when she said she cared for him. But he'd come to despise the word "care." He did not care for it. Nor did he care for the terrible truth that Marla only cared for him.

After two drinks David left the gym. He made his way across campus to Flarety Hall, took the elevator up to his room, removed his trousers and prosthesis, popped a Demerol, popped a half sheet of acid, lay down on the tile floor, and allowed the narcotics to carry him away to a shallow, fast-moving river called the Song Tra Ky.

Ellie Abbott left not long afterward with her husband Mark and with the sound of waterfowl in her head. Harmon would not quit drowning on her. She had dared two affairs in her life, and the second had gone very, very badly, and for almost a year now Harmon Osterberg had been drowning in her dreams. It was something she could never talk about. Not with Mark, not with anyone. The affair had developed by accident, a mild flirtation, never serious, but the consequences were enough to make her believe in Satan. For the rest of her life Ellie would be living with the terror of a ringing telephone, a midnight knock at the door. Secrecy was squeezing the future out of her.

In the cab, as they returned to their hotel, her husband said, "Was it fun?"

"Fun?" she said.

"The reunion. Old friends. What else?"

There was a vacuum, as if a hole had opened up between them, and for a few seconds Ellie wondered if she might find the courage to fill it with the truth.

Instead, she said, "Oh, *fun*."

Almost everyone else partied well past midnight. There were door prizes, and later a limbo contest, and later still a talent show designed for laughs. Marv Bertel was among those who stayed. Bad heart and all, he danced several times with Spook Spinelli, who was already married, doubly, and who divided her time between two adoring husbands and a now-and-then lover on the side. By one in the morning Spook's head was on Marv's shoulder. "I'm a lardass," he told her, "but I'd make a fantastic third husband. Hide me under your bed. Beds, I mean. Plural."

Spook said, "Nice dream, isn't it?"

"Just say maybe."

"Maybe," she said.

★   ★   ★

Dorothy Stier stayed late too. She stood outside with Billy McMann, trying to explain away her mistake, or what Billy called a mistake. She blamed it on religion and politics and the vast differences between them in 1969. "I was Catholic," she reminded him. "I was a Nixon chick. What else could I do?"

"They have churches in Winnipeg," Billy said. "They have tea services."

"At least dance with me."

"No, thanks," he said.

"Please?"

"Can't. Won't. Very sorry." He would not look at her. "So where's Ron this evening?"

"Stop it."

"Let me guess," said Billy. "Home with the kids?"

"Correct."

"You bet correct. Home. Kids. Correct's the fucking word."

Inside, Marla Dempsey still danced alone, down inside herself.

Sixty seconds away, David Todd lay shot through both feet, dumb as dirt, sky high, listening to the sound of everness cut through the tall, bloody grass along a shallow river west of Chu Lai.

Harmon Osterberg was drowned.

Karen Burns was murdered.

In a downtown hotel room, Ellie Abbott lay

20

under the sheets with her husband Mark. At one point Ellie began to reach out to him. She almost said something.

Just after 1:30 in the morning the band stopped playing. The lights came up, people began drifting toward the door, but then someone found a radio and turned up the volume and the party went on.

At the rear of the gym, six former football players ran passing plays.

The twin slide projectors pinned history to the wall. RFK bled from a hole in his head. Ellie Abbott swam laps with Harmon Osterberg in the Darton Hall pool, and Amy Robinson hoisted a candle for Martin Luther King, and a helicopter rose from a steaming rice paddy west of Chu Lai, and David Todd bent down to field a sharp grounder, and Spook Spinelli grinned her sexy young grin, and Billy McMann dropped a fiery draft card from the third-floor balcony of the student union, and the Chicago police hammered in the head of a young man in whiskers, and Paulette Haslo led a pray-in for peace, and *Apollo II* lifted off for the moon, and the President of the United States told heroic lies in the glaring light of day. Out on the dance floor, Minnesota's lieutenant governor and his ex-fiancée, now a Lutheran missionary, swayed slowly to fast music. A chemist explored the expansive hips of a retired librarian. A prominent physician and one of the full-time mothers, formerly a star point guard,

21

made their way toward the women's locker room. Unofficially, this was a thirtieth reunion—officially a thirty-first—and for many members of the class of '69, maybe for all of them, the world had whittled itself down to now or never.

Billy McMann and Dorothy Stier had gotten nowhere. They stood near the bar, apportioning blame.

Paulette Haslo was on her hands and knees, drunk, peering up at the cardboard stars. "All I ever wanted," she was telling no one, "was to be a good minister. That's all. Nothing else."

The chemist kissed the weathered throat of his retired librarian.

Minnesota's lieutenant governor had vanished. So, too, had his ex-fiancée, now a Lutheran missionary.

Spook Spinelli sat in Marv Bertel's lap. Marv was certain his time had come. Spook was certain about nothing, least of all her own heart. After a while she excused herself, got up, and went off to call her two husbands and a now-and-then lover named Baldy Devlin.

At a back table, over the last of their vodka, Amy Robinson was confiding in Jan Huebner about her disastrous honeymoon, explaining how packets of hundred-dollar bills had ended up in her purse. Good luck, Amy said, always came in streaks, and she was afraid she'd used up every last bit of hers on the honeymoon. "It sounds superstitious," she said, "but I wonder if I've got any left. Luck, I mean. For the real world."

"Divorce sucks," Jan said.

"Big-time," said Amy.

Jan looked around the gym. "Maybe we'll strike gold. This whole place, take a look around. Nobody left except a bunch of wretched old drunks like us. People who need people."

"I hate that song," said Amy.

"The universe hates it," said Jan. "Except for my ex-husband."

"Screw the guy," said Amy.

"All the guys," said Jan.

"Cheers," Amy said.

"Cheers," said Jan.

Amy finished off her drink, closed her eyes, blinked out a smile. "Crazy, crazy thing, isn't it?"

"Crazy what?"

"Oh, I don't know, just getting old," said Amy. "You and me, our whole dreamy generation. Used to be, we'd talk about the Geneva Accords, the Tonkin Gulf Resolution. Now it's down to liposuction and ex-husbands. Can't trust anybody over sixty." Amy shook her head. For a few seconds she tapped her empty glass against the table. "And you know the worst part? Here's the absolute worst part. Our old-fogy parents—yours and ·mine, everybody's—they didn't know jack about jack. Couldn't spell Hanoi if you spotted them the vowels. But one thing they *did* know, they knew damn well where we'd end up. They knew where all the roads go."

"Which is where?" Jan said.

"Here."

"Sorry?"

"Right here."

Jan sighed. "True enough," she said. "But look at it this way. Things could be worse. We're not Karen Burns."

CHAPTER 2

JULY '69

It was late afternoon, July 16, 1969. In four days, Neil Armstrong would walk on the moon. But now, a world away, in the mountains west of Chu Lai, Second Lieutenant David Todd lay in the grass along a shallow, fast-moving river called the Song Tra Ky, badly wounded, thinking *Dear God*, listening to people die all around him. Hector Ortiz had been shot in the face. The boy was dead, or seemed to be, but his transistor radio still crackled with the evening news out of Da Nang. *Apollo 11* had lifted off that morning. There were prayer services in Sioux City, progress reports in Times Square, and all across the republic, in small towns and big towns, under bright summer skies, crowds gathered in front of appliance stores to witness updates from Mission Control. Vince Mustin was crying. He had been shot in the stomach. Up ahead, on the far side of the river, Staff Sergeant Bus Dexter yelled something and crawled toward a clump of boulders. He almost made it. David watched the big man push to his feet and begin to run, three or four clumsy steps, then something exploded behind him and lifted him up and jerked him sideways and dropped him dead on the riverbank. Buddy Bond and Kaz Maples had died in the first burst of gunfire. Happy James had been shot in the neck. Doc Paladino had vanished entirely. Minutes ago, during the platoon's rest break, Doc had been kneeling in the grass a few meters behind David, listening to Ortiz's radio, grinning and shaking his head—"Fuckin' moon," he'd said—and then came a crashing sound, followed by a glare, and Doc Paladino had been sucked away into the powdery grass.

Others were still dying. David could hear them making animal noises along the riverbank and in the brush behind him. He had no idea what to do. He had been shot through both feet. He rolled sideways through the grass, toward the river, then covered his head. It was his nineteenth day in-country. He was partly terrified, partly amazed. It had not seemed possible that he could be shot, or shot so quickly, or shot through both feet. The noise amazed him, too, and the way Doc Paladino had been sucked away dead, and how his feet hurt, and how Ortiz's little transistor radio kept playing while people died. Apollo's touchdown was scheduled for 8:27 P.M., Greenwich Mean Time, July 20, at a spot in the universe called the Sea of Tranquillity.

David was too afraid to move.

It occurred to him that he was an officer, and that he should do something, except there was nothing to do, nothing to shoot back at, just the dry, brittle grass all around him.

Ten or fifteen meters away, Ortiz's transistor radio played a transmission from *Apollo 11*.

Somebody near the river was laughing.

There were Vietnamese voices, chattering sounds.

For a few seconds the gunfire seemed to ease off, the way a rain ends, but then it started up again, louder and much closer, and David told himself to move. He took a breath, crawled forward a few feet, stopped, listened, and then crawled again. It seemed absurd to him that he could be shot the way he was. The pain was terrible, but not nearly as bad as his fear, so he pinched his eyes shut and talked inside himself and kept moving until he reached a pair of saplings at the center of the clearing. Oddly, even with the gunfire, he could still hear Ortiz's radio. Vince Mustin was no longer sobbing, and along the river, where most of the platoon had been trapped, the return fire had ceased. The Vietnamese were yipping, sometimes laughing. Now and then a single gunshot rang out. Mopping up, David thought. And it then became evident to him, for the first time, that he would almost certainly die here, and that he would die alone, no buddies, no Marla Dempsey, shot through both feet.

Panic made him move again. He dragged himself through the grass, mostly on his belly, and after what seemed an impossibly long time he reached a thicket of reeds along the Song Tra Ky. The rest

29

of the platoon had to be somewhere downstream. An hour ago he had allowed half his men to march off for a swim; back then the universe had still been a universe.

David wiggled into the muck, hugged himself, briefly pictured his own corpse. He also pictured Marla Dempsey. No doubt she would show up at his funeral. She would drape a flag over his coffin and blink hard and feel guilty. She would do her best to cry.

The pictures made him want to live.

Fifty meters away, barely audible now, Ortiz's transistor radio kept droning on about mankind's destiny, how *Apollo II* had brought the world together. None of it seemed real: not the newscast, not the moon. "Come on, partner, hang tight," a voice said, smooth and Southern, a Texas drawl. Crazy, David thought. The voice seemed to be coming from Ortiz's radio. He pressed himself down into the reeds, trying to think clear thoughts, but all he could manage was the hope that he would not leak to death through his feet, that he would not be finished off like the others.

At one point he heard Vietnamese voices close by. He smelled something fishy and sweet, maybe hair tonic. He imagined a rifle muzzle against his temple. "Hey, don't!" he said, then felt himself slipping away.

Later, he heard himself mumbling about baseball.

Later still, he watched his feet being eaten by ants, a whole colony.

The ants awakened him just before dark. He lay still for a few seconds, and then the pain in his feet hit him hard. He sat up, brushed the ants away, pulled a canteen from his belt, drank it empty, rubbed his eyes, stared up at a purple sky. There were insect sounds, a few frogs, nothing else. The temptation was to sleep again, to float away, and he was surprised, almost frightened, to hear a polished Texas voice say, "Let's go, my man. Move out. Time's tickin', ants lickin'."

David scanned the tropical twilight.

"I'm serious, Davy. Move."

Dark had set in by the time he dragged himself back into the grassy clearing. Already the place had the feel of memory. He followed the sound of Hector Ortiz's transistor radio, which now filled the night with Sly and the Family Stone. Ortiz's corpse lay nearby. Closer to the river, in a rough semicircle, were the bodies of Kaz Maples and Buddy Bond and Vince Mustin and a young PFC whose name David could not remember. They were all dead, pale and plastic, as if they had never lived, but to be sure David examined each of them for a pulse. Afterward, he sat and listened. He was twenty-two years old. He was a baseball player, not a soldier. Part of him wanted to weep, or go crazy, but he was too afraid and too bewildered, even for craziness, and Sly was spooking him.

He switched off the radio, put it in his pocket.

Two notions struck him at once. He knew for a fact that he would die here. He knew for another fact that it was mostly his own fault.

The night passed in fog. Sometimes he prayed, sometimes he surrendered to the pain in his feet. Periodically, when he thought he could tolerate it, David tightened up the laces of his boots, hoping this might stop the bleeding. His thoughts came at him like fireworks: a flash from childhood, then darkness, then another flash opening up into some half-forgotten face from college. He saw Marla Dempsey dancing in the Darton Hall gymnasium. He saw his mother hanging up clothes in the back yard, his father planting a lilac bush, his brother Mickey tossing a baseball at the garage.

Like getting shot, David noted.

None of it cohered.

Late in the night he switched on Ortiz's transistor radio. He kept the volume low, the Sony tight to his ear, and listened to a tired-sounding master sergeant in Da Nang chat about the *Apollo* moon shot. "No potholes, no bumps in the road," the announcer said, "and we got ourselves a nice wrinkle-free trip to the rock. So all you troopers out there, all you wee-hour trippers and dippers and war-wiggies and scaredy-cats, you can take heart in that." The man chuckled. "The technology works, guys."

★　　★　　★

32

At first light David made a systematic search of the grassy clearing. He found what was left of Doc Paladino. It was a quiet morning, perfectly still, like a snapshot of reality. Even the grass did not move. Off to the west, David could hear the frothy bubble of the river. Otherwise there was no sound at all. He opened up Doc Paladino's medical pouch, pulled out seven Syrettes of morphine, jabbed himself once in the thigh, popped a penicillin tablet, taped three square bandages over the holes in his boots, slung the canvas pouch over his shoulder, picked up Doc's M-16, and began the long crawl down to the Song Tra Ky.

It took him well over an hour to cover two hundred meters. Twice, he fell into something very much like sleep. Another time he lay watching a pair of jets passing high overhead, their trails parallel in a neon-red sky.

When he reached the river, the morphine had taken him into a new world. It was no longer a war, and he was not shot and not alone and not leaking to death through the feet.

He almost hoped.

He filled his canteens, took a nap, joined Marla on the dance floor, married her afterward, planted lilac bushes in their back yard.

The midday heat brought him out of it. Presently, more or less with resolve, he decided to move downstream. The rest of the platoon had to be hunkered down somewhere. He could not be the only survivor—his luck had never been that good, or that bad.

After a prayer David slipped into the shallow river. The cold felt good for a moment, then it hit the bones of his feet, and both legs seemed to snap, and something blunt and icy struck him between the eyes. For a few seconds all he knew was his own biology. The river was at most three feet deep, barely a river, but the muscular current spun him over and dragged him face-down along the bottom. He felt himself passing out, and then he did, and it was some time later when David found himself tangled up in a web of tree roots along the bank.

He sat up in a foot of water. Directly to his left, almost touching him, Private Borden Manning bobbed on his back, his nose gone, the current fishtailing him against a big gray boulder. Several others floated nearby, caught up in roots and rocks. Sergeant Gil Reiss lay dead on the bank. Tap Hammerlee, Van Skederian, and Alvin Campbell lay side by side farther down the bank, as if on display, their scalps stripped away, their feet too, the stumps shiny and reddish purple in the lurid sunshine.

There were butterflies along the bank. The corpses were naked and badly swollen. They had been killed naked, frolicking, like a Boy Scout troop.

David pulled himself out of the water and moved into the shade of a little betel palm. The carnage was bewildering. He took a Syrette from his pocket, stuck himself again, wiped himself dry with his shirt. White-and-yellow butterflies circled all around him. He danced with Marla Dempsey for a while, scooped up a ground ball, wept at the pain in his legs and at how alone he was and how afraid of dying. Later, he began to count up the dead. Twenty-four hours ago, when they'd stopped for a break in the grassy clearing, there had been seventeen of them altogether, a stripped-down platoon. Now there was no one. Not even himself, because the morphine had made him into a child, and because he was dying fast. And it was his own fault. He had failed to put out flank security; he had permitted half the platoon to move down to the river for a swim; he had said nothing, and done nothing, when Ortiz turned on his transistor radio to get news about the moon shot. Taken together, or taken separately, these blunders had violated even the most minimal field discipline.

So stupid, he thought.

There was no longer any point in moving. He should be hungry, but he wasn't. He should also come up with a plan, something smart, but all he could do was shut his eyes and wonder when he would be dead.

It was not a war now.

A war stopped being a war, David decided, when you were shot through the feet.

"Seventy-six hours and counting, all systems go,"

35

said the tired announcer in Da Nang. It was late evening, July 17, 1969. Ortiz's transistor radio was still working, even after its passage through the river. "Two days and a wake-up, then we check the place out for little green Communists." The man sighed a heavy, exhausted sigh. "So come on, fellas, let's finish up this two-bit police action. Time to hit the beaches of Tranquillity."

In other news, Rod Carew had stolen home for the seventh time in his career.

Just after dawn, a pair of helicopters swept in low over the Song Tra Ky. Maybe it was David's imagination, maybe the morphine, but for an instant he found himself looking up into the eyes of a young door gunner, rapt, prep-school blue, caught up in the murder of it all. David tried to raise a hand, but the effort made him dizzy. It was all a blur, part of some distant world, and after a few seconds even the blur was gone.

The pain came and went. Sometimes it was nothing. Other times it exceeded physics.

In the heat of midday, David took out another Syrette, punched up, dragged himself down to the river, slipped in, and waited for his feet to quiet down. He tried not to look at the bodies all around him. The smell was enough. He lay on his back in the shallow stream, his shoulders against the bank, and for twenty minutes he let the icy water bubble over his legs and swollen boots. The morphine

36

helped. He was dying, he knew, but his thoughts were baseball thoughts, Marla thoughts, and the sky was a smooth, glossy blue.

He turned on Ortiz's radio, propped it up on the bank, and hummed along to familiar tunes, sliding up and down the scales of his own puny history.

If there was a sad part to this, David observed, it was that his life had gone mostly unlived, all prospect.

Marla, for instance.

Also baseball.

In his junior year at Darton Hall, he'd been scouted by a couple of big-show clubs, the Twins and the Phillies, and with some hard work he might've made it all the way. He had the good glove, the hot bat. For a few minutes, with morphine clarity, David Todd replayed a number of highlights in his head. He was back at shortstop, gunning it to first, and soon afterward he was married to Marla Dempsey, who adored him, and they had a couple of kids and a nice stucco house in Minneapolis, and in his reveries he would not be dead for another fifty years.

In his sophomore year at Darton Hall, David had tried to instruct Marla in some of the finer points of baseball: the intentional walk, the delayed pickoff, the hit-and-run. He had little luck. Marla was an art major. She had trouble caring. "It's what I'm good at," he'd told her. "I can't see why you won't pay attention."

"I do pay attention."

"What's a bunt?"

"A bunt? It's like a dribble, right?"

"Right," he'd said. "Almost."

Sometimes Marla would laugh. Other times she'd mutter a word or two about men and their macho games. "I'll pay attention," she once said, "if you explain how baseball feeds the orphans in India."

"It doesn't," he'd said. "Does art?"

"No. Art feeds something else. Come on now, let's not fight. Tell me about those huge, gorgeous bunts of yours."

And then they'd both laugh. Even so, he could see the dullness in her eyes as he talked about the function of a bunt, how it could be as beautiful and fulfilling as any brushstroke. Marla would listen, and nod, but in the end she would remember nothing.

This frightened him. It made him wonder about their future, what love meant to her, how long it would be before she executed her own hit-and-run.

"The time," said the announcer in Da Nang, "is fifteen hundred hours on the dot, sharp as shitola, and the mercury here in downtown Slope City reads—holy moly, this can't be right—a fuse-poppin' ninety-seven degrees." Then sound effects: the announcer chugging down a glass of water. "What a war—hot as home! So all you boonie rats out there, I want you to gobble down the salt tabs, keep pumpin' in them fluids. That's rock-solid advice from yours truly, Master Sergeant Johnny Ever." The man paused and chuckled. "Which goes double for you dudes up in the mountains, the weak and wounded, poor dumbos like David Todd."

Then came the news. *Apollo 11* was thirty-two hours from touchdown.

In late afternoon David eased off his left boot. Blood trickled from a hole in his instep and from a larger hole just above the toes. He filled his socks with gauze from Doc Paladino's pouch, laced the boot as tight as it would go, took four penicillin tablets, and passed out. He awoke in the deep of night. The pain had moved up through both ankles, into the shin bones, and for a time he listened to himself converse with his feet. He talked baby talk. He made bargains with God.

Later, he tried to sort out the realities.

There were four remaining Syrettes of morphine, which he hoped to conserve for when things got worse. He told himself to wait twenty minutes. He looked at his wristwatch, counting off the seconds, but after one sweep of the hand he shrugged and shot himself up. In the dark, there was the stench of mildew and dead friends. He could smell his feet rotting.

"Here's the straight poop," said the announcer

in Da Nang. "Baseball speaking, you would've made it. Tough rookie year, I'll be honest, but after that . . . I don't want to depress you."

"After that what?" said David.

The announcer made a commiserating sound. "Well, hey, we're talking four seasons in the big circus. Nothing spectacular, I'll admit, but what the hell, it ain't Little League."

David was silent. He turned the tuning knob on Ortiz's transistor radio.

There was static, then laughter.

"Nice try, my man. Thing is, nobody dials out Johnny Ever. I'm like—how do I say this?—I'm network. I'm global. I'm Walter Cronkite gone planetary."

"Right," David said.

"As rain, my friend. Exactly as rain. Anyhow, four sweet seasons, it was in the cards. Real unfortunate, you know? Pity, pity, pity." The announcer sighed. "I ain't your daddy, but you should've finished up that senior year, never dropped out. I mean, Christ, you flat-out volunteered for this sorry garbage." He paused to let the reminder take hold. "What the heck. Water over the dam, I reckon. Anything else you need to know?"

"Go away."

"Want to hear about your love life?"

"Just stop."

"Yeah, if only." Briefly, the announcer seemed to ponder the metaphysics of stopping. Then his voice brightened. "Come on, now. Don't be shy. Ask me questions."

At daybreak David swallowed two penicillin tablets, punched in a Syrette, and waited for the inner music. Today he would move downriver. Probably futile, he realized, yet he needed to pretend he was saving himself.

He spent the morning on his belly, sometimes crawling, sometimes hauling himself down the shallows of the river. Mostly dozing. By midday, when he called it quits, he'd moved less than half the distance of a city block. The effort had made him feverish. He'd lost track of his spiritual whereabouts, his time slot, his place in the overall dream of things. Through the fierce afternoon heat David lay in the shade of triple canopy, listening to the river a few meters to his left, then at twilight he sat up and inspected his wounds. The right foot and lower calf had gone yellow-black. The left leg seemed in better shape—more painful, but not nearly so discolored.

He had two more Syrettes. Once these were gone, David knew, he would no longer be wholly human. Even now it was hard to think beyond the next fix. He took out one of the Syrettes and placed it in the grass beside him.

To make himself wait, he switched on Ortiz's radio.

Apollo II was twelve and a half hours from

touchdown. "Bad Moon Rising" had hit number two on the *Billboard* charts.

"And for you die-hard baseball fans," said the announcer, "it's a season for the ages. Dave, my man, can you believe them raggedy-ass Mets? Bunch of has-beens and never-will-bes, they're surprising all of us, even ol' Master Sergeant Johnny Ever. And I'll guarantee you, this here is one very hip, ten-thousand-year lifer who don't *get* surprised. Spartacus, I guess maybe *he* surprised me. Esther Williams. That's it, though." The man coughed into his microphone. "So listen, Lieutenant. What's the score out there? Down a few runs? Bottom of the ninth?"

Narcotic babble, David thought. He did not reply.

"I don't mean to make light of it," the announcer said, "but you got to remember, man, this dying crud, it's just one more lopsided game. Everybody wants a miracle—like with them shaggy-ass Mets. Got half a mind to help 'em pull it off." Something coy came into the man's voice. "Maybe you, too."

It was a temptation, but David said nothing.

"Not interested? Can't sell supernatural?"

David stayed silent.

"See, the thing is, I got this special sale on today. Two miracles for the price of one. Ask polite, I'll throw in a virgin."

"Are you God?"

The announcer laughed. "Fuck no, I'm not God.

42

Use your head, man. Does God say 'Fuck no'?"
There was a moment of thoughtful silence. "I'm
like—how do you say it?—I'm like a middleman.
Billy Graham without the sugar, Saint Christopher
without the resources. All I can do is put in the
request, ask for a chopper, hope for the best."

David closed his eyes, punched in the Syrette,
and tried not to cry.

"Not that you'd be missing a whole lot," the
announcer said. "Pitiful future, I'm afraid. Face
it—who wants a one-legged shortstop? I could run
the future tape for you, but I think it might end up
real, real depressing. Twenty-two years old, career
finished, nobody gives a hoot about war wounds.
Your bubble-gum cards, Davy, they won't fetch
top dollar. Anyhow, if that's not enough, pretty
soon you start dreamin' the bad dreams. Ten,
twenty years down the pike, here comes the survivor guilt. Ghosts galore. All these dead guys—Bus
Dexter, Vince Mustin—they talk your ear off about
what happened here. Wasn't totally your fault—a
live-ammo war, for chrissake—but try to tell them
that. So one thing leads to another. Did I mention
booze? Trouble on the home front. Tough divorce.
Hate to say it, but that cute Marla chick, she just
wasn't for you. Not for anybody."

David's eyes opened. "What do you mean?"

"Your future, Lieutenant. If you want a future."
The announcer made a snorting sound. "Sorry to
bear the bad news, but you're in for the standard
Jezebel stuff. Old as the crocodiles. Marla tells you

how terrific you are, how you're the love of her life, then one day she takes off with this slick stockbroker on a Harley. Before she goes, though, she bawls her eyes out. Says she can't help herself, says she'll love you forever. Big deal, right? Pow, she's gone, and you waste the next six years waiting for the little lady to change her mind. Every day you check your mailbox. Zip. Not a Christmas card. Tell the truth, could you tolerate it? Your own sorry life?" The man paused. Even his silence carried an edge of mockery. "So here's the deal, friend. Food for thought. Hypothetically speaking, let's say I manage to yank you out of this mess. Send in a medevac, scoop you up, get that right leg chopped off in Japan, retool the other one. Then what? You ready for the heartache routine? You really want that? I mean, do you? Managing some sorry Triple-Z outfit in East Paducah? Chaw stains on your molars? Gum cancer? Eating your guts out over a screwed-up ex-wife? Apocalypse, man, it's a sure bet. Boom, down comes Babylon. Ebola. Plague. That's life, Davy. Everybody dies."

"What happened with Marla?" David said.

"So you *are* paying attention."

"What?"

The announcer sighed in exhaustion. "Sorry, my friend, but I'm not allowed to spill details. Live and learn, that's the theory. Let's just say the gal was born in neutral. No overdrive. No gears at all."

"She never loved me?"

"Your words, not mine. Didn't hear it from Johnny Ever."

Later, after a weather update, the man said, "But Davy, here's the good news. At least she liked you. Liking counts. Liking's right up there with clean socks. Seriously, if more people just flat-out liked each other . . . well, you wouldn't be in this miserable fix. Who needs passion? Give me a choice, I'll take plain ol' lukewarm liking. Not everybody's an all-star."

The announcer made a sound of sympathy. He was quiet for a few seconds.

"Give me an opinion," he said. "If I save the day, send in a dust-off, could you live with it? Would you?"

David lay still. "I'd lose a leg?"

"Yeah, man. Hopalong Cassidy."

"And Marla, too? I'd lose her?"

"The Lone Gimp. Hi-yo, Silver."

David waited a time and then turned off the radio. But there was still an electric hum in the air. Jungle static, jungle gibberish. The announcer yawned and said, "Think it over. No pressure. Either way, pal, nobody'd blame you."

At 0430 hours the next morning, David Todd used his last Syrette. As dawn came, he lay on his back along the Song Tra Ky, not dead, not alive, listening to a delayed broadcast from the moon. "Amazing, isn't it?" said Master Sergeant Johnny

Ever. "All that firepower, all that technology. They put them two peckerheads up there, let 'em jump around, but they can't do shit for us lost souls down here on planet Earth. Pathetic, ain't it? Hell, they don't even know you and me exist. Back in the world, Davy, they're all doin' somersaults, uncorkin' the California bubbly. This whole damn war's on hold." He laughed. "A sad state of affairs."

But for David Todd it was not sad. It was sad plus something else.

His feet hurt, he was alone and scared, he was too young for this. But twelve minutes later he felt a bounce of joy as *Eagle* touched down on the Sea of Tranquillity. It was almost elation, almost awe. He wondered if Armstrong and Aldrin and Collins would make it home.

A year and a half ago Marla had agreed to marry him. Her language, though, had been scrupulous. "I care for you," she'd said, "but I'm not sure it's forever. That seems too much like—"

"Forever?" he'd said.

"I'll try. I will. But I can't promise much."

From the day he'd met her, or even before, David had known that the odds were poison. One in a thousand, maybe worse. But there were no options except to quit.

Now, he smiled at the river and said, "All right."

"All right what?" said Johnny Ever.

"Send in the bird."

"Even if?"

"Affirmative."

"And you understand the deal, Dave? No joke. There's most definitely a stockbroker in your future." The announcer hesitated, then cleared his throat. When he spoke again, his voice carried a mix of compassion and resignation. "Truth is, I'm not supposed to give advice—promise you won't let on to nobody—but in your case, well jeez, I honest-to-God have to recommend bailing. Cut your losses. Check out. Right now, Davy, you don't know what wounded *is*. Wait'll the Marla war starts—all that heartache, all them Harley dreams. You're in for a world of hurt, my friend, and morphine won't do nothin'."

"Understood," David said.

"And?"

"Green light. I'm taking the ride."

"You're sure?"

"I am. Yes."

Johnny Ever chuckled. "Okey-doke. But I'll say this much. You're one brave motherfucker."

CHAPTER 3

CLASS OF '69

It was just after 1:45 in the morning, now July 8, 2000, but a large portion of the class of '69 still caroused in the Darton Hall College gymnasium. The bar remained open, liquids flowed, someone's radio had been tuned to an oldies station, and considerable gray hair and good cheer were afloat upon a bustling dance floor. People had paired off. Moral footnotes were under scrutiny. Out on the dance floor, Spook Spinelli divided her time between Marv Bertel and Billy McMann. She had peeled off her sweater and was down to a metallic miniskirt and bare feet and a blouse that appeared to be constructed of red cellophane. Even so, she had trouble holding Billy McMann's attention. Right now, Billy draped a tablecloth over his head and vamped it up, feigning sexiness, feigning fun, but in his head he was rehearsing all the love-hate lines he would soon deliver to Dorothy Stier. He would definitely squeeze in the word "coward." He had not yet decided among several potent adjectives. At the moment, however, Dorothy stood in an open doorway at the rear of the gym, taking care

51

of Paulette Haslo, who had recently crossed the finish line in a four-hour race toward nausea. "I didn't do anything *wrong*," Paulette was telling Dorothy. "Ask God. Be my guest. Ask. Nothing, nothing, nothing. All I ever wanted in my whole life was to take care of people, be a good minister, make everybody . . . Jesus, did I vomit? I stink. Don't I stink?"

"You don't," Dorothy said.

"I do. Stinkeroo Paulette. Am I crying?"

"Sort of," said Dorothy, "but you don't stink. Tell me what's wrong."

"Nothing's wrong, except I'm a stinky, certified crook. All I did, I tried to be nice. Didn't I? I did. I tried and tried, just kept trying, and now I'm a putrid, barfing criminal. They arrested me."

"Don't be ridiculous," Dorothy said. "You're drunk, sweetheart, but you're not a crook."

"I am!" Paulette wailed.

A few feet away, in a corner, Marla Dempsey danced alone. Her eyes were closed. She wished she had never married David Todd, because in the end she had hurt him so badly, but she also wished that David could find a way to make her love him perfectly. The trouble, though, was that she had never loved anyone, much less perfectly. She'd made the effort. She'd put in the years. It occurred to Marla that maybe she wasn't human, that she was missing some special enzyme or love gene. Always flat inside. Always so gray and tepid and disconnected. And there was also the problem of David's ability to read her mind, to know things he should never know, as if someone were secretly whispering the future into his ear, every rotten detail. And sometimes he'd whisper back. A conversation, almost, or an argument from three decades ago. And for nine impossible years Marla used to lie in their dark bedroom, terrified, curious, listening to him mumble in his sleep—obscenities sometimes, other times begging for his feet to stop hurting. How do you live with that? How do you make a marriage? You don't. You pick a cold, gray Christmas morning, because that's when you can't stand it anymore, and you say the words and walk out fast and ride away on another man's Harley, and then for the rest of your life you despise yourself. You despise the fact that you don't know how to love, not anybody, not even yourself, and the fact that right now, at this instant, you're dancing alone.

Amy Robinson and Jan Huebner had emancipated a fresh bottle of vodka. Their conversation ran a crooked course from divorce to gambling to yeast infection and then back again to divorce. Thirty-one years ago Amy had been slim and tomboyish and cutely freckled; Jan Huebner had been a clown, very homely, swift with a joke.

"Tell the truth, girl, did you honestly love him?" Jan was saying.

Amy said, "What's love?"

Jan nodded, went pensive, then grinned. "Castration. Is that love?"

"Believe so," said Amy. "But here's what I wonder about. Way back when—like a trillion years ago—back then there wasn't a single doubt. Love was love. And we had plenty of it." Amy gazed out at the dwindling crowd. She was still slim, but no longer cute, and at present her consonants were under vodka pressure. "Oh, well," she said. "The world makes circles. One more drink, that's it. Then we take on the football team."

Minnesota's lieutenant governor and his ex-fiancée held fast to each other under the cardboard stars. They seemed paralyzed. She was a Lutheran missionary, he was a handsome, well pickled, newly married compromiser.

A prominent physician and an ex-basketball star, now a mother of three, soaped up in the women's locker room.

Ellie Abbott lay wide awake in a downtown hotel.

Out on the dance floor, a tall, silver-haired chemist, once shy and bookish, stiffened the drink of a retired librarian, once a prom queen. Neither mentioned it, but the years had leveled their bumpy playing field. He had become a Nobel prospect, she had become a recipient of insufficient alimony. Payback was in progress.

Spook Spinelli had given up on Billy McMann, at least for the time being. Spook was now gracing the capacious lap of Marv Bertel, whose star had risen, whose thirty-one years of patience seemed at last to be paying dividends.

Dorothy Stier wiped up after Paulette Haslo. "You'll be okay, give it time," Dorothy said, and Paulette yelled, "Criminal!"

Billy McMann walked over to join Spook and Marv.

Marla Dempsey danced.

David Todd lay dreaming of forever along a river called the Song Tra Ky. He was half tripping, half mad, shot through both feet.

"Call me Cassandra," Johnny Ever was saying. "Crummy pay, no overtime, but I take it super serious. I mean, Davy, what the heck you think déjà vu is? What you think horoscopes are for? Rabbit's feet? Indigestion? Bad breath? 'Red sky in the morning, sailor take warning'—I wrote the friggin' jingle. Irony? Invented it. Same-same with intuition: my own personal brainstorm. Omens, too. Premonitions, *frisson*, clairvoyance, portents, harbingers, all your basic nape-of-the-neck gimmicks. I mean, wake up. You think coincidence is just coincidence? Hell's bells, Davy, that's my day job. Jack-of-all-trades, you could say. Disc jockey. Cop. Duck whittler. Retired colonel, USMC. Not to mention hit-and-run artist and pharmacist and bigshot keyboard player. Even dealt some blackjack in my day." In the dark along the Song Tra Ky, there was a hissing noise. "Believe me, my friend, I could go on. I do. Name's Ever."

★   ★   ★

"And the freaky part is, I waited more than fifty years to get married," Amy Robinson told Jan Huebner. "Lasted two weeks. Barely got through the honeymoon. I remember we stopped at this gas station and I got out and went into the ladies' room and just sat there on the toilet—who knows how long?—half an hour, probably more. And you know what I was hoping? I was hoping he'd drive away. Forget me. Forget it was a honeymoon."

"But he didn't," Jan said.

"No."

"And then?"

Amy stood up and waited for her stomach to settle. "Then nothing," she said. She wobbled sideways, found her balance. "Come on, love. Put on your game face."

"What about our drink?"

"Fourth quarter, fourth down," Amy said. "Billy McMann's wide open, I'm throwing a pass."

Jan grunted and said, "Hail Mary."

CHAPTER 4
THE STREAK

They won twenty-five hundred dollars before lunch. "We should quit," Amy said, and Bobby said, "I guess we should," but by dinnertime they had won another two thousand.

It was late summer, a weekend. They had been married nine and a half days and had stopped at the little lakeside casino on a whim.

"We'll take a room," said Bobby. "Why run away from good luck?"

"Why stay for bad luck?" Amy said.

By midnight they had won fifteen hundred dollars more, taking turns, a blackjack tag team. Amy organized their chips in tidy stacks of black and purple.

"Bet it all," said Bobby. "Six thousand, and we'll go to bed."

They bet it all and won with a pair of jacks and did not go to bed. They bet half their winnings. The pretty young dealer broke on a twelve. Until then, the cards had gone very well, but now it had become a streak.

"Seven in a row," Bobby said. "Put out six thousand."

"If we lose?" said Amy.

"We go to bed."

"For sure?"

Bobby played the hand: a black ace covered by a red queen. There was a warm, dreamy glow at the table. People were stopping to watch. The pretty dealer smiled at them.

"Your turn," Bobby told Amy. "Six thousand again."

"That's too much," said Amy.

"Go on. I believe it's called gambling."

She pushed out sixty black chips. She drew a nine and a four against the dealer's jack.

"Hit it," said Bobby.

"I can't."

"Close your eyes."

She drew a seven. The dealer turned over an eight. Altogether, they had won thirty-three thousand dollars.

"Please, please, please," Bobby said. He was giddy. He put a hand on Amy's hip for good luck, and they won again, another six thousand.

"Very nice," said the dealer, who was perhaps twenty-two or twenty-three, slim-hipped, with braided black hair and black eyes and brown skin. She chopped down the cards and shuffled.

"Newlyweds, that's nifty," the girl said. "I get married myself in October—October first—except with my luck I'll end up honeymooning in my fiancé's Winnebago." She snorted. "As if I don't already know every square inch."

The dealer's engagement ring looked cheap and gaudy against the green felt. Amy tipped her twenty-five dollars.

"What about you?" the girl said. "Big wedding?"

"Pretty big," Amy said.

"Huge, I'll bet. Lucky stiffs like you, I'll bet it was one serious, pull-out-the-stops wedding." The dealer squared the cards and held them out for cutting. "You wear white? You know. Virgin white?"

"Blue," said Amy.

"What was your music?"

"Music?"

"At the wedding."

"Oh, that. One long blur, I'm afraid." Amy cut the cards.

"You should walk," said the dealer, "while the walking's profitable."

"Not a chance," said Bobby. "Six thousand again."

"She might be right," said Amy.

"She might be."

They were dealt a six and a ten. Amy stayed. The pretty dealer broke on a fifteen.

"Just my cruddy luck," the girl said.

Amy tipped her fifty dollars. A crowd had gathered, most of them silent or nearly silent. A man in a plaid sweatsuit giggled when Bobby pushed out twelve thousand dollars in orange chips.

"Can't do it," said the dealer. She stared at

a spot over Amy's shoulder. "Six thousand—table limit."

"Two hands," said Bobby. "Six each."

"That's a real decent used car," the girl said. She waited. "What I'd do right now, I'd go upstairs and pull back the sheets. Start honeymooning."

"Deal the cards," Bobby said.

"I'm nervous," said Amy.

"This is how you win," Bobby said, almost crossly. He tapped the table with the palm of his hand. "Ride your streaks, go where the luck goes."

"But what if—" Amy looked at him. "We can lose, you know. People lose."

"Don't think that way."

He kissed Amy's cheek, a half kiss, then looked up at the pretty dealer.

"Let's play blackjack," he said.

The dealer broke again. They had won fifty-seven thousand dollars since ten o'clock that morning.

"God almighty, I swear, if I only had your luck," the girl said. She pocketed Amy's hundred-dollar tip, closed her eyes, shook her head. "Just once in my putrid life."

She broke the next hand, too.

"Shit," she said.

"Four hands this time," Bobby said. "Six thousand each."

Amy played. She hit a blackjack, a twenty, a seventeen, another twenty. The pretty young dealer broke on a thirteen.

The crowd yelped and applauded.

"I kid you not," the girl said, "my crummy, crummy luck."

"You're supposed to be rooting for us," said Amy.

"Hey, I'm rooting hard, doll. Sweet couple. Ritzy wedding."

Amy was fifty-two, a lawyer, and did not like being called doll. No one had to prompt her to push out another twenty-four thousand dollars, four stacks of orange.

"Win or lose," Amy said, "we quit this time."

Bobby said nothing. He cupped his chin in his hands and leaned low over the table. It was a small, dingy casino, a single square room with a Formica bar, four blackjack tables, and fifty or sixty slots. The customers were mostly locals.

"The thing about a streak," said the dealer, "is that you can use up your luck. Every bit of it—like me. And then there's the rest of your life."

"Which means what?" Amy said.

"Don't listen," said Bobby.

The dealer thumbed the cards. "Waste your luck here, what's left for the honeymoon? What's left for that rainy day in the suburbs?"

"Deal some cards," Bobby said.

The girl let out a breath and dealt. Bobby won two hands, lost two.

"No damage," he said.

"Please, let's take a break," said Amy. "At least a short little break."

"One last shot."

"Yes, but we've made a fortune. We're not here to gamble, are we?"

"You should be happy."

"I am happy."

"You aren't," Bobby said. He gave her a scolding look, as if she were a student in his junior high algebra class. "People don't *get* streaks like this. Let's both just enjoy it, okay?"

"Okay," Amy said.

The dealer shifted from foot to foot, eyed a pit supervisor to her left. The man shrugged.

"Listen to me," the girl said. "Those chips there, that's half a house."

"Now we furnish it," said Bobby.

He played four hands again, six thousand each. The girl dealt him two twenties, a nineteen, a seventeen.

She broke again.

"Piss," she said loudly. "What the hell's *wrong* with me?"

The pit boss murmured something. The girl nodded and said, "Sorry."

"We'll take a break," Amy said.

She began to put out a tip but then drew it back.

"Drinks on the Chippewa nation," said the pit boss, solemnly, with the inflection of a clock.

At the bar, just after three in the morning, they tallied their winnings.

"How long can it last?" Amy said.

"Not forever," said Bobby. "Sooner or later, I guess, the odds grab your throat, start to squeeze." He paused. "On the other hand, you never know."

"That's the math teacher speaking?"

"Yeah," he said.

"So why not quit?"

"Because I'm a lousy math teacher. Because I'm fifty-six years old, because I waited a whole lifetime for this."

"What about me? Did you wait for me?"

"Meaning what?"

"Bobby, we're not a couple of idiots, we don't chase pipe dreams. We settle for . . . I don't know. We take what comes our way."

They looked at each other.

After a second Bobby stood up. He walked to the cage, cashed in, returned to the bar, and dropped one hundred and twenty thousand dollars on the Formica. The bills were strapped and inky-smelling.

"Forty-five goes to Uncle Sam," he said. He flicked his eyebrows, a gesture that irritated her. "The fun thing now would be to bet the bundle. Every dime. Thumb our noses at the numbers."

"All at once?"

"It's pure profit. Their money."

"We'll lose."

"Fun, though."

The casino was now almost deserted. Behind them, a single slot machine made buzzing noises in the dark, harsh and cheerless. Two elderly gentlemen sat dreaming at the end of the bar.

Amy watched the young dealer.

"That girl, she's lovely to look at," Amy said, "but she wanted us to lose."

Bobby shrugged. "I doubt it."

"What then?"

"It wasn't about us losing. She wanted to win."

"Maybe so," said Amy. "But dealers aren't supposed to think that way. It's a job, that's all. A stupid, robot job."

"Not for her. Not tonight."

Amy tried to look away—tried to appreciate the stack of cash in front of her—but again, without willing it, her gaze slipped off toward the dealer. The girl stood alone at her table, arms folded, one hip cocked to the side.

"She *is* pretty, though," Amy said.

"Give it ten years," said Bobby. "Babies and Winnebagos."

"That's nasty. And you don't mean it."

"I don't?"

"You were staring at her."

Bobby chuckled. "I was staring at Lady Luck."

"Not sometimes."

"When?"

"When she shuffled," Amy said. "I'm gabbing away, you're staring."

"I love you."

"You loved winning."

"Well, yes, that is very damn true," Bobby said.

He handed her a stack of hundreds; he winked and did the irritating thing with his eyebrows. "You should be celebrating."

"Then why aren't we in bed?"

"Because we're hot."

"That's why?"

"Don't spoil it," he said.

Amy closed her eyes. Why the image came to her, or from where, she had no idea, but she was picturing the organist at their wedding, a frail old woman in a crepe dress and crocheted white sweater. Bobby had chosen the music—a medley of show tunes—and something about the harmonics and the worn-out old organist now gave Amy the creeps. False sentiment, maybe. Or maybe it was the wedding itself, which had also been Bobby's idea, and to which she had assented out of guilt. They had been together four years. He'd been decent to her, assiduously decent, decent without flaw, and there was no question about Bobby's patience and humor and devotion and kindness and graying good looks. She truly liked him. And in the end, snagged by their years together, she had run out of excuses.

It was not a question of love. Amy was fifty-two years old, almost fifty-three. She no longer expected fairy-tale romance.

"Listen," Bobby said. "What's wrong? Tell me."

"I don't know."

"The money? The girl?"

"I don't know."

★　　★　　★

67

They took a walk along the lake outside the casino, in the dark, which felt dangerous with all that cash in their pockets. Later, back inside, Amy said she was going to bed. Bobby could do what he wanted.

A muscle moved at his jaw.

"In that case," Bobby said, "I want to ride the streak. Doesn't mean we're splitting up."

"It doesn't?"

"No."

"Then what does it mean?"

"Stay with me," he said. "Have fun."

"Bobby, it's not fun. I guess it's me, but even the winning feels dirty."

They were standing at the elevators across from a bank of slot machines. Amy studied the casino. Years from now, she knew, this would all be with her.

"I'm going to bed," she said. "You go wherever."

"You're angry."

"It isn't anger, Bobby."

"What then?"

"Math," she said.

Amy showered, turned on the radio, turned it off, packed her suitcases, sat on the bed, combed her hair, cried, then went out onto a balcony overlooking the lake. Dawn was coming. Something silvery. The lake itself was dark, scarcely a lake yet, but she could hear its fluid movements. To the north, over a great woods, the moon seemed shrunken and far away.

She lay down on the balcony.

Fifty-two years old, she thought. One hundred and twenty thousand dollars.

And then she thought about her wedding day, which had been fine except for the fact that marrying Bobby, or marrying anyone, had never been high on her list of things to accomplish. A year ago, when she'd told him yes, it had seemed such a tiny inconvenience. Now, stupidly, she found herself trying to erase the wedding in her head, subtracting things: the flowers and the old organist and the minister and the music and her blue dress, then Bobby, then herself.

All those winning hands. What incredible, heartless luck.

She was not in love.

Eyes open, Amy imagined her graying new groom downstairs. Maybe he'd fall for the pretty dealer. Save the girl from Winnebagos. Save himself from whatever this was.

She slept for an hour, then dressed and went down to the casino.

Bobby sat hunched over a pile of orange chips. His shirt had come untucked. He had a stale, chemical smell that made Amy back off a step. She watched him draw a pair of kings.

The dealer broke on a sixteen.

Bobby whooped and slapped the table.

"Your hubby," said the young dealer, "officially owns this joint. The man can't lose."

"Can't he?" said Amy.

They drove away with just under two hundred and thirty thousand dollars in cash. For three hours, heading south toward Minneapolis, Bobby would not stop talking about his good fortune, how for once in his life the breaks had gone his way, how he could do no wrong, how they'd just won themselves early retirement and a Mercedes and time to burn and maybe a nice little condo on a golf course in Arizona.

At one point he gave her knee a squeeze.

He laughed and said, "Amazing. We flat-out scalped them. No survivors."

"Right," said Amy.

At noon they stopped at a gas station outside the Twin Cities. Amy went inside, bought a Coke, and called a cab.

She had no plan.

For a time she stood in the doorway, drinking her Coke, watching Bobby tell the attendant about the streak. Both of them were laughing. It struck her that this was a story he would be telling for the rest of his life, which seemed an awfully long time.

Amy went into the ladies' room, locked the door, wiped the toilet seat, and sat down to wait.

She pictured a crocheted white sweater. A condo

in Arizona. Perhaps when the cab came she would explain to Bobby that the marriage had been a mistake, a complete bust, and that his luck had run out. She wasn't sure. She looked for a sign, studied the graffiti. It was written by sixteen-year-olds.

In a few seconds, Amy told herself, she would probably change her mind. She'd probably march outside and get into Bobby's car and finish her honeymoon. Stop on a sixteen. Hope for the best.

CHAPTER 5

LITTLE PEOPLE

After Jan Huebner graduated from Darton Hall College in June of 1969, she performed for several months with a street theater troupe in the Twin Cities area, alerting a distracted citizenry to the horrors of ongoing genocide in Vietnam, or to what Jan saw as genocide—a war of hegemony and dissimulation and free-fire zones and racism and presumptuous Lone Ranger geopolitics. A born clown, funny just to look at, Jan Huebner played Lady Bird to a Texas T. She did accents. She was good with Spiro Agnew's dumb-boy bullyisms, Westmoreland's kill ratios, the parched apologias of the Bundy brothers. She did a terrific Nixon, a prim, slicked-back Robert McNamara. Comedy was Jan Huebner's special gift. "That girl of mine," her mother used to brag. "Ugly as North Dakota, but I swear to Pete, she could squeeze a laugh out of a Baptist."

Comedy or convent? It wasn't hard to choose. Jan had been a jokester since childhood, which kept her sane, and in July of 1969 she was able to wring reluctant smiles from the most ho-hum, is-there-really-a-war-on noontime crowd.

The work seemed important to her. She liked the street, the zeal and fellowship and daily drama. The only drawback, she concluded, was that food and rent were not to be found in the tin cups of guerrilla theater. Jan was broke, dope was expensive.

She felt fortunate, therefore, to be approached one evening by a diminutive, large-headed young man with an offer of fifty easy dollars. It was twilight on Hennepin Avenue. Jan stood smoking, alone, off to the side, watching the troupe put on paper police hats for their Mayor Daley finale. "Fifty for what?" Jan said, although she had an inkling, and the young man, who seemed harmless enough—not five feet tall, not a hundred pounds without the head—looked away and blushed when he said, "What you trying to do, embarrass me?"

"For what?"

"Fine, make me say it. Half hour. Strip naked." He looked up at her with a pair of bulging, bright blue eyes. The man's huge head and tiny body made it hard to tell his age: maybe twenty, maybe twenty-five. "A personal photo shoot. Satisfied? I feel small."

"How personal?" Jan said.

He glared at her, then sighed a light, fraudulent sigh. "Listen, pumpkin, I bet anything you know what naked is. Buff. Birthday suit. Stick your butt in the air, smile pretty, go spend my fifty bucks. You're a virgin, say so."

For a few seconds Jan watched the troupe launch

its police-state assault on a half-dozen pedestrians. She was not a virgin.

"Fifty in advance," Jan said.

"Forget it. Afterward."

"Where?"

"Around the corner," he said. "My studio."

"Why me? 'Cause I'm cute as a button?"

The man averted his eyes. "Not exactly. But you're Snow White, aren't you?"

It was not a studio, it turned out, but the living room of a cramped apartment off Hennepin. The poses were standard. Arched back. Ecstasy. The odd little man kept his hands busy, humming under his breath, paying more attention to shutter speeds than to Jan herself. In a way, although it disgusted her, she could not help feeling flattered. The word "homely," Jan sometimes imagined, had entered the dictionary on the bleak November day of her birth. Her hair was a thin, muddy brown, her jaw sunken, her thin legs jury-rigged to the hips of a sumo wrestler. She had learned early to be funny.

Except for a few curt instructions, the young man said nothing for five or ten minutes. He hummed, played with his lenses, took the pictures, changed film, and then motioned for her to sit on a wastebasket.

"Wastebasket?" Jan said.

"Fifty bucks, you can sit on a wastebasket."

Jan squatted down and mugged for the camera. "Well," she said, "isn't this fun? Ask nice, I'll pass some gas, blow myself off this dumb wastebasket."

She crossed her eyes.

"Cut the monkeyshines," the man said. "My dime, honey. This ain't a circus."

"Oh, wow. Sensitive psycho."

"Mouth closed," he said. "Legs open."

It was a vicious summer: frantic music, frantic sex, chemicals in the sugar, felons in the White House, predators in public places, B-52s dropping death all over Southeast Asia. Jan Huebner expected the worst, and 1969 delivered. At some point, she was almost certain, the young man would put aside his camera and require of her what the times required, which was inordinate risk, and it came as a surprise when he placed fifty dollars in her lap and said, "Good enough."

"That's it?" she said.

"What else you think?"

"Nothing. I don't know."

The man laughed. "I'm a dwarf. I know where the lines get drawn."

Jan put on her bra and panties, unsure where this was meant to go. "I wouldn't say *dwarf*."

"Wouldn't you?"

"No. Short, I'd say."

"Well, gee whillikers, I feel human now." The young man sneered, popped the film from his camera, and slipped it in his pocket. "You're Snow White, I'm Bashful. What's the plan? Plant a smooch on my forehead? Make me see stars?"

"That's ridiculous."

"Girls like you. Free love—what a joke."

It felt awkward to be sitting on a wastebasket, defenseless, unfunny, staring into those brilliant blue eyes. Jan pulled on her jeans and shirt and leather sandals.

"Your attitude," she said, "sucks."

"Sorry for that. Guess I'm Grumpy."

"Yeah, whatever," Jan said. She went to the door. "Thing is, man, you're not a dwarf. You're an asshole."

Jan Huebner had been an English major at Darton Hall, a B student, a dorm counselor, a confidante of pretty girls, a Saturday-night bridge player, a chain smoker, a clown. Until her senior year she had slept with no one at all. She made men laugh, made them into pals. She joked away her own misery. Skillfully, hiding things even from herself, Jan came up with one-liners about all the bucks she'd saved on beauty aids, how nobody ever dumped her, how she was her own best lover and a thoughtful one at that. She wore bib overalls and baggy sweatshirts. She hid copies of *Cosmo* under her mattress. On Saturday nights, after bridge, she would pick up a pizza and lock herself in her room and devote herself to articles on breast augmentation, ten sure ways to land that special guy.

What saved her was the war.

A miracle, it seemed.

In the spring of her senior year, Jan found herself occupying the Darton Hall admissions office, sharing sleeping bags with a number of passionate, very earnest young men. She suddenly had friends—Paulette Haslo and Amy Robinson and Billy McMann—people who liked her and whom she genuinely liked back. A new confidence came over her. She had a knack for the broad-stroked theatrics of peace; she belonged to something. In six weeks Jan dropped fifteen pounds, mostly from her hips, and at times, impossibly, she felt close to pretty, close to desirable. True, she remained quick with a joke, but now she was equally as quick to cry, and on those occasions there were caring people to embrace her and to offer comfort—many of them men, many of them good-looking men. Maybe it was the music, maybe the dope, but for once in her life Jan Huebner felt wanted and appreciated, even loved, for something beyond a laugh.

A morbid irony, Jan realized, but slaughter had given her a life. Napalm had made her happy. She hoped the war would never end.

Word, apparently, got around. Through that white-hot July of 1969, Jan made her bread posing for what the street called "personal photography sessions." The men were losers, one and all—guys with cheap cameras and greasy cash and little else. Mostly old, mostly fat, uniformly creepy. But still it seemed safe enough. Even sanitary: strip, smile, collect. There was a hands-off protocol, a street ethic that promised honor among perverts, and except for a couple of would-be gropers, Jan encountered no dangers worth troubling about. The few problem cases she handled with humor and dispatch.

As a moral matter, Jan entertained only petty misgivings about her new trade. Granted, it was not something she would soon mention to her mother, nor to the college friends she bumped into that summer. But given the copious evil of 1969, a few photographs seemed insignificant. Her body, after all, was no temple. Ramshackle at best, built by a blind man, so why not turn it into a bank? Also, despite herself, there was the undeniable flattery factor. Guys were paying for it. Not even for *it*: just a few ill-focused images of an emaciated, sad-looking woman she barely recognized. At times, Jan thought of the work as artistic modeling. Other times she saw herself as a kind of social worker, a Salvation Army volunteer minus the uniform, passing out Thanksgiving turkeys to the homeless and sexually under-privileged.

In the third week of July, with more than twelve hundred dollars in her savings account, Jan moved out of the apartment she'd shared with six members of her troupe and took lodging in a cheap efficiency on Lake Street. She bought a couple of flashy wigs, new underwear, and a set of secondhand photographer's lights. She also bought a police whistle.

Her business thrived. She took on the street name Veronica. A pretty girl's name, she thought.

In many ways, Jan lived a triple life that summer.

She remained an active member of the troupe and of the antiwar movement in general. Also, at least as far as her mother knew, she was working nine to five as a bookstore clerk in Dinkytown, marking time until graduate school began in mid-September.

But more and more, she was Veronica.

For steady customers, and for those who could be counted on to offer a modest gratuity, Jan began providing her home telephone number. It was risky, she knew, and often a nuisance. Which it was on the twenty-eighth night of July, well after midnight, when she was awakened by a rude, belligerent drunk who said, "If it isn't Snow White."

It took a few seconds to attach a history to the high-pitched, surly voice.

He was at a phone booth down the street. At the present somewhat inebriated moment, the young man told her, he was the proud new owner of a two-inch erection, which for him was enormous. He also had thirty-eight dollars burning a hole in his shorts. Was she interested? Could she find it in her snow-white heart to spot him the missing twelve bucks?

"Shop's closed," Jan said. "Maybe tomorrow, if you learn some manners."

"Yeah, fine. Kiss off a dwarf."

"You're not a dwarf, this isn't a kiss-off."

"No? And what about my record-setting two-incher?"

"Rub it with ice, hit it with a hammer," Jan said. "Maybe it'll grow."

He made a sound that might've been a chuckle. "Okay, you caught me, I exaggerated. Two inches, that's stretching things. Wanted to impress you. Like my mama used to say . . . I mean, she's this normal-size bitch, right? I'm this kid. So she looks down at me, sort of squinting, and she goes, 'Oh well, no big deal.' Get it? No big deal. Mom's idea of a knee-slapper." He hesitated. "Thirty-eight bucks. No cameras. Won't take long. Just talk."

"Talk about what?"

"That," he said, "is what we need to talk about."

Five minutes later, when Jan opened her door, the man stood dressed in a red polo shirt, baggy gray shorts drooping to his ankles, and a blue cap that said TITLEIST. For longer than was comfortable, he peered up at her as if waiting for an invitation of some sort, or perhaps the opposite, and then he made a huffing sound and walked in and sat on the couch. His white sneakers, Jan noted, did not reach the carpet.

"Well," she said. "Back from miniature golf?"

"Miniature, that's hilarious. You mind?"

He pulled a whiskey bottle from his shorts, took a swig, waved the bottle at her. Jan shook her head.

"Here's the deal," he said. "Dwarfs don't fall in love, too risky, end up getting stiffed. Let's just say I've fallen in real serious affection. Landed you some customers, didn't I? Passed the word?"

"You did. Thank-you note's in the mail."

The young man didn't seem to hear this. His huge blue eyes surveyed the apartment, finally settling on the photographer's lights and a large, soiled bed sheet she'd strung up as a backdrop.

"Professional, aren't we?" he said.

"Making ends meet. What do you want?"

The eyes twinkled. "Well, see, there's a couple answers to that. What I did want, what I do want." He seemed to measure her for something, a frame, a future. "All those ads in the paper. Fancy lights. Police whistles. I mean, holy cow, I'm impressed. Pretty darn streetwise, huh?" The twinkle again. "Should I call you Veronica?"

"Sure," she said.

"Sure," he said, mocking. "Take a nip. Won't kill a street girl."

"How'd you know about the whistle?"

"How do I know about everything? Wear it around your scrawny neck, don't you? I see the pictures. Do me a favor—one tiny nip. Old times' sake."

She took the bottle from him, pretended to swallow. Outside, it had started to rain. She felt a little frightened.

"One more time," she said. "You want what exactly?"

"Well, jeez, like I say, there's *did* want and there's *do* want. What I did want, I was gonna prove how smart you are, this hip English major, this strip-naked money machine who thinks she's

Mona Lisa. Gets herself this cool summer job. Other kids your age, they're bagging groceries, detasseling corn. Not you. You're Veronica." He kicked off his sneakers, tipped his cap back, crossed his legs beneath him on the couch. "So what I wanted, see, I was gonna ask for—I don't know—what you got in the bank, sweetie?"

"In the bank?"

"Bank. Like in money. You're so smart, right? That slick education of yours, I figure you got a terrific answer when I say, 'Hey, give me your money.'" He raised his eyebrows. "I bet what you say is, I bet you say, 'Get lost, shorty,' and so I say, 'Yeah, but otherwise I send Ma some juicy pics.' Your ma, not mine. And that's when you come up with that amazing tough-girl answer. That's when you prove what a professional you are."

Jan looked at him for a time, then at the floor. "My mother," she said, "wouldn't give a shit."

"That's your bowl-me-over answer?"

"Pretty much."

He shrugged. "Well, I got news. When it comes to naked, *all* mothers give a shit."

"Not mine."

"No? Tell you what, then." He was cooing, playing with her. "Here's what we do. You and me, we hop a cab right now, show Mom the pics, pop the question. The lady lives . . ." He took out a slip of paper. "Lives in St. Anthony Park, right?"

"Right," said Jan.

"What say we hit the road? No need to get dressed, obviously."

"How much?"

"Sorry?"

"To lay off. How much?"

The man shook his head as if dealing with a problem student, a slow learner. "Zero. Didn't I already say that? What we're talking here, we're doing a shtick on what I *did* want. Guys like me, we exist. And you know why? To fuck Snow White. To put the hurt on cute suburban chicks, think they're half Wonder Woman, half badass. Gonna stop the wars, feed the hungry, get naked with guttersnipes, make a couple quick bucks on the side."

"You planned this?"

"I did. Icky me. What'd you expect? Hit the pavement out of some fancy-dancy school, figure you can skinny-dip in the sewer for a couple months, fraternize with the scum, then hustle back to Main Street with lots of scary stories to tell—you think it works like that? Go lowlife? Walk away clean?"

"I didn't think anything," Jan said.

"Ah. No kidding?" His voice had a mellow, tuneful quality that seemed to blend with the steady rain outside. "Anyhow, lucky for you I turned a new leaf. Fell head over heels in affection. Changed my itsy-bitsy mind."

She looked at him skeptically. "So what's this about? Humiliation?"

"For starters, why not? Humiliation ain't all bad. Look at me, I turned out fine."

"Blackmail," she said. "That's low."

The young man laughed. "It's a living. Dwarfs gotta eat."

"You're not a dwarf."

"Help me out, then. What am I? Extra low, right?"

"Absolutely," she said.

The two of them sat in silence, listening to the rain. In the lamplight the young man's face did not seem so young anymore: black pockets under the eyes, ultraviolet wreckage along the cheeks and forehead. Early thirties, at least. Maybe older. It was his stature alone, Jan realized, that had given the impression of youth, and she couldn't help feeling a twinge of guilt.

She made herself shake it off. "Until twenty minutes ago," she said, "I was doing fine, no problems."

"Were you now?"

"Yes."

"Real hustler, I guess? Working girl?"

"A job. A few dirty pictures, some spare change. I'm not *doing* anything."

"Not doing anything," he said. "Boy, I wonder if Mommy'd see it that way." Again the man's enormous blue eyes flashed, then he shook his head and appraised her with something close to pity. "Listen, I'm trying to be polite. A good citizen, understand? And I'm telling you, sweetmeat, right from my rotten little heart: you're way over your head. Way, way over. I was somebody else—somebody tall, let's say—you'd be in one extremely yucky place right now. Police whistles wouldn't do zip. I mean, who you think you are? Playmate of the Month? Miss July?"

Jan stared at him. Twenty years of ridicule had caught up with her. "Go eat a screwdriver," she said. "Drink poison."

The man laughed. He did Groucho with his eyebrows. "Touchy you," he said.

"You're cruel," said Jan.

"Yeah, well, it gets crueler. Hate like the dickens to break the news, but Brigitte Bardot you're not. Look in a mirror. You got normal going for you, you're not a mutant, and there's the whole sad story. Veronica—makes me giggle. Guys like us, we don't pay for gorgeous, we pay for available. Take my word, you better wake up fast. Get naked in front of street scum, sooner or later some Jack the Ripper decides what the hell, dumb broad's asking for it, she's saying pretty please, she's down on her hands and knees begging for serious hurt. It *will* happen. Guaranteed. Think blackmail's wicked, try a needle in your throat. Try a little back-alley basketball, slam dunk, you're the basket. I know these dudes. Birds of a feather. Far as they're concerned, you're one more pigeon from the burbs. Great big bull's-eye painted on that skinny white chest of yours."

"Mutant?" Jan murmured.

"Hey, I didn't say that. Almost average, I said. Cut or two below mediocre. Count your blessings."

Jan nodded and made a face.

She knew anyway.

"Basically, you're here to insult me?"

"Course not," he said. "Consider the source. Who am I to call the kettle butt-ugly?" He took a hit from the bottle, wiped his mouth, gave her an encouraging smile. "Actually, you were right the first time. What I actually came for, I came here to cash in, to actually extort your ass, maybe even put some actual old-fashioned scare into you. That's what I did want. Now I want something else."

Jan snorted. "I'll bet. I'd rather be blackmailed."

"Whoa. I got feelings."

"Out of here," Jan said. "I already told you, I don't do that."

"I didn't mean—"

"Not if you grew ten inches. Not if you came up to my belly-button."

For a few seconds he glared at her. "What you think, a dwarf can't get nookie? The curiosity factor—you're looking at one hot ticket. Pity factor, too. Pity pays." His tone was still light, but everything else had darkened. "All I wanted, I was gonna invite you to a nice, cheery birthday party. Cake and ice cream. Now I don't know."

"Birthday party," Jan said. "I can imagine."

"You *can't* imagine. Don't be so smart, I've still got the pics."

"Whose birthday?"

"Tiny ol' me, yours truly. It's not like I was hatched, you know. Not like Ma and Pa cracked open a rock, found me there like some puny fossil." He looked away, hands tight in his lap. "So this party, it might be an eye opener, never know. Meet my friends, my brother."

Jan laughed. "This is how you ask for a date? Threaten somebody?"

"Whatever works."

"Okay, I'm curious," she said. "Why?"

"Why?"

"You heard me."

"Well," he said, and the darkness vanished. His eyes went foxy. "Revenge."

"I don't follow."

"Nothing to follow. You get fifty bucks, I get to show off my normal, almost average date. After it's over—my party—we deep-six the porno."

He lifted his eyebrows, waited a moment. "Guess you'll need to know my name, right?"

It was Andrew Henry Wilton. His younger brother—younger by nine years—called him Hanko, or sometimes Andy, or sometimes Little Guy.

Andrew was thirty-two.

He stood four feet seven inches.

He'd grown up in Edina, ritzy suburb.

Ritzy parents, both dead. Ritzy brother, alive, six foot two, smoothie, skier's tan, great teeth.

Anyhow, back to Andrew. Educated at the Blake School and the University of Chicago. Dropped off the map in '67. Tried enlisting, way too short. Tried again, even shorter. Weird thing, but from the time he was a little kid—"And we're talking *little*," Andrew said—he'd always wanted to be a warrior. Not soldier. Warrior. Like in Zulu. Who knew why? Short-guy complex. Audie Murphy movies. "So there's this terrific war on, right? I'm dying to kill people, dying to *get* killed, and guess what? Big bad recruiter morons, creeps take one look, laugh their brains out, tell me to get lost. So I do. Big-time. I get lost."

Cooked hot dogs on University Avenue, buck-fifty each, gouge 'em for sauerkraut, spit in the mustard. Lots of time for reading. Raced through *War and Peace*. Pondered Marcuse, pondered Miss Fonda, yin and yang of nincompoops. Give me a break. Just 'cause you're heightwise disadvantaged, doesn't turn you goo-brain liberal, doesn't make you into Joan Baez, doesn't mean you don't want to go to war and cut off testicles and grease folks every which way.

John Birch Society, mostly dwarfs, bet you didn't know that.

Sold hot dogs, yeah.

Read about Toulouse-Lautrec. Brother pipsqueak.

91

Ladies' man extraordinaire. Hotshot artist. What's to lose? Buy a camera.

Question: You know what most of the silver in the world is used for? Answer: Photography.

Question: You know what makes airhead RFK babes horny? Answer: War and Pity. Should've been the title. Big brawny dude, Tolstoy was. Didn't occur to him.

Sold dogs, snapped pics, got laid like Mick Jagger.

Pretend you're me.

Brother gets drafted. Hates the war, goes anyway, wins medals, comes back with this fab tan, fab teeth, gives you a bear hug, says, Hey, Little Guy.

Except you're eight feet tall. You're Goliath. Zulu, right? Stand on the street all day, sell Oscar Mayer, flash the friggin' peace sign, get yourself a peacoat, watch the Snow Whites go by. Dream about tit for tat. Midget anger, it's big.

Yeah, and keep turning pages.

Dipped into Orwell on the Spanish Civil War, *Homage to Catalonia*, thought about leading a dwarf brigade over to Nam. Like the Lincoln Brigade, you know, except we're all shrimps, chips on the shoulder, scores to settle, out to beat up on Commie peasants even runtier than we are. Impractical idea, pretty much. Gave it up. Gave up hot dogs, too. Peddled pot, got busted, kept peddling, got busted, headed back to grad school. Particle physics, no dummy. Couldn't take it. Dropped out. Peaceniks everywhere, long hair, dipsticks ringing doorbells for Leon Trotsky—hey, what's the country coming to? Back to the street, no big deal. One thing leads to another. Learned the scams. Camera cons. Extortion. Like, for example, how to rip off condescending Snow Whites. How to stick it to politically engaged dimwits who do these clever skits and call it guerrilla theater . . . I mean, Jesus Christ, *guerrilla?* Go bang-bang, scare the shoppers, think you're Che Guevara?

Wasted life.

Feeling blue these days. Awful small.

"There you have it," Andrew Henry Wilton said. "Rainy night. Two-incher. Any pity?"

"No," Jan said.

He chuckled to himself, pulled on his sneakers, and took a bow from the waist. "No sweat. You'll adore my brother."

She did, in fact.

Enough to marry him eight months later, and enough to play the sad-sack clown through twenty-nine years of infidelity, and enough to snap her life in half when he so casually strolled away in the impossibly far-off year of 1999.

But this was Andrew's birthday, July 30, 1969, and except for a polite, excessively gracious manner—a certain CEO slickness, or what might even be called oiliness, perhaps, if one were disposed toward scurrility—Andrew's younger brother seemed nothing at all like the movie-star

93

monster she'd been warned to expect. The man's teeth and tan were unexceptional. He was tall, as advertised, but his overall presence, although scrubbed and pleasant and neatly barbered, would win him no screen tests.

A crinkly smile, true.

Erect posture.

Flirtatious from the first instant.

He looked her straight in the eye when Andrew said, "Babe, this is Richard. Don't call him Dick unless you mean it, like I do."

Richard, with whom she would spend the better part of a nightmare, laughed. He took her hand in both of his. She should've known then, but didn't, because he had Andrew's twinkling blue eyes and his own impeccable manners and all those extra inches.

"And this," Andrew was saying, perhaps too quietly, perhaps with spite, perhaps with fore-knowledge, "is my girl, Veronica."

"Beautiful name," said Richard.

"Thank you," said Jan. "It's not mine."

"Intriguing," said Richard.

The party wasn't much of a party, and near the end, when only four or five guests still lingered in Andrew's pathetically decorated living room, the atmosphere took a turn toward the dismal. There was an uncut birthday cake. There were a couple of balloons, many empty bottles. Jan had done what she had to do—taken Andrew's hand a few times, gone through the motions—but no one had truly bought it, least of all Richard, and after the first hour the pretense had been dropped. It was now a few minutes past midnight. Lights were low, Andrew had vanished, Richard had taken a seat beside her at a cluttered kitchen table, legs crossed, impressively polite, impressively earnest, only an ankle in occasional contact with her left hip as he inquired about the life of a "working model." He seemed undisturbed, soberly spellbound, when Jan said, "I get naked for money."

"Mmmm," said Richard.

"It's temporary. Like a hobby."

"And Andrew?"

"Well," Jan said, and nothing else, which she recognized as a betrayal, a piece of pain she alone had brought into the world, and which would jolt her awake three decades later, in 1999—that word "well," its elusiveness, its invitation, and also, of course, Richard Wilton's ankle so inadvertently against her hip—and how for a short while, as if transported into a story full of gnomes and Prince Charmings, she had forgotten she was a clown, ugly as North Dakota.

In the coming years, this blue-eyed charmer would take great care to remind her of the repulsive verities, relentlessly, without pity, but now, in the early morning hours of July 31, 1969, Jan Huebner felt delivered.

"I'm entranced," said the tall brother, the reptile, the husband-to-be, Richard.

And then, in the same cultured, deeply musical voice that would later come to terrorize her, he talked about his difficulties with Andrew. How much he loved him. How the poor guy could never deal with his height problem—full of rage, full of envy, out to get even with the world, a crying shame—and how he, Richard, heartbreaker, voluptuary, ruiner of lives, fucker of anything, would love dearly to take her to dinner.

The war went on. People ate Raisin Bran. There were new orphans and widows and Gold Star mothers. Three thousand and twenty American soldiers died that summer, and more than seven thousand Vietnamese. People took aspirin for their headaches. People requested doggie bags at fancy restaurants. Dow Chemical made a killing. From sea to sea, along country roads, in great sleeping cities, there were petty jealousies and grocery lists and erotic fantasies and upset stomachs. The earth kept spinning. In the second week of August, Jan Huebner learned that one of her classmates at Darton Hall had been gravely wounded along a river called the Song Tra Ky. Another classmate now lived in Winnipeg, alone and afraid, nursing grudges that would harden into hatred over the coming decades. Elsewhere, in imagination or in fact, the nation's youth began converging on forty acres of farmland outside Woodstock, New York. Sharon Tate had been dead less than a week. Sanitation workers in Manhattan were sweeping up

Neil Armstrong's ticker tape. But for Jan Huebner, as for most others, the summer of 1969 would later call to mind not headlines, nor global politics, nor even a war, but small, modest memories of small, modest things: rumpled beds and ringing telephones and birthday cakes and dirty pictures and catchy tunes about everyday people. There was a fatal Ferris wheel accident in Oregon. There were Krazy Day sales on a thousand sun-drenched Main Streets. Jan Huebner met her husband.

Summer ended, autumn came. Football season. Darton Hall lost its opener.

And while people perished on the far side of the planet, other people had their teeth filled, and field for divorce, and made love in parked cars.

Freshmen were oriented.

The Mets were on a roll.

Small, simple things, yes, but as in some great nationwide darkroom, the most ordinary human snapshots would be fixed in memory by the acidic wash of war—the music, the lingo, the evening news.

In mid-September Jan Huebner abandoned the peace movement. She changed her phone number, dropped out of the street scene, enrolled in graduate school. She gave up personal photo shoots except in the special case of her new fiancé, who seemed charmed by the Veronica in her, or by the abstraction of Veronica. He would not really look at her for another eight months, a full week into their honeymoon, at which point he would suddenly frown and shake his head as if having purchased the wrong brand of cigarettes. They were in Hawaii. They were on a crowded beach. The honeymoon was almost over. Jan wore a new string bikini, posing for him, eyes hooded, one of her practiced come-get-me poses, and for what seemed a long, long while, Richard peered into the viewfinder of his camera as if focus had become a problem, as though some technical malfunction had created a sunken jaw and muddy brown hair and bone-thin legs. Jan was sensitive to this. She crossed her eyes, made a funny face.

A week or so after his birthday party, Andrew had stopped by with fifty dollars.

His mood was chipper.

"An actress you're not," he said, "but who's to complain? You showed up. Got to meet that incredible brother of mine."

Jan shook her head and tried to decline the money. A few nights earlier she had slept with Richard for the first of what would become a good many humiliating times. She would sleep with him again in four hours, and after eight months she would marry him, guileless, never suspecting, and then she would spend the remainder of the twentieth century as a captive to ridicule and dirty pictures. She would live in a three-bedroom house in Eden Prairie. She would drive a Chrysler. She would watch her husband flirt at cocktail parties.

She would endure jokes about plastic surgery, and even make a few herself, and try to clown her way toward a happy ending.

"Just take it," said Andrew. He pressed the cash into her hand, stared up at her, then winked. "My brother, you adored him, I bet."

"I did, I do," Jan said. "Very sweet."

"Sweet you think?"

Jan nodded. "Everything's relative. He treats me like a person."

"Yeah, well," Andrew said. "Give it time."

He flashed her an odd grin, a little wicked, as if he'd just run one of his street scams, exacting revenge for some uncommitted crime.

"Which means what?" said Jan.

"Who knows? Wait and see."

Again Andrew gave her that strange, mechanical, almost malicious grin, and for the next thirty years, off and on, Jan would find herself wondering if this had been a setup from the start.

"Gotta run," Andrew said, "and so should you. You won't, though. And that's fun, too." He gazed up at her with just a trace of longing. "Can't say I never stuck it to Snow White."

CHAPTER 6

CLASS OF '69

It was 2:15 A.M. when they left the dance floor and made their way up to the bar.

"Vodka on ice," Spook Spinelli told the bartender. "Two shots. Big glass. Squeeze in a lime—the whole lime—then crank it to the top with tonic."

"Always the glutton," said Marv Bertel.

"Always thirsty," said Spook. She moved a hand to his rump. On her ring finger, almost overlapping, were two large and pricey-looking wedding bands. Though past the half-century mark, Spook looked terrific in her metallic skirt and frosted hair and pricey rings.

"Your hand," Marv said gravely, "appears to have found my fanny."

"It *has.*"

"You're a married lady."

"More than most," she said. "Hurry up, now. Place your order."

Marv's chest hurt, and he was badly winded, but he tried not to show it. "Bourbon," he told the bartender. "Two shots, big glass, hold the lime rigmarole."

"You all right?" Spook said.

"Fat, not dead."

Spook looked at him. "All the same, we'll sit out a couple. And no more fast dancing."

They had been close friends in college. A one-way romance on Marv's part. Now, three decades overdue, there were signs that she might finally be returning his love. Things had flamed up at an afternoon cocktail party, developed over dinner, ripened on the dance floor.

When the drinks came, they toasted each other.

"What about the wife?" Spook said.

"Denver," he said.

"Think it's worth it?"

"Love?"

"No," Spook said. "The other part. The part with my hand on your butt."

Marv laughed and said, "Dream come true. It's worth it."

"You're positive?"

"Pretty sort-of positive."

They carried their drinks over to a table near the dance floor. The mood had long since dampened, and now an echoing, lonely-sounding radio provided the only music. Just over two dozen exhausted members of the class of '69 still moved to memory in the Darton Hall gym.

Beneath the table, Spook snaked a hand into Marv's lap. "Well, now," she said. "I suppose I should behave myself, shouldn't I?"

"Not essential," said Marv.

"You don't mind, then?"

"I do not."

"Thank you, sir. But you'll be sure to warn me if I accidentally start tugging?"

"I will."

"Is that the correct word? Tug?"

"Very close."

"And you *will* warn me?" said Spook. "Won't let me make a total tramp of myself?"

"I'll raise the red flag," he said.

Spook laughed and looked out at the dancers. Thirty-odd years ago Marv had gotten nowhere. They'd been the best of pals, as close as people get, but at times it had seemed that he was the only man on campus to be excluded from her romantic orbit. Still, Spook had always been a grab bag, full of endless mini-Spooks, and now she beamed a beguiling smile at him. Her teeth looked either capped or false. "What I don't understand," she said, "is why this didn't happen a long time ago. Before all the complications."

"Because you were in love with Billy McMann," said Marv. "And because Billy loved what's-her-face."

"Dorothy."

"Right you are. Dorothy. He loved Dorothy."

"And Dorothy loved—?"

"Her mirrors," Marv said.

Spook laughed again. "Fair enough. Even back then it was pretty complicated."

"Always is."

"Always, yes. Like now, for instance. This happy business in your lap."

"Happy lap, happy me."

"With Billy watching us. Dorothy, too."

"They're jealous," said Marv. "Three decades—who'd believe it?"

"Yes, but here's the question. Should we go to your room?"

"Why not yours?"

"James might call. Or Lincoln."

"The husbands?"

"Indeed," said Spook. "Married as all get-out. Well-wedded woman."

Marv leaned back in his chair, used a cocktail napkin to wipe the sweat from his forehead. He could feel the drums in his chest. "In that case," he said, "I guess we'd be smart to forget the hanky-panky. Like you say. Complicated."

"Your wife. Another fly in the ointment."

"Excellent example."

"And that sick heart of yours."

"The heart's fine," Marv said, though it was not fine. Six months ago things had been touch and go. He'd seen the famous tunnel up close, very impressive, which in part was what had brought him to the reunion. And Spook. For more than thirty years he'd speculated about the possibilities. Fantasy, of course, but over a lifetime he'd encountered no one like her, a woman so aware of her own force field, so unaware of what she wanted from the world. Even as a college kid Spook had taken huge emotional risks without knowing why, gambling on instinct, man after man, betting big, mostly winning, always trusting in chance and the purity of human motives. In 1969, just before graduation, she'd been suspended for appearing topless on the cover of the Darton Hall yearbook. A week later, after considerable controversy, the provost had seen fit to reinstate her on a freedom-of-the-press issue, plus Spook's very persuasive threat to display the remainder of her assets in a special issue of the campus newspaper. Marv had been editor that year. He'd supervised the photo shoot, personally delivered a packet of black-and-whites to the provost's office.

Through two troubled marriages, off and on, give or take, Marv had loved Spook Spinelli.

"So what we'll do," Spook was saying, "is we'll just pretend. No conjugals."

"It won't kill me."

"Won't it?"

"No. Anyway, I could use the magic." He looked at her. "I'll tell you a story. Promise not to laugh."

"I won't."

"Swear it."

Spook lifted her glass, took the oath.

"All right, then," Marv said. "Ludicrous story, I guess, but back in college, senior year, I got hooked on that dumb card game solitaire. I couldn't stop. This weird obsession or something. I'd tell myself, 'Marv, if you win this game, you win Spook, she'll come running.' A thousand times I did that. Ten thousand."

"Ever win?"

"Of course I won. No payoff. Too fat."

Spook shook her head. "You were my friend."

"Friend, thanks. Always a comfort."

"Sorry," she said. "It *is* complicated, isn't it?"

Marv stirred his drink for a time. "I'll say this. Those two hubbies of yours, they get high grades for tolerance, tough skins, all that. Don't mean to butt in, but if you ever need to talk about it ... The dough boy, he's still your friend."

"Not tonight. Boring."

"Only if you want to."

Spook put a thumb to her mouth, nibbling on it, gazing across the dance floor at Billy McMann. She seemed to be calculating something, time or distance. Plump flecks of mascara dotted her eyelashes.

"What's to tell you?" she finally said. "Fell in love. Got married. Fell in love with number two, forgot to fall out of love with number one." She chuckled to herself, closed her eyes, sighed and made a little what-the-hell motion with her head. "Give me credit, though. I'm loyal. And I won't stop loving you either."

"No?"

"Never. But you'd have to lose weight, clean out those arteries. Stop drinking."

"May I finish this one?"

"Down the hatch. Then we decide about the sleeping arrangements."

"Thought it was decided."

"Was it?"

"No," he said.

"One more drink," said Spook. "Then we decide."

They sat in silence, remembering things, imagining things, then Marv said, "Lincoln and James. Sounds like an English jam."

"It does, doesn't it?" Spook pulled her hand from his lap and massaged her temples. "Christ, I'm drunk."

"Let's disappear."

"Oh, let's," she said. "Except not quite now. I've promised Billy a dance."

"Naturally you did."

"Stop it. He's got Dorothy to deal with."

"You've got husbands."

"Marv, that's childish."

He looked down at the table and said, "Sorry," but he wasn't. A long time ago he'd been a fat college boy, now he was a rich and unhappy and much fatter manufacturer of mops and brooms. All-American fat cat, he reminded himself, with an inflated, failing heart. He could not help how he felt about Spook's two husband and Billy McMann and all the other eat-what-you-want bastards in her life.

"One question," he said. "Tell me how you manage it. Two houses? Two cocker spaniels?"

109

"You don't need to hear this."

"I sort of do."

Spook stared at him. "I'm not apple pie, Marv. Two houses, yes. Two beds. Two diaphragms—at least until a few years ago. Not necessary anymore."

"Both guys know?"

"Sure they know." She hesitated. "Listen, I'm screwed up, I realize that. Miserably and out-of-my-head screwed up. And sometimes—this is the truth—sometimes I just want to make a run for it. Anywhere. Escape." She looked across the gym. "There you are. Haywire. I'll go dance with Billy, then we're out of here."

"Go do that," Marv said.

"One dance. Two max."

"Right."

She clasped his hand, kissed it, smiled, then stood up and moved across the dance floor toward Billy McMann. Marv did all he could to avoid watching her. Eventually, he knew, she'd be back, though not for a while, and probably not for a long while. Both of her husbands, he was sure, would vouch for that.

He went to the bar, commandeered a bottle of bourbon, danced a few times with Amy Robinson, told broom jokes, laughed, made other people laugh. He was jolly. At one point he removed his shirt to allow old friends the pleasure of remarking on his enormous white belly, which was the belly that had preceded him through life and would no doubt precede him to his grave.

At 3 A.M. he called his wife in Denver.

A nightmare, he told her. No more reunions.

"Nothing," he said. "*Nothing's* wrong."

Later, he found himself in a men's room, woozy, examining a soiled square of floor tiling. What the place needed, he concluded, was a good, expensive mop.

It was almost four in the morning when Spook came up behind him. He sat alone at a littered table near the bandstand.

"Marv, Marv," she said.

"No late-night nookie?"

"Next time around, for sure. Thing is, I need to please the whole damn world. Everyone, no exceptions. Man, woman, child, beast."

"Billy McMann. Need to please Billy too?"

"It's my nature."

"What happened to Dorothy?"

"Husband, kids. I'm the sub."

"Many congratulations."

"Marv, don't hate me."

"Pals forever," he said.

Marv tried to stand but couldn't manage it. He dropped back into his chair, looked up at her, made a goofy face that was meant to convey standard fat-guy hurt.

"Keep a secret?" he said.

"For you, I sure can."

"Those pictures I gave the provost, remember?

Bareass Spook. So naked. So young. I've still got the negatives up in my attic."

Spook kissed his forehead.

"Enjoy," she said.

CHAPTER 7

WELL MARRIED

S pook Spinelli lived in an expensive brick house at 1202 Pine Hills Drive in White Bear Lake, Minnesota, a suburb of the Twin Cities. She also lived in a more modest house at 540 Spring Street in the same suburb. Spook was married to Lincoln Harwood, an attorney; she was married to James Winship, an associate professor of philosophy. Both husbands were aware of the arrangement and more or less accepted it. Spook had married Lincoln in 1985, James a year later. "I love you guys dearly," she'd told them, "and I don't see why we can't invent our own rules. I'll be faithful to both of you."

They were intelligent, open-minded children of the sixties. There was almost no contention. Initially, to be sure, Lincoln had articulated some displeasure at Spook's desire for a second husband, yet he adored her and realized that the alternative was to lose a wife he deeply cared for. Just as important, and much to his credit, Lincoln understood that relationships require fine-tuning, that Spook loved him no less, and that he wasn't losing a wife but gaining an in-law. On July 3, 1986, at a meeting convened in a coffee shop in downtown St. Paul, the three of them had hammered out an informal covenant. James, the philosopher, reviewed the ethical issues. Lincoln, the attorney, discussed problems of law. It was decided that Spook's second marriage, to James, would have to go unaccredited in the strictly legal sense; it would be a marriage of spirit and of domestic fact. Spook would split her time between the two households. She would reclaim her maiden name.

When the meeting adjourned, Lincoln clasped James's hand and said, "Welcome aboard."

By convention, and perhaps out of psychological need, we too often interpret the bizarre facts of our universe as mere farce, beneath belief. *Man Marries Pet Bengal Tiger*. Every day, in every newspaper, a reader's eye will fall upon some such headline, sometimes less peculiar, sometimes more so, and by and large the average good citizen will chuckle and congratulate himself on his own ferocious realism, his own more modest eccentricities, forgetting that for a man who loves his tiger—and who is to say he does not? you? your adulterous spouse?—the union between man and beast is in no respect whatsoever farcical or absurd or less than wholly solemn.

Whether we choose to credit the bizarre, to take it seriously, is finally irrelevant. The world does its work. The Holocaust. The Amazing Mets.

And so, defying at times their own credulity,

116

Spook and her two husbands made it through thirteen and a half years. There were instances of doubt and jealousy, even outright rivalry, yet both husbands were willing to adapt, willing to pay a price in return for Spook Spinelli's divided attention. They were good men. They loved her. They were also a trifle afraid of her, and afraid for her. They recognized the fragility at the core of Spook's personality, the tenuous grip she had on her mental health and perhaps on life itself. It would have been easy to say, as friends did say, that the arrangement couldn't last, that in the most fundamental sense it violated human nature. But it did last. And it was no farce, not for the principals. Their three-way union was relentlessly real, relentlessly pedestrian, with double the difficulties of any standard marriage: housework, meals, head colds, vacations, quarrels, reconciliations, car repairs. On Spook's part, life was exhausting, almost always hectic, but over time she learned to husband her resources. By nature, she was a woman who could handle it: self-confident, sometimes crafty, dexterous since girlhood in the art of making the men in her life feel desirable and at ease. She was a risk taker. She loved a challenge.

Bizarre or not, the arrangement might have endured indefinitely.

But at a party on the eve of the new millennium, when Spook fell for a young attorney named Baldy Devlin, her genius for romantic calibration collided with common sense. Enough became too much.

Four years out of law school, Baldy was a new hire in Lincoln's firm. He was half Spook's age, a long-distance runner, cowboy-rugged, smart, well spoken, far from bald. The nickname, apparently, was someone's idea of irony. "We're in trouble," Lincoln told James in the early morning hours of January 1, 2000. The two husbands, now somewhat testy cronies, stood near a fieldstone fireplace in Lincoln's living room. The party was at its peak, libidos at full burn, and Spook and Baldy had set up shop on a large white sofa Lincoln had purchased only a week earlier.

"She's smoking," said James, "on your new sofa."

Lincoln scowled. "Same crap when she met you. First thing she does, she lights up."

"Not on a sofa. Not with me."

"Right, in my Chevy," Lincoln said. He gave James a look. "That's not the point. Three's a crowd, four's a nightmare."

"Well," James said. "We could intervene."

"Spook Spinelli?"

"Right. True."

Lincoln laughed bitterly. "Look at that head of hair. Baldy, my ass."

Decades earlier, in 1969, Spook had campaigned vigorously to end the war in Vietnam, standing in candlelight peace vigils, occupying the Darton Hall admissions office during the spring of her senior year. Though politics bored her, at least in the abstract, Spook had loved the action of it all, the intimacy and the danger and the high passion. Ten of her fourteen collegiate sexual encounters had involved members of the movement, a statistic that did not include a janitor and a politically confused assistant chaplain. She had posed topless for the Darton Hall yearbook; she'd escorted six baffled young men to the senior prom. Not that Spook was promiscuous. Broad-minded, yes, and physically generous to the point of philanthropy, but without exception her heart remained in rough accord with her loins. She had a conscience. She'd loved them all. Yet it was also true that from the time Spook was a girl, she'd had great trouble with the word "no." She did not like disappointing people. She adored men and took pleasure in the knowledge that men adored her.

In the light of history, then, Spook could foresee no real difficulties in regard to Baldy Devlin. She'd been there before, numerous times, and knew how to keep a good many balls in the air.

"What we'll do," she announced on the morning of New Year's Day, "is play it by ear, see how things develop."

The four of them were seated in Lincoln's living room—Spook and Baldy on the new sofa, James in an armchair, Lincoln presiding from a barstool. None of them had slept. The room was cluttered with ill will and the debris of a new millennium.

"It might be a good idea," Spook said, "if we

all took a nice, deep, healthy breath. There's no reason to be hasty."

"You spent the night with that man," said James. He flicked his head at Baldy Devlin. "I'd call *that* hasty."

"Oh, for crying out loud," Spook said. "It's 2000, isn't it? Let's be adults."

"James *is* an adult," said Lincoln, "and he's pissed."

Spook nodded. She was making this up as she went along.

"Maybe so," she said, "but that just proves he's a male." She snuffed out a half-smoked cigarette and immediately lit up another. Her lime-green eyes were flashing. "I'm no history expert, but women've had to tolerate this sort of thing forever. What about Brigham Young? The Bible? Abraham and Jacob and David and horny old Solomon—it goes on and on." She sighed. "I thought we were enlightened about this."

"The issue isn't enlightenment," said James. "The issue is your heart."

Spook hooted. "My heart, you think?"

"I do," James said. He looked at Lincoln for support. "How far can you spread love—how thin—before it stops being love?"

"And becomes fucking," said Lincoln.

Baldy Devlin blushed, wiped his forehead, and put his mind to retying a shoelace. Spook gave the man's knee a pat.

"I hope I'm wrong," she said, "but it seems

there's a pride-of-ownership issue here. I'm not somebody's convertible." Again Spook attended to Baldy's knee. She was out of control. She knew that. She needed that. Risk made her the Spook she was, something more than the sad, mute Caroline she had been christened. Risk kept her away from household poisons. "Our new partner," she said, "wants to give this a chance. The four of us, I mean. Isn't that right, darling?"

"Four?" said Baldy.

"In for a dime, in for a dollar," said Spook.

Lincoln snorted. He was a tolerant man, low-key to the edge of drowsy, but now he found himself reaching for sarcasm. "What the lady means is," he said, "she means the more the merrier."

"Wants her cake," said James. "Wants to eat it too."

"Three cakes," said Lincoln.

Baldy Devlin rose to his feet. "Look," he said, "I'm no swinger. To tell the truth, I didn't know she was married at all. Name's Spinelli, right? No kidding, I didn't make the connection until—you know—until all those drinks got drunk, until it was too late." He glanced at James, then at Lincoln. "I'll just head for the door. Let you folks work this out."

"Don't be ridiculous," Spook said. She smiled and tapped the sofa. "Have a seat now."

"I'd rather—"

"Sit."

Baldy sat down.

"Here's an honest fact," Spook said. She was still smiling, but her smile had gone icy. "I won't be bullied, not by anything. If it's heart we're talking about, or love, or affection"—she paused and stared at James—"well fine, I care about each of you. And I won't let my emotions be dictated to me by some mom-and-pop idea of good behavior." She smiled again. "Am I pretty clear?"

"Pretty," James said. "Except sooner or later people make choices. Nobody gets it all."

"Who wrote that law?" said Spook.

"Common knowledge."

"Precisely. I'm *un*common. Got a problem with that, any of you, you're free to walk."

"In that case," Baldy said, and began to rise.

"Not you," said Spook.

As it turned out, Baldy Devlin did leave—rapidly, permanently—and he took with him Spook's unblemished record for sovereignty over the male gender. Over the next several weeks her phone calls to Baldy went unanswered, her e-mails vanishing into deep cyberspace. She had trouble sleeping. She gained four pounds and kept on eating. She could not summon the energy to visit her gym. For the first time in fifty-odd years, Spook noted slippage in her once stylish mix of charm and magnetism, an erosion of her womanly appeal, which until then had seemed both a blessing and a birthright. Small, ugly dimples pocked her buttocks. Her breasts seemed closer to the floor.

122

More than once, Spook broke down in tears. Meals arrived late at two tables. She began losing at canasta. Even her sex drive, once ravenous, disappeared entirely. Both marriages suffered.

Her unhappiness, Spook realized, had little to do with Baldy Devlin and very much to do with her own self-esteem. The man was handsome, yes, but hardly *that* handsome, and in other circumstances she might already have filed him away under "conquest" or "good fun." As it was, she could not evict Baldy's face from her thoughts.

She was sick of spirit. She was also frightened. She wanted no more lithium in her life, no more hospitals, no more dead people whispering in her ear.

Spook's husbands offered little help. Through the dreary days of January, they spent more time with each other—drinking, sulking—than with Spook herself. On an afternoon in early February, Lincoln moved out of the house on Pine Hills Drive, renting a small guest bedroom in James's more humble residence on Spring Street. "Until this gets settled," he told Spook, "it's obvious you need time alone. James and I, we'll batch it for a while."

Spook nodded. "Is he all right?"

"I guess. Doesn't feel much like a husband."

"No, I meant Baldy," she said. "You work with him. Does he ever—"

"Oh, *stuff* it," said Lincoln. He picked up his suitcase, strode to the front door, then turned and studied her. "A word to the wise," he said. "People who want everything, they end up with nothing."

Spook shrugged. "That's out of your stud handbook?"

"No," he said, more gently than she deserved.

It was not as if Spook had never known disappointment. On occasion, the extraordinary events of our universe can be explained by the purely conventional, the bizarre by the banal, and so with Spook Spinelli.

She had been born a twin—Caroline to her sister's Carolyn—both blond and lime-eyed, identical except for their kidneys. At age five Carolyn had fallen ill with renal disease. Seventeen months later she died, and over the next year Caroline stopped speaking: a word here, a word there, little more. She was in and out of hospitals, subjected to the probings of child psychologists, but in the end her muteness seemed willed, entirely volitional, a product not of disease but of some fierce internal stubbornness.

Her father nicknamed her Spook: to joke her into speech, to make light of the distanced, otherworldly quality that seemed to carry her through that terrible year.

She heard voices sometimes, mostly her sister Carolyn's. She reverted to thumb-sucking. She giggled in her sleep. She was kept out of kindergarten and a good part of first grade.

And then abruptly, just after her seventh birthday, Spook began talking again, whole sentences, as though she'd never stopped, and for the next five and a half years she was a normal, cheerful girl. People remarked on her lovely lime eyes, her sunny smile, her devil-may-care stance toward the world. Boys developed crushes. Teachers chuckled. An outrageous flirt, her father said. A born heartbreaker.

At age twelve, on a rainy August afternoon, Spook dug a shallow grave in her back yard. Her mother found her there, lying face-up in the rain, eyes closed, hands folded at her waist, soaking wet, pretty as a picture. Spook did not speak again for eight months.

Again there were hospitals, and this time drugs.

Again, too, the recovery was sudden.

"I didn't *need* to talk," she told her parents, and turned away, and said nothing more about it.

She was sweet. She didn't want to frighten anyone.

Except for one or two instances, Spook Spinelli's high school and college years passed with nothing more serious than a kind of charming exhibitionism. Public thumb-sucking, bared breasts in the yearbook, affairs with an assistant chaplain and a Marxist janitor and a wide assortment of very grateful students. She was well liked. She received excellent grades, shrugged off two abortions.

After graduating from Darton Hall in 1969, Spook left Minnesota for Los Angeles, where her beauty and zesty appetites soon brought her to the bed of a forty-one-year-old screenwriter known for his uneven work in the dying genre of the western. Within weeks she had traded up for an actor, succeeded by a busboy, succeeded in due course by the keyboardist for a wildly successful rock band. Spook's future looked promising. Her name appeared twice in *Variety*. She was photographed beside Ryan O'Neal at a charity event in the Hollywood Bowl. But in the end L.A. went sour, which was partly her own fault. The keyboardist had no patience for Spook's courtship of a marginally more famous, marginally richer, marginally better-looking drummer for a competing band.

"Chicks like you," the keyboardist told her on the night she was sent packing, "are what I write my saddest songs about."

Spook returned to the Twin Cities. In less than a year she was engaged to Lincoln Harwood. Fourteen years later she married him. A long engagement, but worth the wait. Lincoln was financially secure, receptive to her eccentricities, and took pride in being the sequel to a rock star. Beyond anything, he loved her. Absolute and unqualified love, which was what Spook Spinelli required.

In late February, a few weeks after Lincoln moved in with James, Spook hosted a strategy session with her two best friends, Jan Huebner and Amy Robinson. Amy had been divorced for just over a year, Jan for only a month, and their combined bitterness and realism brought wise counsel to the table.

They met in the Pine Hills Drive residence. Coffee was served. "You know where this Baldy guy eats lunch," Amy said. "Take a job as a hostess. Show him your menu."

"Work?" said Spook.

"Forget it," said Amy.

Jan Huebner cried. Then she said, "Spook, you're still beautiful—God knows how you do it—so why not be direct? Go to his house. Wear something slinky."

"Exactly," Amy said. "Same sly crud you did in college. This coffee's delicious."

"Kona," Spook said. "He won't see me."

"E-mails?" Jan said.

"Poof. Gone," said Spook. "As if I never wrote them."

For a time they sat thinking.

"Tell us more," Amy said. "Habits. Likes. Dislikes."

"Weaknesses," said Jan.

"Stuff we can use," said Amy.

Spook did her best to recall the New Year's Eve conversation, but it was now an obscure buzz of innuendo and rising expectations. "Well," she said, "he's a Vikings fan. Football, you know?"

"There you *are*," Amy said.

"Where?" said Spook.

"I'm not sure," said Amy.

Jan Huebner teared up again. Her ex-husband had been a Vikings fan.

"What about cartwheels?" Amy said. "A cheer-leader, just like the old days, except now you're—what?—fifty-three, fifty-four years old. A novelty act, it'll knock him dead."

"Fifty-three," Spook said crossly. "And I was never a cheer-leader."

"No?"

"No," said Spook. She got up and stiffened their Kona with shots of bourbon.

"Well, gosh," Jan sniffled, "you sure dressed like one. Everybody else in blue jeans, maybe a T-shirt, you show up in tinfoil shorts."

"Not *tinfoil*," Spook said sharply.

"Tinfoil," Amy said. "Tight tinfoil."

"Metallic," said Spook. She smiled in recollection. "Flattering, I thought. Guys loved them."

"Speaking of which," Amy said, "you owe me an apology. Billy McMann. Flash the tinfoil, steal him away."

"That was love," Spook said.

"This coffee *does* rule," said Jan.

Amy's voice rose. "Give me a break. You didn't have to wreck it with Billy. My one chance."

"Let's not fight," Jan said.

"Let's," Amy said. "Unless she apologizes."

"Apologize," Jan said.

Spook shrugged. "Fine. I'm sorry. Billy loved me, though, and I loved him."

"For six minutes," Amy said.

"Stop it," said Jan, "or I'll cry." She pinched the bridge of her nose, blinked away the sting of a bitter divorce, a bitter marriage. "Listen, here's what Spook should do. She should march right into this guy's office—this Baldy manipulator—and she should pin him right to the wall and pry out some answers. He slept with you, right? On New Year's Eve?"

"Pretty much."

"Pretty much?" said Amy.

Spook gazed into her coffee as if searching for something. "Lots of booze," she said. "I'm not sure he completely understood—you know—what happened."

"Which was?" said Amy.

"Cut it out. I needed the action. I'm *married*, for Pete's sake."

"I'll say," said Jan.

"In other words," said Amy, "the guy was in dreamland?"

"Not totally."

"I'm about to puke," said Jan.

Amy Robinson took Spook's hand, held it for a second, then tapped her twin wedding rings. "This'll strike you as simplistic," she said, a little pompously, "but those two husbands of yours, they're nice people. More than nice. They're terrific. Jan and me, we've got zero. Try an empty house. Try going without."

"Try loneliness," said Jan Huebner.

"Try a vibrator," said Amy.

Spook spread out her hands in exasperation. She wanted to speak, wanted to stand up for herself, but a deadening fatigue had come over her. Almost always desperate. Almost always afraid. Something sad and familiar was happening in her head, like a curtain coming down.

Baldy Devlin was no longer the point. Spook wasn't sure if there was a point. She could scarcely recall the man's face, or what had so attracted her, or how she had ended up at this empty place in her life. She felt the horrifying press of middle age, plus the bourbon and the ghosts and the guilt and the endless pursuit.

Nothing Spook could do. She let herself slide away.

At one point she giggled.

At another point, late in the afternoon, she put a thumb to her mouth and said, "Oh, hi," but no one heard her, and after that she said nothing at all.

It lasted less than a month this time. James and Lincoln helped her through it, attentive and forgiving, and even Baldy Devlin showed up one day with flowers and good wishes. Spook watched the sunlight come and go. She ate meals, did some housework, allowed her husbands to hold her on alternate nights. If she had wanted to, she could've spoken much earlier, could've laughed and risen out of her silence and plunged headlong into some new and exhilarating affair of the heart. Instead, she claimed those days as her own. She allowed herself to be loved, found refuge in a doubled domesticity. What to an ill-informed, self-congratulatory stranger might have appeared peculiar or even bizarre—Lincoln pouring her morning coffee, James spooning in the sugar—was to Spook Spinelli a matter of the highest exigency, as essential as fresh meat to a Bengal tiger. Not that there weren't tradeoffs. There were many. And sooner or later, Spook knew, the curious circumstances she'd been given, or perhaps had chosen, would almost certainly lead to terrible things: a rainy day, a backyard grave.

On a morning in late March, as she neared the end of her silence, Spook was visited by Jan Huebner and Amy Robinson. Both friends, like both husbands, were solicitous and understanding, their voices pitched low in deference to a larger, more catholic quiet. They kept Spook entertained with talk about their recent triumphs and troubles, news from old friends, an approaching college reunion. "I think it's sometime in July," Amy Robinson said, "so you've got a few months to get yourself together, plug up the leaks."

"So to speak," said Jan Huebner.

"Go shopping for tinfoil," Amy said. "Billy'll be there, I bet anything."

"All six-three of him," said Jan.

"Lying down," said Amy.

Spook smiled a dreamy smile. Right then, she could've spoken, and almost did.

She closed her eyes, put a thumb to her mouth.

Already, in her rich imagination, Carolyn and Caroline were gliding hand in hand into the Darton Hall gymnasium, toenails blood red, hair highlighted, decked out in their matching bronze-and-silver miniskirts—maybe spike heels, maybe those sexy push-up bras to lead the way.

Maybe Lincoln and James might come along. Maybe Baldy Devlin as a backup.

Or maybe no one.

Maybe this once she'd go alone.

CHAPTER 8

CLASS OF '69

I have breast cancer. I'm fifty-two. Fifty-three in a week."

"All the same," said Billy. "Still gorgeous."

Dorothy Stier shook her head and looked away. "One never says, 'I had cancer.' One says, 'I have cancer.' It's like with brown eyes or a birthmark. You carry it to the grocery store. You take it to the cemetery."

"I'm sure," said Billy.

They stood, half facing each other, at the edge of the dance floor. It was well after 4 A.M., and the gym was deserted except for nine or ten die-hard members of the class of '69.

Billy tried to hurt her with his eyes.

"Ron?" he said.

"Fine. Rich. Pair of Volvos. Waxes the steel out of them."

"And those boys of yours?"

"Not boys anymore," Dorothy said, and laughed. "They're terrific. You'll probably meet them tomorrow."

"No."

"It wouldn't be a problem."

"Still no."

"Billy, that's absurd. Nobody cares what happened a whole lifetime ago."

"Nobody, nobody," he said.

"I didn't mean nobody."

"I think you did."

"Billy, be sweet. Meet the boys."

"Thanks," he said. "Not my cup of tea."

Dorothy frowned. "Dance, then?"

"Too little, too late. Maybe a drink."

"What's that in your hand?" said Dorothy. "Come on, please. One happy dance."

"Cancer?"

"Eight nodes, three years ago. I've got a chance. You used to adore dancing."

"I used to."

"Do you hate me?"

"It helps."

She rotated her jaw slightly, in the old way. Her makeup was thick and unconvincing. She looked ill. "Listen, I did what I had to do. My God, Billy, when does it stop?"

"What's the 'it'?"

"Hate," she said. "Wanting to hurt me."

"No kidding?" he said.

"Billy, let's dance."

"Can't do it. Dance with Ron."

Billy turned and moved to one of the tables in the darkness beyond the dance floor. For some time he sat alone, watching the tired faces bob above their name tags. Later, Dorothy came up to him and said, "Do you really want to leave it like this?"

"Like what?"

"May I sit down?"

She sat on his lap.

"Better?" she said.

"Erases everything," he said. "Those two boys of yours. Do they have my eyes?"

"Billy—"

"Big blue eyes?"

"Your eyes," she said, "are not blue."

"Right. They are not fucking blue."

"You do hate me."

"Ron's eyes," said Billy. "What shade of blue should we call Ron's eyes?"

"I don't see the point."

"No. You don't."

"Maybe I shouldn't sit here."

"Maybe not."

Dorothy pushed to her feet, not gracefully, and looked down on him. She took his glass from the table. "I can be drunk too. I can be cruel."

She drank up his whiskey. Then she drank the remains of three other glasses that had been left on the table.

"What good is it to hurt me?" she said. "I was young. I wanted some things, like a normal life, and you were just . . . You were gone."

"Gone. Odd word."

"He wanted to marry me. He adored me."

"And I was gone."

"You were."

"It's not Siberia," he said. "Indoor malls. Not so gone."

"Well, it felt that way, Billy. Like Siberia." Dorothy stepped over to an adjacent table and came back with someone's drink. "Do you dare me?"

"Go ahead."

She drank it fast. "You know what the statistics say? Eight nodes—five to seven years. Like a manslaughter sentence."

"Ron can afford the funeral."

"Will you please, please dance with me?"

"Please, please," he said.

"I'll dance alone, Billy. I'll take my shirt off."

"Brave you," he said.

"You think I won't?"

"I think you won't."

She went off somewhere. Later on he saw her dancing alone. It ought to have been embarrassing, which it partly was, because she was drunk and loud and fifty-two, almost fifty-three, with a husband and two grown boys, but it was also true that Dorothy was a sensible woman and kept her shirt on.

CHAPTER 9

WINNIPEG

Billy McMann left the country on July 1, 1969, eighteen days after graduating from Darton Hall. He had waited as long as he dared. At 11:30 that morning, after twice changing his reservation, Billy boarded an Air Canada flight that arrived in Winnipeg in early afternoon. His life was packed in three small suitcases.

At immigration he declared himself a tourist, showed his passport, picked up his bags, and cleared customs in under a minute. There were no questions. There were no cops, no FBI agents waiting with handcuffs. He took a cab to a downtown hotel, where he checked in, showered, put on jeans and a T-shirt, stared into the bathroom mirror. A tall, scared kid with a ponytail stared back. "God, please," he said. Then he called his parents in southwestern Minnesota. Billy had practiced his speech many times, searching for an efficient way to say things, yet he found himself in emotional trouble as he explained to his mother what he'd just done.

She was bewildered at first, then angry.

"It's your life," his mother said, "and I suppose

you're entitled to ruin it." There was a buzz of static. "I'll put your dad on."

His father understood. He would wire money. He would talk to Billy's mother.

"It's the right thing," Billy said.

"Sure it is."

"I'm sorry."

His father made a coughing noise and tried to laugh. "Well, hey," he said. "The right thing. Your own words. Now where do I send the dough?"

When he hung up, Billy gathered himself and dialed Dorothy Stier's number in St. Paul. There was no answer. Dorothy was terrified, no doubt—afraid of the telephone, afraid of the poignant and very sensible excuses she would invent for having missed their flight.

Billy waited an hour, tried again, then went out for a walk toward the river. Hard to believe, he thought. Still July 1, 1969. Still Billy McMann. All around him the world seemed impossibly ordinary: people eating ice cream cones, people chatting on street corners. It was hard for Billy to know what to feel. Relief, yes, but also guilt and fear. At times he seemed to slip outside himself, hovering there, a spectator to his own life. Other times he felt like an outlaw.

He had supper in a Chinese restaurant on Provencher Boulevard, returned to the hotel, and again tried Dorothy Stier's number in St. Paul. She did not pick up until well past midnight.

"Just listen to me," she said.

He laughed.

"I was packed, Billy. Actually jumped in a cab, made it halfway to the airport. I'm a coward, I guess."

"I guess you are," he said.

"Don't."

"Don't what?"

"You *know* what," she said. "This is killing me, I can barely breathe, and I wish you'd just listen. I can't stop crying. All day, all night. It feels like—I'm not sure—it feels like my brains are jumbled, like I'm inside a cement mixer."

He pictured Dorothy at her kitchen table: those smart brown eyes, the year-round tan, the well-bred, well-schooled sorority-girl smile that could mean almost anything. She would be reading from notes, keeping her story straight.

"I'm twenty-one years old, Billy, and I can't just run away from everything. It's too dreamy, too romantic."

"Too romantic?"

"I didn't mean it that way."

"I believe you did."

Dorothy cried, or pretended to cry. Afterward, she said, "You don't *want* to understand, do you? All I meant, I meant it was this impossible, dumb fantasy. Wearing peasant dresses. Living in the woods."

"Winnipeg," said Billy, "is not the woods."

"But *you* know."

143

She wasn't crying now. She was thinking. "Anyway. When I got in that cab, I couldn't make myself believe anymore. We're different people. I'm a Republican, Billy. I'm an American. I can't help it."

Later, as an afterthought, she said, "It's not that I don't love you."

Then she said, "I could visit sometime. We could talk."

He knew what was coming next.

"Billy, I'm sorry," she said, with feeling, but in a tone that was more exculpatory than apologetic.

Curiously, Billy did not picture Dorothy's face. What he saw instead was a silver bracelet he'd given to her on Valentine's Day. She had hugged him and teared up. But he had never seen that bracelet again, nor had she ever mentioned it. Which was her way. With Dorothy you had to pay attention to things that were never said, the erasures and elisions.

Right now, for instance, she did not say, "Billy, I love you more than anything," because she did not love him more than anything. She loved cashmere. She was a good person in many ways—witty and bright and visceral and generous and tough-minded—but all that goodness sometimes got smothered by privilege and caveman politics.

Billy wanted to weep. Instead, he seized his anger. "I canceled two flights," he said. "Called a dozen times, two dozen. No answer."

"I was afraid."

"I know very damn well you were afraid."

"Don't swear at me. And don't be cruel or I'll hang up."

He snorted. "Cruel was three nights ago. Under the sheets. When you forgot to mention I'd be flying off alone."

"I wasn't sure then."

"It sounded sure. All those promises."

There was a whirring on the line, as if an air conditioner had clicked on inside Dorothy's head. "I guess you're right," she said, but her tone suggested that he was only partly right, that promises were contingent. "I shouldn't have been so definite. I've admitted that. It was a mistake."

"What about the getting married part?"

"Billy, I wish—"

"That brick house. Those babies you wanted?"

Dorothy's tone went petulant. "Well," she said. "It's obvious you despise me."

"That's insane."

"Is it? Always so high and mighty. Never wrong about anything."

Pretty city, but Winnipeg played with his head. Dreams of exile: Nixon in hot pursuit, numerous sirens and searchlights and barking dogs. Even by daylight, just walking along the river or sitting alone in a park, Billy had the sensation of being watched by an unknown authority on issues of right and wrong—the Mounties, maybe, or his mother, or a smiling Buddha. In a restaurant one morning, over boiled eggs, he started crying. On other occasions a kind of paralysis came over him, a spiritual shut-down, and he'd close the hotel room drapes and lie in bed, staring at the television. He had no friends in the city. He had no job. He had no ambitions that reached beyond the next sunrise.

For months, during his senior year at Darton Hall, Billy had been fantasizing about this, coordinating things with Dorothy, but in the end it had come down to impulse. The draft notice had arrived eight days after graduation. He had cleaned out his savings account, purchased a pair of one-way plane tickets, packed his bags, and waited at the airport until he could wait no longer.

Billy called her again after two weeks. He tried to keep things hopeful, but the conversation soon weakened. They listened to each other's desperation. Dorothy finally said, "I will try to visit. Maybe in a month or two."

"Where's the bracelet?" he said.

"Bracelet?"

Billy nodded at an open window. There were elm trees and telephone wires. "Forget it. Are you dating someone?"

"I wouldn't call it dating."

"You wouldn't?"

"No."

Dorothy started to add something, probably a qualifier, but in his head Billy could already hear all the other names she might call it.

"Ron?" he said.

"Not just Ron."

"Fine. Mainly Ron?"

"Mainly, I guess."

"How mainly?"

"Just mainly," she said. "Stop it."

Billy looked out at the telephone wires.

"Sure, come visit," he said. "Mainly bring Ron."

The first month had the feel of a dream. Impossible colors, vulgar shapes and vulgar sounds, a horrifying new weight to the world.

Billy cut off his ponytail.

He stopped brushing his teeth.

Sometimes he laughed at himself. Sometimes a pointless rage swept over him: rage at Dorothy and at his country and at smart people who came up with smart reasons to kill other smart people. There were always reasons. Attila had reasons. Once, when he'd tried to express this to Dorothy, she had asked what he would do if someone tried to rape her—wouldn't he fight back? wouldn't he kill the creep?—and Billy had said Yes, if a VC rapist showed up at Darton Hall, flew in from Hanoi, in that case he'd hustle right over and dispatch the little pervert. This had gotten him nowhere. Dorothy was patriotic and abstemious of thought. Irony was not in her repertoire. "That's absurd," she'd said, and Billy had grinned and said No, it was one of those excellent reasons to kill people, the old Greek reason.

He worried that he might be going mad.

Movement was a problem. His body had become stone. On many mornings he had trouble prying himself out of bed. He watched TV. He talked aloud to Dorothy. He delivered long, intricately argued lectures to God, defending himself, explaining his motives.

Hey, you, he'd say.

He'd say, *Come on, I'm just a kid.*

In early August, down to his last hundred dollars, Billy made himself do something. After two days he found a decent job in a branch of the Winnipeg public library system—part clerk, part janitor.

To remain in Canada, he was told, it would be necessary to secure something called "landed immigrant status," which meant crossing back into the United States and then recrossing again into Canada with evidence of employment. The prospect terrified him. For a week Billy found excuses to put it off, but on August 17 he rented a car and headed south down Highway 7. Three hours later he was waved across the border outside a little town in Minnesota. He had lunch there, thought about calling Dorothy, decided against it, and checked into a motel for his final night as an American.

He slept an hour at most.

On the morning of August 18, 1969, at 10 A.M., Billy McMann took a seat in a small, pine-scented office on the Canadian border. He presented his employment papers and birth certificate. An immigration officer brought him a cold Pepsi.

Altogether, it took just over two hours.

Midway through the paperwork, when Billy wept a little, the officer said, "Tough thing—it has to be—so if you're not sure . . ."

"What's sure?" Billy said.

The man shook his head and said, "Don't know."

A week later, Billy rented a cheap apartment in the St. Boniface district of Winnipeg. It was the place he and Dorothy used to imagine for themselves: oak floors, high ceilings, a big bay window over-looking a boulevard shaded by giant elms.

Billy bought a camera, snapped photographs of the apartment, and mailed the undeveloped film to Dorothy Stier.

Four years passed. Dorothy never called.

Billy's pain hardened into resentment, then into something close to hatred.

In 1974 he became a Canadian citizen. In 1975 he married a librarian from Calgary. He opened a hardware store, bought a car, had a baby girl. But the bitterness remained with him. There were times when he'd lie in bed beside his wife, feeling dark and restless, full of guilt, full of anger, wondering how things might have turned out if he had gone to the war and died politely.

Not that Billy doubted his own judgment. He had done the right thing, or what he believed was right. But without Dorothy the right thing often felt wrong.

Billy was careful not to mention any of this to his wife. He stayed silent, which seemed necessary, but which increased the guilt. He wanted to be a family man, to give himself completely, but all he could do was pretend. He expanded his hardware store, bought a modest three-bedroom house, feigned contentment at the dinner table. By and large he got away with it. Now and then, though, his wife would stop whatever she was doing and just look at him. The corners of her lips would move.

"What?" he'd say.

In April of 1985 Billy's wife was killed by a hit-and-run driver.

Three months later Dorothy called.

"It was in the alumni bulletin," she said. "I'm sorry."

"How's Ron?" Billy said, and broke the connection.

She called back in twenty minutes.

"Did that help?" she said. "Hanging up?"

"It was a try," he said.

"I can't undo things, Billy. I can't go backward and get on that airplane."

"You didn't say how Ron's doing."

"Ron's fine. He feels terrible too—about your wife, the accident." She seemed nervous, but not too nervous. "Did they catch him? The driver?"

"No. How's Ron?"

"Stop that."

"Stellar human being. The guy married yet?"

"You know very well he's married."

"Right, think I heard. Fancy wedding. And who's the lucky, lucky gal?"

"Billy, what do you want me to say? Do you want me to say it was all my fault?"

"Yes."

"It was my fault."

"You forgot a word."

"All," she said.

He hung up again and waited the rest of the night, and then he waited another eighteen months. When she called again, Billy said, "I'll bet he's rich, isn't he? I'll bet you live in a house with a swimming pool. Huge lawn. Big white columns out front. Statues of Agnew."

He had been rehearsing these lines for a long while, not just the words but also the brightness in his voice.

"You wouldn't believe the progress up here," he told her. "Running water. Canned goods."

"Are you finished?"

"Tanning salons."

Dorothy waited.

When he'd exhausted his playbook, she said, "I hurt you. What do you want me to do?"

"Do?" he said.

"I thought you might want to talk." She made a soft, releasing sound in her throat that he recognized from years ago. He could imagine her stately posture. "You have a little girl?"

"Susie," he said.

"Susie. Pretty name."

"Yes."

"And she's—"

"Ten going on a hundred," Billy said. "Very cute, very everything good. Like her mother."

"I'm sorry. Losing someone you love."

"Nothing new," he said.

He looked over at his daughter, who stood scowling at him.

He turned his back and said, "Anyway, there was always this cold shadow in the way. Imagine the shame."

"I'm not cold."

"What are you, then?"

"I'm Dorothy. Nothing else." She made the releasing sound again, not quite a sigh. "I'll stop calling, Billy. Except nobody should hold a grudge this long."

Billy laughed. "Where's the bracelet?"

"Which bracelet?"

"There's my answer."

Dorothy's voice turned brittle, almost snappish. "I think you'd better see someone," she said. "All that bitterness. It isn't healthy."

"Give Ron a big wet kiss for me."

After he'd hung up, Billy's daughter stared. "Well," she said. "Now you're kissing men?"

By 1991 Billy owned a chain of four hardware stores, plus a lumberyard and a successful roofing company. He was vice president of the Winnipeg Rotary Club, secretary of the Winnipeg Arts Council. He had not remarried.

In October of that year, Billy hired a young woman to handle his accounts. She appeared one day, vastly overqualified, wanting a job. Her name was Alexandra Wenz. Right away, Billy felt an attraction, something mysterious, something beyond biology. She was tall and quiet and smart, very efficient, very grave, with slate-blue eyes and red hair. After a few months they began dating. On their fourth night out, when he tried to kiss her, Alexandra confessed that she had killed Billy's wife. "I was seventeen," she said. "I've been wanting to . . . Christ, I don't know what. Talk to you."

Billy's hands were still clasped against the small of her back.

"Seventeen," Alexandra said, "and scared."

They were standing on her doorstep. It was just after midnight. There was a bright half-moon, the sound of crickets in the grass behind them.

"So I drove away," she said. "Had the car fixed in Kenora. Didn't talk about it, not to anybody. No one ever knew." Alexandra swept her red hair back, looked at him with a question shaping itself

153

at her forehead. "Sometimes I'd call your house. You'd answer and I'd take a big breath and start to talk, explain what happened, but I couldn't get the words out, not a sound, so I'd just listen for a while. Must've done that a hundred times."

Billy nodded. He took his hands from her waist.

"You can turn me in," she said. "I don't care anymore."

She unlocked the door to her apartment, looked at him briefly, made a strange slashing gesture with her hand, and went inside. Billy followed. They sat in her kitchen, on barstools, facing each other across a countertop.

Billy still heard crickets, even with the windows closed.

"All that time went by," Alexandra said, "and then one day I had to do something. Saw your help-wanted ad in the paper. Walked in. Asked for the job. Because—who knows—because finally I couldn't stand it anymore. I had to face you, or it, or whatever." She looked up. "Please say something."

Billy shook his head.

"You can turn me in," she said again.

"I won't turn you in."

"But you can. Should, I guess."

Alexandra sat still, watching him, waiting. "Do you want to kill me?"

"No," said Billy.

"I wouldn't blame you."

She pushed to her feet, filled two glasses with water, carried them over to the countertop. "This is hard, but I'll say it. She jumped. Your wife, I mean. On purpose. One second she was on the curb, just standing there, then she sort of lifted up one of her hands, sort of winced, sort of smiled, and then she was right there in front of me. Jumped. I'm seventeen years old—poisoned my life."

Billy wasn't surprised. It made sense.

"Well," he said. "I poisoned hers."

"You did something?"

"Yes. Or didn't."

They were quiet for many minutes. They listened to the crickets. Alexandra drank down her water and looked at him. "You want to sleep with me?"

"I do."

"Will it be evil?"

"I don't know. Maybe."

He called his babysitter, and Alexandra put a frozen pizza in the oven, and they took off their clothes and had sex at the kitchen counter. Later, they ate the pizza in bed.

Alexandra told him about her childhood, about an absent father and a mother who wanted her daughter to be a majorette. "That's all my poor, nutso mom ever talked about," Alexandra said, "all that majorette twaddle, like it was a life goal or something, like it was some special career. Crazy, you know? My mother. She called me Allie, not

Alexandra, because the last thing she wanted was a *complicated* majorette."

Billy talked, too.

He talked about Dorothy Stier, and about obsession. He explained how his wife used to stare at him, maybe intuiting, maybe knowing, and how in the end a ridiculous grudge had destroyed both her life and his own, as if he'd murdered her, as if he'd pushed her in front of the car.

"You didn't," said Alexandra.

"Almost."

"This Dorothy, you should call her up. Tell her what happened, what she's involved in."

"It's three in the morning."

"What's the number?"

He gave Alexandra the number and she dialed and passed the phone to Billy. It was a surprise when Dorothy answered. Her voice came from 1969, girlish, untouched by what time can do to voices.

Billy listened for a moment and hung up.

"Answering machine," he told Alexandra.

A few seconds later the phone rang.

"Star sixty-nine," said Dorothy. "A different world, Billy. Can we finally talk?"

"Not now."

"When, then?"

"Someday," he said.

There was a hesitation. "Billy, I can't see why . . . We're getting old."

"You'll survive."

"*Old*, Billy."

"I suppose so," he said. "How's Ron?"

Billy and Alexandra saw each other for five months. They shared the burden of guilt, which was a comfort, and over time Billy came to appreciate Alexandra's sad blue eyes, and her courage, and her tentative smile, and the way she approached the world from the inside out. In the end, however, there was too much between them. Sometimes it was as if Billy's wife were sitting on the couch with them, or curled up at the foot of their bed. There was Dorothy, too.

"Maybe I'll head for Dallas," Alexandra said. "Become a Cow-girl. Not quite a majorette, but close. Develop a cleavage. Make my mother happy."

Billy said, "You made *me* happy."

"A little, I hope."

"A lot."

"Well, that's good," she said. Her eyes were ancient and sad and wise. "Except we both know too much. Sometimes it's best not to know things."

"We could keep trying," said Billy.

"And Dorothy?"

"Forget Dorothy."

"Lovely thought," Alexandra said, and shook her head. "But it's like somebody died and you're still hugging the corpse. She must've been pretty phenomenal."

"No. Pretty ordinary."

"Too bad for me. I'll work on ordinary."

Alexandra smiled. She was very beautiful, Billy decided, and very, very kind, and it crossed his mind that on top of everything else he had now lost the rest of his life.

"The thing is, I love you," Alexandra said. "But I need a guy who can look at me."

Billy's mother died on September 19, 1992. Two days later, with his daughter in the car beside him, he crossed the border at International Falls.

"Your eyes seem weird," Susie said, and Billy said, "Are they?" and after a moment his daughter flicked her eyebrows and said, "Weirder than weird. Old-man weird."

They attended the funeral in Billy's hometown, stayed a few days with his father, then drove north to the Twin Cities.

Billy called Dorothy from their room in the St. Paul Hilton.

"Let's have a drink," he said. "Meet at the airport."

"You're after symmetry?"

"No," he said. "Show up."

Dorothy laughed a deft little laugh, flirtatious but meaningless, the way she laughed in college. "Well, fine, but I'm too smart for stacked decks. Anywhere else. Not the airport."

They met in the hotel's coffee shop.

It was no surprise, really, but Dorothy looked just about as he'd imagined: expensively dressed, expensively tanned, her hair cut short and colored to the ivory blond of her college years. She tried to kiss him, but Billy wouldn't allow it.

They sat in a curved corner booth, which made it easier to avoid excessive eye contact, excessive emotion.

"Ron knows you're here?"

Dorothy's gaze went to the table. "Well, no," she said. "Not yet."

"Do me a favor," Billy said. "Don't tell."

She moved her jaw slightly, that rotating action, then unfolded her napkin and spent a few moments spreading it in her lap. Her eyes were glittery and shrewd.

"All right, fine," she said.

"Fine?"

"I won't say anything."

Billy nodded. It struck him that he was fortunate not to have married this woman.

They ordered vodka tonics, their old drink, and then for what seemed a very long while he listened to Dorothy chat about their Darton Hall classmates, about her two boys and Ron's triumphs at Cargill. The whole time, though, Billy had trouble concentrating. For more than twenty years he had envisioned this conversation, all the ways he'd make her hurt, but now he was unclear about what he wanted. He couldn't locate the bitterness. As Dorothy discussed her insomnia—how she'd get up at two in the morning and bake bread—Billy found himself gazing at the smooth, glossy tip of her nose. It was as if he were watching a muted TV, a close-up of some familiar, weathered actress in a skin cream commercial.

At one point, after she'd thoroughly explored the topic of vacation homes, Billy reached out and pushed a thumb against her nose. "Let me ask something," he said. "Do you mind?"

She shook her head. He took his thumb away.

"One question. If you look at your life, the whole ritzy deal, can you think of anything—I mean, anything at all—that you regret? One item? One mistake? Anything?"

She looked at him sourly, puzzled, as if he were administering an exam for which she'd forgotten to study.

She sighed. "I guess you're talking about water over the dam."

"I guess I am," Billy said.

Dorothy crossed her legs and beamed at him; she had already composed herself. "Ron's been a dream, if that's what you're getting at."

"Not exactly."

"What then?"

"Nothing," Billy said. He beamed right back at her and raised his glass. "Salute to Ron."

"Do you want me to say I made a huge mistake? That I should've run away with you?" She gave him a look he couldn't decipher. "I don't wish for that, Billy."

"My loyal buddy Ron."

"Well, he was."

"Was."

Dorothy glanced away. "You've made a point. Maybe now you feel better—I hope so—but it doesn't change anything." She stopped for a second. "I'm happy."

"A committed woman?"

"Of course."

"No affairs, then?"

"Me?"

She laughed.

She was lying.

It didn't matter now.

Billy let her maneuver the conversation back to her kids, who were fantastically and terrifically astounding.

After ten minutes he said he had to go.

Dorothy took his arm as they crossed the lobby, erect posture, smiling, looking up at him as if she expected an invitation. It was not a come-on, Billy realized. It was sexy and rigid and empty; it was Dorothy's way of being polite. She asked if his daughter was upstairs, and Billy told her no, that Susie had gone off to a movie, and then again there was a meaningful void while Dorothy waited for the opportunity to be both nostalgic and perfectly content with her life.

"Billy, if you're ever in town again—"

"I sure will," he said.

"Come to dinner. Seriously. Ron likes you."

"Ron would."

He walked her outside, said goodbye, went

up to his room, took a shower, turned on the TV, lay down, and thought about all the squandered years.

It was an hour before his daughter returned from the movies.

"So how was it?" Susie asked.

Billy said it was fine.

"Tried to seduce you, right?"

"Unh-uh."

"What does 'unh-uh' mean?"

"It means no. She wanted a tennis partner."

For a few minutes Billy stared at the television, a cartoon of some sort, then he chuckled and asked his daughter if she'd like to take a road trip, maybe see something of her father's country. Maybe the Grand Canyon. Maybe Texas.

"You're Canadian," Susie said.

"That's true."

"Why, then?"

"No special reason," Billy said. "Because I lived here once."

CHAPTER 10
CLASS OF '69

A T 8 A.M. on Saturday, July 8, 2000, a scant eighteen members of the class of '69 assembled for a buffet breakfast in the Darton Hall student union. Among the absent were Spook Spinelli, Dorothy Stier, Billy McMann, Marv Bertel, Amy Robinson, Jan Huebner, a prominent physician, a mother of three, and the morning's breakfast speaker, Minnesota's lieutenant governor.

Paulette Haslo arrived late, haggard and regretful. She sat down with Ellie Abbott and Marla Dempsey. Only Marla had an appetite.

"About last night," Paulette said. "I'm really, really sorry. What a nincompoop."

"Sorry for what?" said Marla.

"God," Paulette said, "I'm not even sure. That's what I'm apologizing for."

They laughed and sipped their watered-down college coffee and made small talk, sliding from topic to topic, avoiding the hazardous. After twenty minutes, David Todd rattled a spoon in his glass. He stood up, steadied himself, and delivered a short, mostly comical talk as a proxy for the scheduled speaker. He said he regretted dropping out of Darton Hall after his junior year, but there was a war to win and he'd felt obligated to bludgeon to death myriad VC with his amazing right leg. Lethal leg, he said. Westmoreland had offered big moola for the patent. In any case, he'd finally graduated with the class of 1992, whose reunions he also attended, but whose females were decidedly inferior to those of '69. A fraction younger, he said. A fraction lighter on the scales. More acrobatic, by far. But all in all, he said, the class of '92 was not blessed with a single female graduate who could compare with, say, just for example, Marla Dempsey. "As you know," David said, "I majored in Marla here at Darton Hall, and then for almost ten years afterward. Mostly got D's, I'm afraid—ended up with a big fat F—but I'll love her forever."

People applauded. When he sat down, Marla excused herself and went over to David's table.

"Pity," Paulette said. "What's it take to be *happy* these days?"

"Happy?" Ellie said.

The two women exchanged a look. Neither of them had slept much.

"Listen," Ellie said, "you're a minister, right?"

"In a manner of speaking. Unemployed at the moment."

Ellie nodded, drew a breath, and said, "Want to take a walk?"

★　　★　　★

Just after 9 A.M. Spook Spinelli woke up in a tiny, concrete-walled dorm room on the top floor of Flarety Hall. Billy McMann lay snoring beside her. For a few minutes Spook watched him sleep. She felt some regret, and mild embarrassment, and a strange sadness just behind her eyes. Pity, she thought. Even dear Billy—bless his heart, bless his willie—even this sweet, wonderful man could not relieve the pressure on her heart, the need to drink from a fire extinguisher, to become a dead sister. For years the fantasies had come and gone. Now they were constant.

She kissed Billy's forehead. She got dressed and took the elevator down to the ground floor and walked across campus toward her own dormitory. Fifty-blank years old, she thought. Options running out. In the pale light of morning she felt bleak and ugly, a little ridiculous. She wore last night's metallic miniskirt and spike heels and see-through red blouse. Her head hurt. She wondered if her husbands had called, and if tonight she would find someone new to sleep with, and if there was anything at all she might do to stop from destroying herself.

It was a hot morning, midsummer, very still, and the campus had a silent, sleepy, suspended air, lifted above history, as if all the clocks had stopped.

Paulette and Ellie strolled past the gymnasium, past the new science building, and then turned onto a gravel path that wound up into a small wooded park above the school. Years ago, in these same urban woods, they had built bonfires and plotted peace and sung folk songs to the accompaniment of guitars. Time had annulled all that. Their dreams were now middle-aged dreams, their politics personal. Neither woman said much. They left the gravel path, turned up into the trees, and stopped in a little clearing where Ellie and Harmon Osterberg had once wrestled with problems of innocence and desire. Out of the blue, Paulette said, "You talk, I'll listen."

"I don't think so," Ellie said.

Paulette took her hand. "One thing I've noticed. Men these days, it's blow job first, let's get acquainted later."

"Not always," said Ellie.

"No?"

"Harmon."

"Right," Paulette said. "Time to talk."

"I can't."

"You can. One word, then another word."

"In a minute. I'll try."

But then Ellie cried.

David Todd and Marla Dempsey lingered over coffee in the student union. They'd been divorced since 1980, yet for all their history they still loved each other. David's love was fierce and excessive, Marla's was dispassionate, which was the subject

168

when she said, "I used to wonder if maybe I was gay or something. You know, because I couldn't seem to—what's that expression?—I couldn't get my hot water turned on." She looked at him. "Did you wonder?"

"Sometimes," David said.

"I'm not."

"Not?"

"What I just said. Girls don't do it for me either."

"Excellent," he said. "That's an important thing to know." David tilted back in his chair and grinned at her. "Speaking of which."

"Yes?"

"It's personal."

"Too personal?"

"So-so. Medium."

"All right, go ahead. That's why we're sitting here. To be personal."

David nodded. "That's why."

"Ask away."

"It's a hypothetical," he said. "If I begged you—if I told you I'd hang myself or maybe jump off a roof—I mean, if it were life or death—I need to know if you'd marry me again."

"*Is* it life or death?"

"No," he said.

She grinned back at him. "Then sure. The answer's yes—I'd marry you again. Life or death, though. Which I gather it's not."

"Marry me hotly?"

169

"Of course hotly. Steamy Marla."

"May I ask something else?"

"It depends."

"Well, see, here's the program," David said. "Tonight. I plan to set up a launching pad between your legs, set off rockets, fly to Jupiter, go bowling with your ovaries."

"That," said Marla, "is not a question."

"It's all right now," Paulette said.

"Nothing's all right," said Ellie Abbott. Her breath came in quick, messy spurts. "My God, I can't stand a single second more. Never quits. All day, all night."

"What?"

"I'm afraid to go to bed, afraid to wake up. It won't ever, ever stop."

"What?"

It was 10:30 A.M. when Marv Bertel finished shaving. Flarety Hall had no air conditioning, and already the morning had gone sticky hot. Marv inspected himself in the mirror, thinking of Spook, wondering if he should shower again, but instead he sprayed on some deodorant, popped three tiny pills for his heart, and shuffled back to his room. Spook's face waited for him there—in the closet, under his pillow. Tonight, he thought. Screw the heart. Screw solitaire.

"Look, I'm single," Paulette Haslo said. "Never

been married, never even close, but if you want to take a chance on me, just talk things over, I'm pretty sure I can identify. I've got tons of time, sweetheart."

Ellie shook her head. "It's not my husband. It's me."

"Fair enough."

"I just can't—I don't dare. That's what makes it so terrible."

Ellie shook her head again. "Did you ever have to keep a secret? Really *have* to?"

"Probably so," Paulette said. "I'm not sure."

"For me it's always. Every time the phone rings, every time a car drives by. Never goes away."

"A man?" said Paulette.

"Worse than that."

Paulette looked up at the vigilant July sky. A secret of her own had just returned to her. "Well, that's bad," she said. "Worse than men. I honestly didn't think it got that ugly."

"It does."

"I'm listening. Convince me."

"I really can't," said Ellie. "That's what a secret *is*."

Dorothy Stier lived with her husband and two kids in a fancy section of St. Paul, a half mile south of the Darton Hall campus. Dorothy had arrived home just before sunrise. She had slept fitfully, two hours at most, but she was up by 8 A.M., preparing breakfast for the troops, cheerfully lying to her husband about the reunion, how boring it was, same old faces, the standard gripes and jokes and bragging. She did not mention Billy McMann, nor her own late-night threat to remove her shirt. As a practical matter, Dorothy had no doubt that she'd come to the correct decision many years ago. Ron was thoughtful and kind, a fantastic provider, good with the kids, and Dorothy knew in her bones that she had chosen the only life that could satisfy her. She required comfort. And so what? She would not apologize for sending the boys to good schools. Billy could say what he wanted—call her names, make nasty comments—but there was nothing evil or depraved about a decent home, a decent income, summer excursions to London or Venice or Nassau. Truffles were not immoral. Besides, Dorothy would've rotted away in Winnipeg. She loved her country. Loved her flag. She'd canvassed the neighborhood for Bob Dole. "What gets to me," she told Ron over toast and skim milk, "is that they're still spouting that same wasn't-it-beautiful, wasn't-it-so-pure-and-perfect garbage about the stupid sixties. All of them—Spook, Amy, Paulette, Jan—they're back in the dark ages. I mean, everybody's doing fine, they've got money—God knows Amy Robinson does, our own little Ho Chi Minh—but it's like they all feel guilty about it, they refuse to be happy, they won't grow up. Honestly, what's so terrible about right *now?* We're adults. We're allowed to be snug."

Ron looked at her thoughtfully. "Was Billy there?"

Spook Spinelli peeled off her metallic miniskirt, wrapped herself in a big blue towel, decided against it, removed the towel, slipped on a pair of heels, and made her way down a humid hallway to the women's lavatory on the second floor of Collins Hall. Ordinarily, Spook would've felt some disappointment at the deserted bathroom, no girl talk, no envious stares, no backhanded compliments about her well-preserved ass. What she felt instead was disgust and fear. She kicked off the heels and stepped into a shower stall. The disgust could be washed away, as always, but the fear was beyond soap and water. It had been baked in since she was a girl: afraid of being alone, afraid of not being alone.

As she scrubbed away Billy McMann, Spook hummed a tune that had once generated truckloads of cash for her ex-key-boardist out in L.A. She thought about giving the man a call, which made her chuckle, and then she thought about drinking from the red fire extinguisher at the end of the hallway. Slip the nozzle down her throat. Squeeze the silver trigger.

It was almost noon when the July heat finally awakened Amy Robinson and Jan Huebner. Jan had passed out on Amy's bed, and the two of them now lay side by side, roommates again, taking turns complaining about inferior vodka and middle age. Jan confessed she'd gone through menopause a few months earlier. "Dry as the Pecos," she said. "And that creep Richard, the bastard takes one look and leaves me for wetter waters. Gives me this wave. Smiles. Strolls away."

"Stop, stop, stop," Amy said.

"You're right, I'm being preposterous." Jan moaned and sat up. Her smudged Midnight Plum lipstick matched the puffiness beneath her eyes. "Important question. Is the Pecos dry?"

"Got me, honey."

"The Sahara, how's that?"

"Better. Don't believe it's a river."

"Not a river?"

"Think not."

"Holy poop." Jan wagged her head. "Anyhow, a bummer. Dripped my last drop. We're talking bone-dry. Parched."

"Listen, babe," Amy said wearily, "I need a tremendous favor. My head's killing me, plus I didn't get half close to laid last night, plus—and here's the main thing—plus it's way too early for divorce talk. Promise me you won't cry."

"Done deal," Jan said. "No crying. But I'll need a drink."

"You just woke up."

"And?"

Amy nodded.

She got up, padded over to her dresser, retrieved

174

a bottle of vodka, and carried it back to the bed.

"Mud in your eye," she said.

"Mud yourself," said Jan. "Do you think we drink too much?"

"Without a doubt. Let's stop this instant."

"This right-now instant?"

"Down the toilet," said Amy.

"Well," Jan said. She cast around in her head. "Here's my take on it. We don't necessarily have to go teetotaler insane. There's the whole question of crying."

"True," Amy said.

"We wouldn't want that, I assume?"

"We sure as heck wouldn't," said Amy.

"You're positive?"

"I am. Drink."

Jan reached for the bottle, took a swallow, and lay back in bed. She examined the ceiling for a time. "You know something?"

"Oh, God."

"I'm old. I think I'm lonely."

"Stop."

"No, I mean *really* lonely."

"Please, please don't cry," said Amy.

In the same dorm, three floors down, a well-known physician stood brushing the snarled gray hair of a mother of three, formerly a basketball star. They had just ordered champagne from a delivery store on Snelling Avenue. They were naked. At that

175

memorable July instant, the mother of three was giggling over a comment she'd just made regarding the physician's bedside manner.

The physician nodded.

"Nice to hear," he said. "That'll be three hundred dollars."

Neither of them had given thought to the future, or to the miraculous happiness they felt.

"Tell the truth," said the mother of three. "Will I require additional surgery?"

"You well may," said the physician.

Two doors away, Minnesota's newly married lieutenant governor was outlining political reality to his ex-fiancée, who had not yet mastered the plain facts.

A half mile from campus, Dorothy Stier said, "I'm pretty sure he *was*."

When Spook returned to her room, she found Marv Bertel waiting on the bed. He wore a blue suit, a maroon tie, buffed black shoes.

"You're looking naked," he said.

"Thank you, dear," said Spook. She covered herself with the towel, did a model's spin. "What about the heels?"

"The heels," he said gravely, "add a dimension."

"And the towel?"

Marv shrugged. "I'll be straight with you. The towel I don't care for."

"I'm exhausted, Marv."

"No sweat," he said. "I'm fat."

Spook took off the towel, put on blue jeans and a white shirt, and then sat with him on the bed. "You were right. Billy McMann . . . giant mistake, one of my doozies. Very sorry."

"Oh, well, fat but smart," Marv said. "Patient as a goddamn glacier."

"You are patient," she said. "You're wonderful. And you make mops."

"I do indeed. Damn near perfect mops."

She put her head to his shoulder. "We're spectacular friends, aren't we?"

"Yes, we are," he said.

"So if I need you to stick around here while I take a snooze—?"

"Staying," he said.

At 12:30 P.M. Marla Dempsey and David Todd left the student union and walked to a florist's shop on Snelling Avenue. They bought a pair of long-stemmed white roses, one for Karen Burns, one for Harmon Osterberg. A memorial service was scheduled for later in the afternoon. On the walk back to campus, David put a hand on Marla's hip and said, "I'm a cripple, slow down," and Marla swatted his hand away and said, "*You* slow down."

In the wooded park above campus, Paulette Haslo and Ellie Abbott had reached an agreement on how to proceed. A secret, they decided, would still be a secret if everyone involved swore to absolute, on-your-honor secrecy.

"You go first," Ellie said.

CHAPTER 11

HEARING

Just after 11 P.M., in a western suburb of Minneapolis, Mrs. Janice Ketch turned off the Leno show, removed her hearing aid, flung Rudy's pillow from the bed, pulled up the covers, switched off her lamp, and lay muttering to herself in the summer dark. Janice was furious. So angry, in fact, it made her stomach bubble. A trillion times—probably ten trillion—she'd told Rudy to cut out the steaks and whiskey, to stop gallivanting every weekend with his boring, blowhard American Legion buddies.

Now he was dead and Janice was alone. Stranded, she told herself. High and dry. Sixty-three years old, mostly deaf, no husband, no handyman, no one to prepare her evening tea or mow the lawn or fix that broken lock on the back door.

Moron, Janice thought.

And then she said it aloud, bitterly, right to Rudy's dead, waxy, irresponsible face. He had been in his grave almost a full week, but still, in Janice's thoughts, day and night, she remained hostage to that half-wit grin of his, the way he'd chuckle at some foolish thought and wiggle his false teeth and then stare into the dusty, uninhabited regions of his own fatuity.

"Idiot!" she snarled.

Janice closed her eyes, scolding him, finally drifting off in a haze of disgust.

Maybe she slept for a time, maybe not. But very soon, after what seemed only minutes, she found herself coiled up in bed, stiff with terror. She had been startled by a noise at the rear of the house—metal against metal. She lay listening, turning her better ear to the bedroom door, but all she could make out was the sound of her own deafness, a fluid rush at the center of her head. A number of thoughts came to her at once. This was the suburbs. People did not get murdered in their sleep. She had just purchased a new thirty-six-inch television set.

Janice slipped out of bed, groped in the dark for her robe and slippers, patted her hair, moved to the bedroom door. Again she strained to hear, but there was only that underwater rush in her ears.

Absurd, she told herself. She had lived in this house for thirty-eight years without the slightest trouble, except of course for the Kepler twins next door, a pair of budding ax murderers who could not seem to understand the function of a sidewalk. How Rudy could've tolerated such brats she would never know—a pitiful excuse for children of his own.

Janice grunted. Tommy and Eddie Kepler: those

two freckled felons were definitely at the bottom of this.

With an exasperated sigh, emboldening herself, Janice nudged the door open and stepped into the living room. She was an overweight woman, thick in the waist and thighs, and these late-hour exertions brought a wheeze to her breath.

There now, she thought. Perfectly normal.

But in the next instant, even without her glasses, Janice registered the silhouette of a tall, slender figure standing in the glow of a flashlight at Rudy's old walnut desk. Almost immediately, she recognized the intruder as her own pastor, Paulette Haslo. The woman was dressed in black bicycle shorts, white sneakers, a skimpy white halter. Janice felt her heart go tight. It was Paulette Haslo who had bungled—positively mutilated, in point of fact—the rites over Rudy's grave; it was Paulette who had been unable to conduct a simple interment without the gush of tears and ostentatious sentiment; and it was Paulette Haslo, an overzealous, overpaid woman of the cloth, who had failed to mention the Lord Jesus Christ or even a saint or two in the course of Rudy's flagrantly expensive funeral. Ultraliberal was one thing, godless was another. But this was burglary. Janice's terror dissolved in a mist of indignation.

"Well, now," she said sharply. "Moonlighting?"

Paulette Haslo bowed her head, her face picking up streaks of red and yellow from the flashlight. A few seconds passed before the minister said, "Oh, Janice."

"Well, yes. I live here. And I'm quite positive you don't."

"No."

"Speak up," Janice snapped. "This isn't one of your Sunday sermons."

"Correct," said Paulette. "I don't live here."

"Wonderful. That's settled." Janice nodded and crossed the room. An exhilarating surge of power shot through her veins. She had not felt such mastery over the world since the day Rudy died. "If you don't mind," she said, "I suggest we turn on some lights, make ourselves comfortable, and consult with the police." She paused and glared. "You should be ashamed."

"Oh, I am," Paulette said.

"Louder. Try to enunciate."

"I am. I'm ashamed. Very much."

The minister's voice was muffled, the consonants spongy and slurred. Janice sniffed the air. Bourbon, she decided—the same poison that had dispatched Rudy to an early grave.

"Well," Janice said.

She switched on the overhead lights. For a few seconds they stood facing each other, calculating, making adjustments. In Paulette's two years at St. Mark's, there had been substantial friction between them, differences of dogma and temperament that sometimes flared up in open hostility. Not that Janice accepted the slightest blame. She considered

184

herself as broad-minded as the next person, tolerant to a fault, but it didn't seem to be asking too much that one's own pastor should believe in God, or that a Sunday homily be something more than freethinking Democratic propaganda, or that Christian charity should not automatically encompass the indolent, the perverted, or the plain revolting. It was Janice's conviction that a pastor's first quality had to be toughness of spirit, an uncompromising moral stamina. Decorum, too. Some self-restraint. Not the soft-headed, anything-goes radicalism of Paulette Haslo.

Now, as Janice surveyed her new opportunities, the notion of revenge began to form. Also, the words "sitting duck." Already she was imagining how she would report this incident to the board of deacons, the outfit she would wear, the new white gloves she would purchase for the occasion. The prospect tickled her. For an instant Janice felt a joyful fizzing in her heart. True, dress gloves were hard to find these days, but with perseverance it could almost certainly be done. Perhaps that snooty antique store down on Seventh Street.

A crease came to her forehead. She had nearly forgotten the minister.

"I don't suppose," Janice said, "that you'd care to explain yourself? Unless, of course, you plan to tie me up and gag me. Slash my throat? Chop up my bones, make a nice pot of soup? Is that the idea?"

"No, I hadn't considered that," the minister

said. She seemed calm—far too calm—and looked at Janice with a steady, unchastened gaze. "I suppose we should talk."

"Talk? I can barely *hear* you."

"I said—"

"I know exactly what you said, I'm not handicapped. And I'm not some liberal do-gooder ignoramus." Janice made a brusque click with her tongue. The new power was thrilling. "If there's talking to be done, we'll do it in front of the police. Honestly, look at yourself. A flashlight, for God's sake. The dead of night, skulking through people's houses. In a *halter*, I might add. A so-called woman of God." Janice punctuated the moment with a pause. "Let's be frank. You've been drinking?"

The minister shrugged. "A few, yes. To work up the courage."

"Courage?"

"I was desperate, Janice."

"Oh, I'm sure you were."

Her own tone of voice, Janice realized, was a trifle smug, yet it felt good to have rectitude on her side. Here at last was a moral edge, no room for theological double talk. Out of good breeding, and to retain the high ground, Janice offered a thin smile.

"I'll be back in one moment," she said. "If you remember the words, now might be an excellent time for the Lord's Prayer."

Then she marched across the living room toward the telephone.

"Janice, don't. Please."

"Too late for please. You should've thought of that before—"

"Put down the phone. Now. I mean it."

The minister's voice was suddenly quite audible. Janice pulled her hand from the telephone.

"What I want you to do," said Paulette, "is go find your hearing aid. No moaning. Just do it. And then I want you to sit down and listen to me. Ears open, mouth shut. Understand?"

"Well, if this isn't Satan talking . . ." Janice blinked and wrinkled her forehead; she'd lost her train of thought.

"Where's the hearing aid?" said Paulette.

"The bedroom. My nightstand."

"Make it fast."

Janice glared at the woman. "Now listen, Miss Halter Top, you can't order me around like . . . My God, you *do* plan to murder me, don't you?"

"We'll see," Paulette said.

"What?"

"You're a Presbyterian, Janice. Good behavior, good deeds. Everything depends on it." The woman smiled dangerously. "Go get the hearing aid."

Janice edged away. She was now genuinely afraid for her life. In the bedroom, to buy time, she stood fiddling with her hearing aid. It occurred to her that no fewer than five members of the congregation had passed away over the last year or two. All of them had been elderly, all in ill health, but even so their deaths had come out of the blue. And now Rudy. Instantly, a combination of dreadful thoughts arose. Over the past month, as her husband deteriorated, Janice had twice found the minister sitting alone at his hospital bedside. No nurses, not a doctor in sight, just the fragile hum of a respirator. On both occasions the woman had seemed jumpy, quick to rise, quick to depart. And it was Paulette herself who had eventually called with the news of Rudy's passing.

The facts seemed indisputable. Janice was in the hands of a serial killer, a ruthless preacher in bicycle shorts.

The realization caused Janice to glance up at a window over her bed. Swiftly, she ran the numbers. A good five-foot drop to the lawn. Sixty-three years old. One hundred and eighty-two pounds. An unpleasant equation, but better than dismemberment.

Janice climbed up on her bed, unlatched the window, pulled it open, tightened her robe, and prepared herself for the plunge.

It was a shock when Paulette Haslo gently slapped her bottom.

"Janice, Janice," the minister said.

"Don't butcher me!"

"Just give me your hand."

"My God, I don't deserve this, I'm a churchgoer, I haven't missed—"

"Janice. Stop it."

Paulette helped her off the bed, gripped her arm, and escorted her back to the living room.

They sat facing each other, Janice on the sofa, Paulette in Rudy's leather recliner. Janice felt weak. In part she was exhausted by her trials with the window; in larger part it was as if a faucet had been opened in her heart, bleeding out every last droplet of her once justly famous spunk. Hopeless, it seemed. She watched the minister lean back in the recliner, tug at the strap of her halter top, and cross her long, ill-shaven, almost entirely naked legs. There had been a time, not twenty minutes ago, when Janice would've summoned up a pungent remark about the matter of clerical dress: what was appropriate and what was not. Now she sat mute. Even her tongue would not function.

Paulette sighed. "Look, I'm sorry, Janice. It wasn't planned this way."

"Planned?"

"Tonight. In and out, I thought."

"In and out. Very considerate." Janice folded her hands in her lap. Already she felt better. "And you actually thought you'd get away with it?"

"Who knows?" said Paulette. "The lights were out. You're hard of hearing. Like I said. Desperate."

"And how did you manage to—what's the term?—how did you break and enter? I believe that's what they call it on *Law and Order*."

Paulette made a slack movement with her

189

shoulders. "Not a problem. Broken lock. Rudy mentioned it."

"Rudy?"

"We talked sometimes."

"Blabbermouth," Janice muttered. "And now he's killed me."

The minister gave her a searching look. "Oh, well," she said.

"Oh well what?"

"Nothing. Stay put, Janice. Don't budge."

Paulette stood up, went across the room to Rudy's desk, and began opening and closing drawers. The woman now seemed anxious, almost panicky, as if she'd misplaced an important set of keys. What Paulette was looking for, Janice could not tell, but she took satisfaction in the knowledge that her silver was safely tucked away at the rear of a utility closet, her best jewelry in a flour canister on the kitchen counter.

Janice smiled at her own cleverness.

"A word to the wise," she said. "If you expect to get rich, you'd best hope for one of those Bible miracles you don't believe in. The resurrection, for instance. A figure of speech, I believe you called it." Janice rolled her eyes. "Trust me, you won't find a dime. Not in that pigsty of a desk. Lord knows I tried to get the man to clean it up—don't think I didn't mention the subject a time or two—but he'd just wiggle his filthy teeth and . . . Excuse me! What are you doing there?"

Janice sat forward on the sofa. Without her

glasses it was hard to be certain, but Paulette seemed to be stuffing a sheaf of documents into her bicycle shorts.

"Now, look here," Janice said. "Return those papers. This instant."

The minister slammed a drawer shut, pulled open a filing cabinet, tucked something else into her shorts.

"Well, I knew it," said Janice. "The day they hired you—a female pastor, for crying out loud—right then I told them there was something fishy in Denmark. I said it. Point-blank. 'Fishy in Denmark,' my exact words."

Paulette Haslo did not glance up. The woman was reading something, one hand on her hip, the other gripping a piece of yellow notepaper.

"I beg your pardon!" Janice yelled. "Are you *deaf?*"

The minister turned and studied her. "Lovely thought," she said. "Would've made my job so much easier."

"Easy?" said Janice. "You work one day a week—two hours, tops—which hardly justifies that preposterous salary of yours. Let's just say it keeps you in plenty of halters and bunny tails. Which is another matter. Prancing around like Mata Hari. I mean, you're not some spring chicken, Paulette. Forty-five, I'll bet, if you're a day."

"Over fifty," Paulette said.

"Ha. There you are."

To Janice's eye, the minister was a plain,

altogether asymmetrical woman, and it seemed
ludicrous that certain male members of the congregation couldn't pry their eyes off her bulging
vestments. Even old Rudy, for whom the word
"infidel" was first invented, had managed to sit
immobile during the woman's Sunday sermons.

Disgusting, Janice thought.

For a few seconds she looked at the minister.
"Well," she said, and then made a demonstra-
tion of clearing her throat. "Whatever your age,
Reverend Cat Burglar, I suggest you return those
documents. Now would be ideal."

"Sorry," Paulette said. "They're mine."

"They most definitely are not yours. That desk
belongs to Rudy, and every squalid item—"

"Relax, Janice. It's for the better."

"I don't see how—"

"Better for all of us. Even Rudy." The minister
made a slow, weary gesture with the sheet of yellow
notepaper. "Sit back now. I'll be out of here in a
minute."

"I should hope so," said Janice. "And I should
also hope . . . Lord, I'm feeling faint. A glass
of ice water. I'd like to be conscious when you
slaughter me."

The minister hesitated, put down the sheet of
notepaper, and went off to the kitchen.

Immediately, Janice pushed to her feet. She
stood still for a moment, undecided, more apprehensive than afraid, and then she clicked her
tongue and marched over to Rudy's desk. The

sound of running water came from the kitchen. Janice bent forward, squinting down at the sheet of paper. Without her reading glasses, she could make out only bits and pieces. The word "cutie" caught her attention. Also the words "happy hunk."

Whoever had authored this bald pornography, Janice told herself, had obviously never studied penmanship; most of the letter was a blur, barely legible. Still, it seemed improbable that Rudy could be the recipient of such trash. The man could barely read. And there was nothing remotely cute about him. Even on their wedding day, at his scruffy best, Rudy had reminded her of a large circus seal waddling down the aisle, frisky and disobedient, a straggle of whiskers dotting his chin. Right now, decades later, she could still see that funny gray top hat he'd worn for the ceremony. How he'd put his head back and bellowed "I do," and how his eyes had twinkled, and how he'd come to her bed that night like a bashful little boy, reeking of cologne, his thinning brown hair slicked back as if for his first day at school. Amazing, she thought, what time could do. Back then the man had seemed so clever and witty, even charming. But over the years, especially after she'd lost her second baby, Rudy had become more a ghost than a husband, rarely uttering a complete sentence for days at a time. Always putzing in the garage. Always carving those silly ducks of his. There had been numerous occasions, in fact, when the man's silence seemed part of a crafty thirty-nine-year plan to drive her mad.

Again Janice looked down at the piece of yellow notepaper. She was puzzling over the word "cutie" when Paulette came up behind her.

"Your water," the minister said. She put the glass on Rudy's desk, then reached out and ran a finger across the notepaper. "I wish you hadn't looked at that."

"'Happy hunk,'" Janice said. "Hunk of what, may I ask?"

Paulette shrugged. "An expression."

"So I gather you're responsible for this slime?"

The minister lowered her head. She seemed on the edge of tears.

"Well, I suppose there's an explanation," said Janice. "Something outlandish." She paused. Paulette's shoulders were shaking. "Honestly, I'm embarrassed for you. He was a sick old man, for God's sake, not to mention half daft."

"No," the minister murmured. "He was smart."

"Smart?" said Janice. "We're talking about Rudy, is that correct?"

Paulette said nothing. She swallowed and put a hand to her eyes.

"Let me remind you," Janice said, "that I lived with that imbecile for thirty-nine years, closer to forty, and I'm here to tell you that 'smart' does not apply. Try dull. Try foolish. And one more thing: I wish you'd compose yourself—*I'm* the victim here." She arched her eyebrows in a manner she'd perfected during countless Sunday services. "Now what about this pen pal nonsense?"

Paulette Haslo made a short deflating sound, as though one of her lungs had malfunctioned. She gazed straight at Janice for ten or fifteen seconds. "All right, but try to listen to me. It wasn't an affair."

"I beg your pardon?"

"Rudy and I, we'd talk on the phone, write letters now and then. We liked each other. Nothing else."

Janice blinked. "Affair," she said. "Well, of *course* you didn't have an affair. The man was seven hundred years old."

"He was sixty-four."

"I know his age, thank you."

"Janice, for once in your miserable life, turn up that hearing aid. He was a good man, we had things in common. Sometimes on Saturday nights we'd get together. Have drinks. Talk. Laugh. He liked to flirt. Stupid of me, but I thought if I slipped in here and took those letters . . . I thought you'd never find out, never have to worry." Paulette shook her head. "And I'll admit it, I wanted to protect myself, too. My job, my life. I know you, Janice. How vindictive you can be, the way you jump to conclusions. I was trapped, I just did it. So goddamn dumb."

"You," Janice said, "are a foul-mouthed lunatic. For one thing, Rudy *couldn't* flirt. Second of all, Saturday was his Legion night."

"Right," said Paulette.

The minister's eyes shifted. Her voice carried a covert quality that made Janice glance up.

"You're telling me I'm not right?"

Paulette balked. "It's not what it seems. He'd spend an hour or so with his friends, maybe two hours, then we'd meet somewhere. Usually the Holiday Inn. Sometimes—"

"You met Rudy at a Holiday Inn?"

"The bar, Janice."

"I see. And presumably liquor was involved?"

"Oh, come on."

Janice made a quick, angry motion with her hand, swatting at the air. "Let me tell you something right now," she said. "Your days at St. Mark's are numbered. Bang, you're out of here. Defrocked, booted out, whatever they call it. And I doubt you'll ever work again, not in any church."

"I know that," Paulette said quietly. "For a fact."

"And you deserve it," Janice said. "Believe me, I could see it coming. At that first interview of yours, the way you were dressed. Boots and blue jeans, spangles on your blouse. We might just as well've hired some oversexed ranch hand." Janice growled at her own sarcasm. "Anyway, what a load of rubbish. Holiday Inn, my foot. Rudy would've told me."

"I'm sure he tried," said Paulette. "Hearing was never your strong suit."

Janice made a dismissive cluck at the back of her

throat. Already, though, she was reviewing the past several months, seeking clues amid the ruins of a cluttered memory. Only a few ragged images came to her, nothing coherent. Rudy painting polka dots on his decoys. Rudy straining orange juice through a paper towel—"Pulp is for losers," he used to say. Rudy at a church picnic, dressed in a straw hat and Bermuda shorts, dancing with someone's German shepherd. Rudy playing hopscotch with the Kepler twins. Rudy clutching his chest. Rudy in a hospital bed, unshaven, skinny, bald, his Adam's apple twitching as he scanned the pages of a lingerie catalogue. Rudy on a respirator. Rudy in his coffin.

A strange creature, to say the least. But for Janice the most peculiar image of all was of Rudy whiling away the hours in a Holiday Inn with Paulette Haslo. For his whole life, certainly for as long as she'd known him, the man had scoffed at anything associated with the church, preachers in particular.

"Well," Janice muttered, "I don't know what you're up to, but I don't believe a word of this. Holiday Inns. Love letters."

"They weren't love letters," said Paulette.

"What then?"

"Just—I don't know—just affectionate. He needed someone with ears."

Janice tightened the belt on her robe. Inexplicably, she was struck by a protective instinct toward Rudy, a sense of ownership. "In other words," she said, "you're not just a burglar, you're a home wrecker? A husband thief?"

"No," Paulette said, "I am not." She folded her arms as if to restrain herself. Her eyes were angry. "I've already told you, it was nothing physical, not even close. But I'll tell you something else. I wish to God it *had* been. I wish I'd run off with him, made him happy. I wish we'd checked into one of those rooms he kept talking about."

"Rudy suggested—?"

"Sex, Janice. Skin. He was getting old, for sure, but he wasn't dead." The minister's voice dropped to a low, graveside register. "You're right, I'm as good as fired, so why not tell the truth? The man was a human being. Heat, you know? Passion? I've heard the history, Janice. The empty cribs, the disappointments. But it wasn't Rudy's fault. Not yours either. Nobody's."

Janice pushed herself off the sofa.

More swiftly than she would've thought possible, she took three paces toward Rudy's desk, stopped, pivoted sideways, and flung her glass of water at the minister. Her marksmanship surprised her. The glass seemed to hang in midair for an instant, upright and sparkling, and then it struck Paulette Haslo just below the right ear.

Janice spun around and ran. A moment later she was out the back door. She crossed the patio, ducked into a juniper hedge along the garage, got down on her hands and knees, and crouched there in the dark. Instantly, the mosquitoes were at her. She pulled her robe tight and tried not to swat at them. All around her, the night seemed fiercely mundane: frogs, stars, a hazy quarter-moon over the garage. Ludicrous, Janice thought. There should be bonfires in the sky, it should be raining rabbits. For a second or two she considered praying, but the world had gone upside down and even the notion of God struck her as eccentric and foreign.

After a short while Paulette came out the back door. She stood at the center of the patio, scanning the lawn.

If the woman spoke, Janice did not hear it.

Several minutes passed before Paulette turned and went back inside, but even then Janice refused to leave the safety of the hedge. She tugged her robe down, struggled against an urgent need to weep. She wasn't sure why. Terror, of course. The shock of it all. But there was also a fuzziness inside her, cognitive disarray, a sense that she no longer recognized her own life. The house. The stars. The whole back yard—trees and garden and picket fence—it was an alien landscape, brand-new to her. This very hedge. She'd walked past it a thousand times, or ten thousand, never paying the slightest attention, and here she was inside it, blended in, breathing its dust and chlorophyll. Yes, and Rudy too, the man she'd so mistakenly called a husband. Who was he? Or what? All those years, minute sliding into minute, and now his face had dissolved into little more than a blur. It was as if she'd been on a four-decade train journey with the man, sharing a compartment, watching the miles go by, never speaking. In the end they'd collected their baggage, nodded farewell, and gone their separate ways. Total strangers, Janice realized. The man's very identity would forever remain the purest guesswork: a bumbler, a child, a cheat, a hopscotch player, a lifelong whittler of ducks.

Janice felt something fracture in her chest. She tried not to cry, but she was crying, tentatively, in little gasps, as if for the first time.

A while later Paulette Haslo came out the back door and moved into the grass beyond the patio.

"Janice, I'm leaving now," she said to the dark. The woman's voice was husky and strained, so slurred Janice wondered if she'd discovered the key to Rudy's liquor cabinet. "I've written out a resignation, it's on the desk inside. You'll get a kick out of turning it in for me. Doesn't matter. Nothing matters. Tell the board whatever you want." Paulette looked up at the night sky. For more than a minute she was silent. "You know, it's weird thing, Janice, but ever since I was a girl, five, six years old, all I ever wanted was to be a minister. I'd put on my father's bathrobe, pretend I was preaching. Take up collections. Pass out wafers and grape Kool-Aid. I mean, this is before there *were* female ministers—not many, anyway—but for me it was this natural thing, this perfect Paulette dream. Other girls, they wanted to be nurses or ballerinas or who knows what. Not me. My whole life, I never considered anything else, not once, and now it's finished. God knows what I'll do with myself. Maybe just . . . Listen, I'm sorry, Janice. You're right, I made a mess of things. Thought I was being a minister."

For a few seconds Paulette stood motionless in the dark. "Janice, he missed you," she said. "He wondered where you'd gone."

Then she turned and crossed the lawn and disappeared into the shadows beyond the garage. There was the sound of a car starting.

Janice waited ten minutes before crawling out of the hedge. She stood, brushed herself off, and looked up at the sorrowful yellow light streaming from her bedroom window.

She felt no need to rush inside. In the morning, of course, she would make a number of phone calls, but for now she was having trouble with reality. Her hearing aid produced a sizzling in her ear. She shook her head and tried to ignore it, but Rudy's thin, fluty voice filled her head with chatter from years past, all nonsense. "Hey, Blades," he was saying—a nickname she had despised and eventually bludgeoned from his vocabulary. "Hey, Blades, you're lookin' feminine tonight, real extra female."

Too much stress, Janice thought.

She moved to the patio, sat on a lawn chair, and removed her hearing aid. But there was still that sizzle in her ears, an electric buzz that seemed to come from a transmitter deep in the Milky Way. "Blades!" Rudy yelled. Briefly, for reasons she couldn't fathom, Janice found herself sliding back to the occasion of her second miscarriage. It was August 1964, and she was telling Rudy that enough was enough, no more bedroom horseplay, that he would have to find something new to occupy his time. In the summer dark she watched Rudy think about it, how his eyes went hard for an instant and then softened forever. After a time he chuckled and said, "Ducks'll do it." He never mentioned it again. He became a jester, a do-it-yourselfer, a dancer with German shepherds. "Blades!" he kept yelling. He wouldn't quit. Not then, not now. Janice stood up. Ridiculous, she thought, and began to move inside, but the buzz in her ears stopped her and she was taken back to another silky summer night, forty years ago. An amusement park, Independence Day, and she was watching Rudy drop to his knees in front of the roller coaster, a big, stupid grin on his face—"Super feminine, if you follow my drift, so do we get hitched or *what?*"—and then he slipped the ring on her finger and squealed like a ten-year-old. "Blades!" he kept yelling, because she'd worn a scooped-back dress that night, and because he admired the smooth, graceful slope of her shoulders.

Janice went inside. She washed up, changed into a clean nightgown, got into bed, and turned out the light. There was still that distant sizzling sound, and in the dark of memory Rudy sang,

"Buffalo gals, won't you come out tonight, come out tonight," and then he yelled, "Blades!"

Janice refused to listen.

She shut her eyes, shut her ears, and began planning her morning activities, the white gloves she would buy, the revenge she would exact. As Janice drifted off, it occurred to her that she should say a little prayer, except she'd quit praying many years ago. She was a believer, yes, but she hated God. Idiot husband, two unborn babies.

CHAPTER 12

CLASS OF '69

Well, it's sad," Ellie Abbott said, "but I don't understand. All you did, you had drinks with this henpecked old man. Gave him some attention, flirted a little." Ellie hesitated. "To be honest, I'm not really sure why you broke in that night. I mean, *why?*"

Paulette Haslo swept a hand across her eyes. "No choice, it seemed. Thought I'd lose my job. My whole life."

"Except you did lose your job."

"Oh, yes."

They sat together on a concrete bench in the small wooded park above campus. The morning was hot and quiet.

"All right, listen," Ellie said. "Here's what I'm getting at: what about your own feelings? This isn't a criticism, Paulette. Please don't take it that way. But I really didn't hear much about *you*. Plenty about that old woman, Janice what's-her-name, but hardly a word about Paulette Haslo. And she's what I care about. Why you did it, everything that happened afterward. It had to be horrible."

"It was. It was horrible."

"So?"

Paulette pushed to her feet, looked up at the July sky. She was a tall, shapely, almost muscular woman—a swimmer, a bicyclist. There was just a sprinkling of gray in her hair, no fat at all on her hips or stomach. More than any of them, Paulette had kept a grip on her youth.

After a time she laughed to herself, started to say something, then stopped and moved her tongue along her teeth as if to retrieve an elusive scrap of language. "I did love him, you know."

"Love?"

"Rudy. No sex, no affair, but he was just this . . . He was a good man. Never any pretension. No agenda, no subterfuge. Loved him a lot."

"I thought he was—"

"Old?"

"I suppose," said Ellie. "Old."

Paulette smiled. "Sixty-four. And once upon a time I guess that would've seemed ancient. Not anymore." She smiled again. She seemed embarrassed. "Been single my whole life, Ellie. Lived alone. Thirty years, two boyfriends. Six months each. Trust me, the preacher thing scares men off."

"I can imagine."

"Can you?"

"I think so."

"The price, I guess," Paulette said. "Men think you're this pious, press-your-knees-together non-entity, this nobody, not even a woman. Rudy was

208

different. A peculiar guy, no question about it, but he put the Paulette part first, the minister stuff second. Made me laugh. Made me feel like a girl. Almost pretty. Almost beautiful sometimes."

"You should feel that way," Ellie said. "Beautiful face, beautiful figure. God, that chest of yours. I'm jealous. Women pay a fortune for boobs like those."

Paulette rolled her eyes. "Not what they used to be. But Rudy liked them."

"You just told me—"

"Right, I know. And we didn't." Paulette stared down at the sunlit campus, and then chuckled to herself and looked up at Ellie with a happy grin. "If you're interested, there's a story."

"I'm interested."

"I'll make it quick," said Paulette. "Couple of years ago Rudy and I went off on this retreat together, this place up north, an old tourist camp in the middle of nowhere. My idea. Thought it would do him good. God knows where Janice was—laid up with bad temper or something. Who knows, who cares? Anyway, the retreat was run by this retired hippie. Guy named Larry Tabor, absolute lunatic. Larry Tabor's Funny Farm, that's what Rudy ended up calling it. The point is, neither of us had ever been there before, no idea what to expect, and it turned out to be this neoreligious place, very avant-garde. The first morning, before breakfast, we all troop out into this big meadow, maybe fifty of us, and everybody starts doing yoga.

Rudy, too. Give him credit: sixty-some years old, not the yoga type, but he's game, he jumps right in. So after a few minutes people start taking off their sweatshirts. No problem, I think. It's hot. But then they whip off their T-shirts, then their pants, and before you know it they're down to nothing, not a stitch. Fresh air and mother nature. Doing *yoga*. Rudy looks at me—you know—kind of puzzled. I'm mortified, I had no idea, but he figures I knew all about it, thinks I'm into this naked yoga thing. So he shrugs. Peels off his clothes. And I'm stuck, no options. Next thing you know I'm bare to the wind. Lotus position, headstands. You know me, Ellie. I don't take showers nude. And the whole time, Larry Tabor stands up front like this crazy cheerleader or something, egging us on, all these chants and mantras, and then he yells, 'Come on, people, let's everybody cavort with nature.' Cavort? I'm a minister, right? Except no way out of it. What the hell, I cavort. Grab my boobs, start prancing around that field. Later on, when we sit down for breakfast, Rudy can't stop talking about how graceful I was, how he never knew religion could be such fun. And then he grins. Looks right at me and grins. And suddenly he's . . . he's a new person. He's thirty years old. No fool, no buffoon. And there's this incredible electricity in his eyes, this glow, like he could look right inside me and see every detail, everything I am, everything I ever did. This absolute burning aliveness. And I'll tell you something. Right then

I would've married that old coot. Would've loved him forever."

Ellie laughed. "Man of your dreams?"

"Oh, he was. My prince." Paulette rubbed her nose, smiled. "Now he's dead. Your turn, Ellie."

CHAPTER 13

LOON POINT

In the summer of 1999, when Ellie Abbott lied to her husband and flew off to meet Harmon in Minneapolis, she felt some guilt and malaise, and considerable terror, but very little remorse. She did not contemplate turning back. All she wanted was to get away with it. At O'Hare, before catching a connecting flight, Ellie called her home outside Boston and spoke to the answering machine. "Mark," she said. "I miss you." Then she stopped and listened, imagining the flutter in her voice, the betrayal. After a second she said, "Hey, kiddo, I love you lots," which was true.

Ellie was fifty-two years old. It was her second affair. She had only a dim sense of the protocol.

"Kisses," she told the machine.

Harmon met her at the Twin Cities airport and they drove north for several hours, to a resort called Loon Point, where they spent five days and four nights. It was not a luxury resort, but the cabins were comfortable and newly painted, and there was a nine-hole golf course and a big lake with growths of pine and birch pushing up against the shore. They had a good time, mostly. They fished for walleyes, played golf, sunned themselves on a pebbled beach, talked in a vague way about whether they would ever live together and how it might be made to happen. There was no real romance between them, no heat, but there was affection and good humor and the trust of co-conspirators. And there was also a shared history—the sticky ideals and illusions of 1969. After graduation, Harmon had gone on to become a dentist. Ellie had become a waitress, then a dance instructor, then the wife of Mark Abbott.

Now, she was not sure what she was.

An adulteress, to be sure. A liar, a cheat.

More than anything, though, she was a mix of the many things she was not: not content, not hopeful, not fixed to any moral destiny, not the person she had imagined she might be back in 1969.

On their fifth day up north, after breakfast, Harmon drowned in the waters off Loon Point. Ellie witnessed it from a reclining beach chair. Harmon raised his arms up high, the morning sunlight gathering all around him, his hands closing into fists. He looked once at the sky. He went down and came up and then vanished. There was no drama to it. Ellie waited ten minutes, thinking she'd lost him among the waves.

It was nearly two hours before Harmon was brought to shore in a boat. His eyelids were half open, his pupils like thin wafers of quartz. His arms and legs seemed oddly shrunken, out of proportion to the heavy chest and stomach, and on his face there was an impatient, almost harried expression, as if he were working on the teeth of an unhappy six-year-old. He had lost his distinguished good looks. While the paramedics leaned over him, Ellie wondered how she'd ever come to care for such a man, someone so wet and dead, whose swimming trunks had slipped below the knees and whose buttocks looked wrinkled and fishy white in the bright morning sunlight. Her own transgressions, of course. Her own gross stupidity. She understood that. But despite herself, Ellie couldn't push away a peculiar sense of anger. She felt betrayed. As the medics secured Harmon to a stretcher, she tried to imagine how she might explain things to Mark, sorting through amendments to the truth, testing the possibilities, but in the end nothing persuasive came to her. She felt caught. A snagged sensation. It all seemed so radical, so unfair and unnecessary, and as the medics lifted Harmon into a shiny white ambulance, Ellie wished he were properly alive so she could scold him.

Later on, she almost cried. Someone handed her a Kleenex. There were boats on the lake, many waterfowl, and the morning was warm and pleasant.

After the ambulance took Harmon away, a young policeman folded Ellie's beach towel and led her by the elbow up to the cabin. The man's grip was without sentiment, almost casual, and Ellie felt steadied by his presence. He

217

seemed at ease with tragedy. When they reached the porch, the policeman handed her the beach towel. "There'll be things to take care of," he said. "I'll wait right here, give you a lift into town."

Oddly, then, he winked at her. Or maybe not. Ellie couldn't be sure.

"No hurry," the policeman said. "Take your time."

Ellie showered and changed into a skirt and blouse. It was not yet noon. As she used Harmon's hair dryer, Ellie contemplated calling Mark and blurting out the truth. A full confession. Names and dates and places. The notion tempted her, but Ellie sighed and shook her head. She dialed her home number, narrowed her throat, and informed the answering machine that her flight had been canceled, that she would be delayed a day or two. The call helped only a little. She pulled on a pair of sandals, devoted a moment to her lipstick and mirror.

Outside, the policeman stood fingering an unlighted cigarette. He smiled apologetically and returned the cigarette to its pack.

On the ride into town, Ellie rolled down her window. "Go on," she said. "Smoke."

The man shook his head. He was a careful driver, alert, both hands on the wheel. For several miles Ellie watched the trees go by, little flashes of open lake, then she put her head back and released a surrendering sigh.

"I should explain," she said. "We weren't married. Harmon and me. Not to each other."

"Oh, yes?" the policeman said.

"You understand?"

He nodded, just barely. "It's a tragedy. Sad world."

"What I mean is," said Ellie, "I mean—here's the point—I hope this can be kept confidential."

"Confidential?"

"You know."

The policeman seemed to think it over. He had a pleasant way of squinting into the morning sunlight. "Well, see, I guess it depends on what you're asking for." His voice was low and fluid, almost a drawl, misplaced in Minnesota. "The man's drowned, of course."

"Yes, he is."

"That's a problem. We don't often hide bodies."

Ellie sat up straight. "I wasn't suggesting anything of the sort. Common sense. Ordinary discretion. It's not illegal or anything."

"I guess not."

"Basic decency," said Ellie. "I don't see why someone else should get hurt."

"You mean—"

"I mean my husband."

The policeman stiffened slightly, as if his back were bothering him, then he pulled on a pair of sunglasses. "Well, there's the risk," he said. "People play games, people get hurt."

"It wasn't any game," Ellie said.

"No?"

Ellie sensed the man was mocking her, or something worse, and for the rest of the ride she went out of her way not to look at him. She paid attention to her breathing. In front of the courthouse, when the policeman tipped his hat, Ellie pretended not to notice, lashing back with silence. As she walked up the courthouse steps, the man called out to her.

"Lots of luck," he said.

There were interviews with the county coroner and sheriff, two formal statements, several periods in which she sat alone in a cramped anteroom and drank coffee and waited. At times Ellie felt a kind of nerve sickness. The world seemed aligned against her. She would picture Harmon's face, then Mark's, and instantly her stomach would cramp up. She couldn't see a way out. There was some sorrow, to be sure, but mostly she felt mistreated by circumstance. She blamed the lake and Harmon and the raucous waterfowl. A conspiracy of nature, it seemed, and there was no sense of moral participation. The affair itself had started almost by accident. An exchange of Christmas cards, a few casual letters. And now, after seven months, it had ended the same way, without choice or volition, as if she were strapped into the back seat of her own life. And the odd thing, Ellie thought, was that poor, dear Harmon had once seemed so safe. A married man. No demands. A solid, plump, slow-moving dentist with a grown daughter and a big modern house on the outskirts of Minneapolis. They'd been sane about it. All the precautions, all the safeguards, and everything had seemed so logical and foolproof.

Now, glancing at her wristwatch, Ellie found herself wondering if anything on earth was proof against her own foolishness. Somewhere in the building, Harmon was stretched out on a cold steel gurney, and all the fine logic and safeguards could not flush the lake from his lungs.

Again she had the urge to call Mark. She loved him and wished she could remember why.

In late afternoon, after what seemed many years, the coroner stopped by to ask if Harmon had a history of heart trouble. Ellie shook her head. She had no idea. There was a short silence as the coroner studied her legs. The man blinked once, nodded crisply, and said it was something he might better discuss with the immediate family.

"Sure," Ellie said. "They'd know."

It was nearing dark when the policeman drove her back to Loon Point. Tiny beads of rain dotted the windshield. A wind was blowing, which made the car shimmy, and the sky had swollen up fat and purple. Neither of them spoke much, except to note the occasional lightning off to the west.

At her cabin door, the policeman offered a vague smile. "Considering everything," he said, "you might want to pack up soon. Guy's wife and daughter come in tomorrow morning. You probably don't need to be here for that."

"Probably not," Ellie said.

"There's an early bus. Six-fifteen, I think."

"Thanks. Good night, then."

"Night," the young man said. He gazed out at the storm beyond the lake. "Look, if you need anything—a few bucks—it's no problem. We've got vouchers."

"I'm not a whore."

The man's eyes crinkled. "Well, fine, that's a good chunk of information. Easier for everybody."

"Anything else?"

"I guess not." He made a small, conciliatory movement with his hand. "Unless I could help you pack. Brew up some coffee. People don't need to be alone."

"In my case," Ellie said, "that's all I need."

"We could talk."

"About what?"

"Everything," he said. "No shortage of subjects."

He was still smiling. When the wind picked up, his upper body seemed to bend toward her.

"In the car this morning," Ellie said, "I thought you were making fun of me. Disapproving."

"No."

"It felt that way."

"Not at all, ma'am. The world does its nonsense. One thing I know for a fact: approve or disapprove, it don't count for zip." He swiveled and faced her. "What about that coffee?"

There was no coffee, but Ellie made hot tea, and they went out to the porch and sat on a wicker sofa and watched the storm move toward them from across the lake. The man kept his hat on. He was in his mid-twenties, Ellie guessed, and something about his youth made her aware of her own weakened spirit, her melancholy, how empty she had become. She pictured Harmon wet and dead, all that flesh. The image frightened her. It made her feel cruel.

"I did care for him," Ellie said, too quickly, conscious that it was not the full truth. "Harmon, I mean. I knew him years ago, in college. A wonderful guy, loads of fun, always laughing, and when we—" She wanted to stop herself. "It wasn't a fling. He would've married me. It was out of the question, of course, just impossible, but for some reason I couldn't come right out and admit it. Not even to myself. I suppose it would've ruined the fantasy."

"Which fantasy?"

"The trite one. Running off together. Such a strange, ridiculous thought."

"So you strung him along?"

"Probably. Or myself."

The policeman shook out a cigarette, twirling it between his thumb and forefinger. "And your husband?" he said. "He doesn't suspect?"

"No," Ellie said. "Not a clue."

"And you love him?"

"Mark?"

"Mark. Yes."

Ellie closed her eyes and began to say something, but then stopped, because there was nothing she could say that was entirely true. Out in the darkness, the first droplets of rain made a soft, random patter in the trees, a sound that seemed to come from a time when she was a little girl. The desolation was overwhelming now. Fifty-two years old. Harmon was dead, and Mark was on his own planet, and it was hard to imagine a future for herself. Ellie wanted something. She wanted it very badly, but she did not know what.

She finished her tea and stood up. "The truth," she said, "is that my husband is a fabulous man. Better than fabulous." She tried to smile. "I hope you'll keep him out of this."

The young policeman studied the dark. He seemed to be humming to himself, except there was no sound. "You know what I think?" he finally said. "Don't take this the wrong way, but I think you'd sleep with me in a flash. Down and dirty."

For a few seconds Ellie said nothing. She was not shocked, not even surprised.

"Go away," she said.

"Oh, soon enough." He leaned back comfortably in the wicker sofa. There was something illusory about him, something not wholly connected to the world of lakes and trees and rocks and drowned human bodies. "Right now," he said, "you wouldn't dream of it. Sex, that is. Because I brought it out in the open. Now you can't. But if I hadn't spoken up . . ." He looked at her brutally. "I guess we'll never know, will we?"

"We won't," she said. "Go."

"I didn't mean it in a bad way."

"How, then?"

"Well, most people in your shoes, they try to hide the betrayal. Not you. You want to hide the actual freakin' body. Now, that's pressure, a walking nightmare, and I figure you need to make sure it's all real. Make sure *you're* real."

"I'm plenty real," said Ellie. "I don't require proof."

"Then I apologize."

His voice, however, was not apologetic. It had a bitter, singsong quality. In a way, Ellie thought, the man did not seem to be speaking to her at all, but to himself, or to someone in the dark behind her.

He stood up, touched his cap.

"I'll do what I can to keep a lid on," he said. "But not for you. For me, really. So I'll know for a fact you're wide awake at night, chewing up those gorgeous rich-lady nails." He smiled. "I'm what you've got instead of a conscience."

"Why can't you just—?"

"Bad luck, I guess. Wrong cop."

"Listen," Ellie said. "I'm not evil."

"Heck no, ma'am. You're just so terribly, terribly unhappy." His smile was courteous, almost solicitous. "Here's the thing. I knew this lady once, loved her a bushel and a peck. Reminds me of you, kind of. Real unhappy. Spiritual emergency, she tells me, then she grabs her hair curlers and trots out the door. Week later—oh, hell, not even a week—two days, three days later, she's off with some other guy, this dumbass Spartan, and I'm stuck with my own spiritual emergency. Never forgot, never forgave."

"Spartan?" Ellie said.

"Yes, ma'am."

"I don't follow."

The policeman made a harsh, predatory sound. "Nothing to follow. Goddamn Spartans. They'll eat you alive."

"Who are you?"

"Me?"

"Officer *what?*"

The policeman chuckled, stepped off the porch, and stood in the rain. His face was little more than a smudge.

"I'll be in touch," he said. "Conscience and all that."

Ellie took the early bus to Minneapolis, then a half-empty jet to Boston, then the 4:05 commuter train out to Sheffield Farms. She was amazed to find her car parked exactly where she had left it a week ago, in the lot behind the train station; somehow, without realizing it, she'd been expecting rearrangements in the most banal details of the world. But the car was there, unmoved by

226

events, and so was the road to her house, and the bright green mailbox out front, and the giant oak trees, and the gravel driveway up to the garage.

It was a little after 5. The house, too, seemed complacently unchanged. There was a fresh woodsy scent in the air, as if the furniture had been sweating, and in the kitchen she found a blue Mason jar full of cut flowers from the garden. Ellie put down her suitcase. She stood still for a moment, almost calm, then she moved to the den and switched on the answering machine. There was a whining noise before she heard herself say, "Kisses." Later her voice said, "A fiasco, Mark. The whole stupid flight was canceled. Nothing I can do. Miss you a whole bunch."

She replayed the tape once, listening for the lie, but her voice seemed sturdy and expansive, like the house.

Ellie fixed herself a drink, carried it upstairs, filled the tub, slipped in, and sat soaking. More than anything, she now craved sleep. A four-month nap, then wake up to find matters settled. She could not focus on the practicalities. At some point things would have to be said, but the logic of it all seemed far too intricate. When she thought of Harmon, it was to think of him in the abstract, like a problem in geometry. The old passions struck her as something quaint and foreign. She remembered how they had gone dancing one night at Loon Point, how adventurous it had seemed, how the music and starlight and danger had stirred her to feel close to him, giddy with pleasure, and how in a curious way it was not really Harmon in her arms, it was the idea of happiness, the possibility, the temptation, a slow, tantalizing dance with some handsome future.

Ellie slid back in the tub, her lips just above the surface of the water. For a few seconds she drifted away, half dreaming, half awake, listening to the loud, mindless din of waterfowl, wild ducks and geese and loons, many thousands.

At six o'clock she went downstairs to start supper. A half hour later she heard the garage door crank open.

When Mark walked into the kitchen, Ellie fixed her lips in an expression of savage domesticity. She adjusted the heat on the electric skillet, used a spatula to drop on three hamburgers.

Mark came up behind her. "The globetrotter," he said, and kissed her neck, his fingers squeezing the inch or two of loose flesh at her waist. This was a habit Ellie disliked—it made her feel fat—but now she let herself lean back into his hands. She felt a rush of gratitude. Immediately, by the pressure of his fingers, she knew he had no inkling.

"You're late," she said. "Again."

"Wow, I didn't realize—"

"An hour late," Ellie said. "More than an hour." It was not quite true, but it transferred the burden of explanation.

Mark stripped off his tie and sat on a stool beside her. He did not look at the clock.

"Usual nonsense," he said wearily. "Nancy brings in this pile of contracts, the Earhardt deal, except she's got the addresses all scrambled. A first-class bollix job. Christ, if I hadn't spotted it—" He made a sound that was meant to convey frustration. In fact, Ellie knew, he was pleased with himself. "Anyhow, I straighten it out, but by then it's almost five, so I end up driving the damn contracts across town. I'm a mailman. I'm a six-figure delivery boy."

Ellie flipped the hamburgers. "But you settled it?"

"The Earhardt thing? Signed, sealed. Professionally well delivered."

"My warrior."

"Right, babe. Call me Tonto." Mark grinned and stood up. He glanced at the evening newspaper. "How was the trip?"

"Fine," said Ellie.

"Well, great. Give me the whole happy scoop at dinner."

They ate in their bathrobes in front of the TV. The evening news was dominated by the economy—lagging exports, a proposal for retaliatory new tariffs—and Mark's posture went rigid as he watched footage of small, brightly colored Korean cars rolling off a ship in Seattle. At one point he muttered, "Sick." A moment later he said, "Criminal." During the commercials, in a tone Ellie recognized as politely forced, he asked questions about her trip. He was interested in the airline food, the weather, the friends she'd been visiting in the Twin Cities. Ellie kept her answers short. The friends were a bore, she said. The weather was hot, the food was poisonous.

Mark nodded at the TV screen. His eyes had a far-off shine. Apparently it had not occurred to him that in the past six months she had accumulated a good many frequent-flier miles. Not that it was Mark's fault, Ellie realized—it was her own—yet she found herself riding a quick wave of irritation.

"Listen, I'm sorry about the snafu," she said. "Nothing I could do about it."

Mark was scanning channels with the remote control. "Snafu?" he said.

"The canceled flight."

"No kidding?"

Ellie glanced at him. "Mark, I was due in yesterday. I explained how I couldn't . . . You didn't get the message?"

"Oops," he said, and frowned at her. "Never checked the machine."

Ellie stared at her plate. The hamburger had left a fleshy, rancid taste in her mouth. Stupidly, without calculation, she was seized by a need to strike back. What she should've done, she thought, was call in a message describing how her lover had drowned in the waters off Loon Point. All the details. She should've talked about Harmon's wet corpse, and how she was feeling pretty soggy herself, and how she'd been numbed by the terror of growing old and silly and insignificant. Even now, maybe, she could unburden herself. Interrupt the broadcast. A personal bulletin.

Instead, Ellie took her tray to the kitchen, rinsed the dishes, and moved out to the back patio. The evening was humid and still. In the leaden twilight, she once again had the desire to lie down and sleep, just collapse, and it required an act of glacial willpower to hold herself together. From beyond the oak trees came the brain-dead drone of someone's leaf blower.

Ellie loosened the belt on her bathrobe. The hamburger was not resting well.

Barefoot, moving with new caution, new knowledge, she walked out to a bed of flowers she'd been nursing since spring. Ellie spent the last minutes of twilight there, admiring her astilbes and phlox, recalling the many ceremonious, unconscious hours she had devoted to this tidy patch of suburbia. It seemed bizarre and gallant that she'd once taken such pleasure in the growth of things. The happy farmer, Mark always said. And it was true: she *had* been happy, or whatever happiness was when it came without joy. Her life, she observed, had fallen into the cycle of a nasturtium, uncomplicated by desire. She loved Mark, yes, and perhaps in a vague, nostalgic way she had also loved Harmon, but the reality of love was not what she'd once imagined it to be.

Ellie reached down to pull a weed. Then she stopped. Something awesome, something approaching grief, suddenly flooded her stomach.

In the evening air, like a blank tape, there was the hum of a terrifying question—What next?—which then deepened into the sound of an imperfect, infinitely approximate answer: Who ever knows?

She pictured Harmon on the dance floor at Loon Point. She pictured herself as a little girl in a frilly blue dress and white shoes.

And then one other image came to her. On a New Year's Eve eighteen years ago, a few months before they were married, Mark had presented her with a huge corsage, then they'd taken a cab to a late-night party, where they had danced and sampled exotic drinks and looked at each other with the apprehension that love was happening. At one point, well after midnight, Mark had led her outside. He'd put his hands on her shoulders. "Please, please, love me forever," he'd said, "just keep on loving me, always and always and always and always and always and always, please, please, and don't ever, ever, ever stop, not ever," and when Ellie bobbed her head, when she began to cry, Mark Abbott had grinned like the man he was, a simple, romantic, courageous man—so good, so hopelessly guileless—and he kissed her lips, kissed her throat, leaned down and ate the corsage off her breast.

Ellie opened her robe to the garden and let herself be bathed by the humid night air.

She would never tell.

She would brace herself. She would endure the terror of discovery. She would flinch at each ring of her telephone, at the approach of a mailman, at every knock on the door. For the remainder of her married life, maybe beyond that, she would be pulled into the deep by the weight of a drowning man. Even now, on the street opposite a neighbor's lawn, a car had just stopped. A slim, neatly dressed young man got out, locked his car, seemed to hesitate, and then walked away into the shadows.

It was not the policeman. Probably not. But someday, Ellie knew, it surely would be.

A little later Mark came up behind her.

"Hey, gorgeous," he said. "How's the crop?"

Ellie tugged her robe shut. "It's fine," she said.

CHAPTER 14

CLASS OF '69

S o what you're afraid of," Paulette said, "you're afraid of getting blackmailed? By that policeman?"

"A little," Ellie said. "Not much."

"Conscience, then?"

"If I have one. But sometimes it feels like—this'll sound completely nuts—it feels like that snotty, holier-than-thou cop's actually spying on me. I look up, he'll be there. Then he's not there. And then he is."

"Whatever it takes," said Paulette.

Ellie Abbott looked up at a passing airliner. The morning was hot and muggy, very silent, but now a shroud of clouds had started to pile up over the Dakotas, still distant, still many hours away. There was the scent of a coming storm.

"I'll tell you what else it feels like," Ellie said. "It's like this heaviness inside me. The secrecy. It weighs a ton. I wake up with it, lug it around all day. Can't ever relax. I'll be watching TV, having dinner, and then boom, it's not dinner anymore, it's Harmon, and he's drowning. How do you hide this big, white, dead body? Won't ever stop."

"You can't hide it," Paulette said. "You don't. You told *me*, Ellie. Tell your husband."

"What if he turns around and—"

"Oh, I know," Paulette said quietly. "Problem is, what if *you* don't?"

Ellie almost nodded, not quite.

She looked at her wristwatch and tried to smile. The smile didn't come off.

"We should get back," she said. "The service starts at three, I've got to pick up flowers, change clothes, try to make myself—"

"Harmon's dead," said Paulette. "So is Karen. You aren't."

"Christ. All right, then. I'll try."

"Don't say try, honey. Promise me."

"Okay," said Ellie.

"Is that a promise?"

"I don't know."

They turned and headed back toward campus, holding hands. For some time neither of them spoke. Then Ellie said, "Did I mention the loons?"

"You did."

"Well, good. Do you mind if I stop a minute and cry?"

"Let's both," said Paulette.

At 2:15 P.M., Spook Spinelli's alarm went off. She nudged Marv, who slept face-up beside her. His tie had been loosened, nothing else.

"Hi, there," he said sleepily. "Did we do it?"

★   ★   ★

Marla Dempsey and David Todd dropped off their flowers at the Darton Hall chapel. It was a circular brick-and-glass building, the venue of their wedding thirty years earlier, but neither of them had the courage or discourtesy to bring that up.

"Off to change clothes," Marla said. She pecked his cheek. "You all right?"

"A-okay."

"You're positive?"

"Yeah."

"I'll stay if you want."

"Not necessary," he said. "Change."

When she was gone, David sat in a front pew. The chapel was empty except for a teenage organist setting up her sheet music.

Outside, the temperature was approaching ninety-four degrees. Inside, it seemed warmer.

David popped some Darvon, popped some Demerol, folded his hands, leaned back, and listened to Johnny Ever scold him about lost causes. "Ancient story," Johnny was saying. "Old as the protons. Seen it once, seen it a zillion times. We're talkin' grand illusion here. Fairy tales. Fuckin' *Hair.* Your whole wacked-out generation, man, it got turned around by all that *tooby ooby walla starshine* crud. I mean, in all flat-out honesty, what the fuck? Greek to me, Davy, and I *know* Greek." Johnny sighed. "Naïveté, my friend, it's health risk number one. Romantic fantasy, it ought to be covered by your HMO. Give it up, partner.

239

All them cockeyed Marla dreams. Remember the Alamo."

A half mile away, in an affluent section of St. Paul, Dorothy Stier stood before a mirror in her master suite. She was dressing for Billy McMann. She was also explaining to herself how happy she was, how the cancer had been mostly beaten—eight nodes, knock on wood—and how her boys were the two best kids on earth, and how Ron was completely devoted to her, very Catholic, the ideal partner, always supportive and punctual and full of wonderful ideas about home air filtration and automobile maintenance.

Dorothy decided against ostentation. She would wear a simple blue blouse over her prosthesis. No pearls. Glass earrings. That cheap perfume Billy used to like.

"So?" Marv said.

"My secret," said Spook, "but I'll tell you this much. You *are* a fathead."

"Thank you, thank you," Marv said. "Not just the head, the whole well-marbled shebang." He looked at her. "Took advantage of me, then?"

Spook said, "In my dreams."

Marv said, "Maybe tonight? Say maybe."

"Maybe," said Spook. "Straighten up that tie, unstraighten the hog. We've got funerals to go to."

"Hog?" Marv said.

"Under your pants."

"You mean this fat thing?"

"That's what I mean," said Spook.

"Say maybe again."

Spook laughed and said, "Don't press it."

Jan Huebner fluffed up her close-cut bleached hair, applied a coat of Midnight Plum lipstick, painted on a pair of blue-black eyebrows, and said to Amy Robinson, "No place like a church to get lucky. How do I look?"

"Fucking awful," Amy said.

The new bride of Minnesota's lieutenant governor, twenty-six years his junior, watched the big old houses on Summit Avenue slide by. She was not interested in reunions. She was not interested in funerals. And she was most especially and most definitely not interested in that crowd of alcoholic, pot-bellied, whatever-happened-to-us old folks. She'd had her fill the day before. Claimed a headache, left midway through last night's dance: crappy songs about barricades and paranoia.

She looked over at her husband, who was driving.

"Whose funeral is it?"

"Memorial service. Two old friends."

"Who?"

"Karen somebody, Harmon somebody."

"Loved them dearly?"

"Names," he said. "I'm getting old."

"You are old," said his new bride. She sat restlessly for a time. "That fiancée of yours, will she be there?"

"Ex," he said.

"And?"

"Probably."

"Certain times," Johnny Ever said, "you gotta bite the bullet. Take your medicine, hope for the worst. Ask my opinion, Dave, them Irish folks got the right idea. Expect the world to break your heart. Somebody burps, begs your pardon, it's a sunny day in Tipperary."

David Todd closed his eyes, let the drugs carry him off. Quiet, he thought. This is church.

Johnny chuckled.

"Bet your sweet soul, it's church. So listen up, I got this riddle for you. What came first, chicken or the egg? Answer: The old man sneezed. Tried that once on Robespierre, fella just blinked at me. But you get the point, I hope. No point. Like with that lost colony at Roanoke, the one that up an' vanished into thin air. Bunch of change-the-world dreamers, sixties all over again, everybody full of spit and vinegar: 'Hey, let's start a commune!' Next thing you know, bam, they're the lost generation. Ring a bell? I mean, come on, take a good look at things. Brand-new millennium. Now you got cable. Twenty-four-hour chitchat, the Desperation Channel, all the Joyce Brothers you can stomach. New world, huh? And what about Thorazine?

Didn't even exist back then. Chat rooms. 1-800-SABBATH. Tape your own porno. Plenty of sweet new potions to ease the soul, help shake off them late-night losties. Progress, hey? You bet! No need to dwell on that lost-love hooey. She's passé, Dave. Old hat." Johnny's voice softened a little. "Believe me, man. I'm an angel. She'll crush you all over again."

Dorothy Stier drove the half mile to campus, parked on Grand Avenue, and hurried into a neighborhood drugstore to look for the perfume Billy used to like. The brand name eluded her. Adoration, Amour. Something cheap as dirt. She spent a few minutes sniffing the wares, studying bottles, and then asked a bald, natty-looking pharmacist if he had any ideas. "Something with an A," she said.

"Allure?" the man said.

"No. It's ancient. Adoration, I think."

"Adoration?" He clicked his tongue. "Don't know it. We got Allure. We got that Anaïs Anaïs junk, smells like my brother."

"Maybe Amour," said Dorothy.

"Never heard of it. Anaïs Anaïs, though—take a whiff of my brother, you'll know what I mean." The pharmacist pushed his glasses up over his small, bald, perfectly round head. "If you want, I can check in back. Something A, you said?"

Abruptly, the man turned and went through a door. Dorothy looked at her watch. It was six minutes to three. A dumb idea, she thought. Perfume, for crying out loud, what was wrong with her? Then she wagged her head and looked up at a big black-and-white poster behind the counter: TEN WAYS TO PREVENT BREAST CANCER.

A great deal of time went by before the pharmacist returned.

"No luck," the man said. "Allure, Anaïs Anaïs, that's it. Take my advice, stay away from Anaïs Anaïs. Allure, I don't mind."

"Nothing, then," said Dorothy. "I'll pass."

"Good choice."

The man studied her pensively, boring in, and then he seemed to smile without moving his lips.

"Anyhow," he said, "perfume won't do it."

CHAPTER 15

HALF GONE

On a balmy, sunlit afternoon in midsummer of 1997, a Saturday, nine and a half months after her surgery, Dorothy Stier removed her shirt, removed her bra, adjusted her wig, slipped into a pair of sandals, finished off a glass of lemonade, cursed, muttered to herself— "Enough of *this!*"—threw open the back door, passed through it, marched across the patio and down a slate sidewalk that led to the driveway at the side of the house, where her husband Ron, a senior vice president at Cargill, had just finished washing and waxing his two prized Volvos. The twins, he called them. Inanely, Dorothy thought. One was an aqua-blue station wagon, the other a boxy, oversize, much-gadgeted silver sedan. Since acquiring the vehicles a few weeks back, in what he too cleverly, too repetitively called a "package steal," Ron had lavished upon his new automobiles a preposterous mix of time and labor and paternal love. Which struck Dorothy as perverse. The man was already father to two spiffy boys. Not twins, perhaps, but well polished and mechanically sound. And he had a wife, too. A terrific wife. A wife, for that matter, who herself had once been awfully damned sporty, awfully sleek, a vintage Bentley amid a fleet of utilitarian SUV housewives.

Dorothy was angry. Beyond anger, in fact. She had been contemplating departure. The "where" was irrelevant: Paris or Hong Kong or Duluth or even the frigid streets of Winnipeg. No matter. At that particular instant, which registered in the suburban heavens at just after 2 P.M., July 19, 1997—and which found Dorothy Stier twelve tipsy strides down the cement driveway, now bare to the waist, now committed, now pinned to the glaring present by the bewildered gaze of her gardener Jimmy—at that radiant, savage, remotely noble moment, Dorothy feared she might vomit. Her stomach wobbled. She was propelled down the driveway by four or five vodka lemonades. Not quite drunk, perhaps, but she'd done her best. To steady herself, Dorothy lifted a hand as if to grasp the summer air. She nodded briskly at Jimmy, who glanced down at his hedge clipper, inspected it, then looked back at her again. The man grinned but said nothing. Nor did Ron, whose attention was fastened on a sparkling hubcap and a pad of steel wool.

But on the adjoining lawn, behind a low, freshly painted picket fence, Dorothy's dear friend and next-door neighbor, Fred Engelmann, a retired Marine Corps colonel, had plainly taken notice. Only a moment earlier, Fred had raised his garden hose by way of greeting. He had started to say something, started to wave, but his jaw had locked midway through a curious smile. The hose shifted in his hands. He was watering his collie's doghouse.

"Freddie, darling!" cried Dorothy.

She released her grip on the air and fluttered fingers at the man: thoughtful neighbor, confidant, ex-assassin, domestic adviser. Cheerfully, in a magnified, somewhat slurry across-the-fence voice, Dorothy cried, "Gorgeous day!"

"Roger that," Fred said.

"Wet doghouse!"

"Affirmative again," he said, and redirected the hose. Crinkles formed at the man's eyes. He had decided, apparently, to treat this with humor. "Catching rays, I guess?"

"That I am!" said Dorothy.

"Good, then. Good for you."

"Goodie for me! One second, I'll pop right over."

"Do that for sure," said Fred.

All this had consumed little more than a few moments of Saturday, July 19. Ron had not yet turned to encounter his future. He knelt alongside the aqua-blue station wagon, his forehead puckered in concern over a scarred hubcap. Dorothy was six strides away, closing fast. Two or three elongated heartbeats elapsed: Jimmy pruning, Fred watering, a buzzing lawn mower, a child squealing, a radio playing Wagner, the two waxed Volvos gleaming like precious stones under a flagrant summer sun.

Ron pivoted on one knee.

He began to rise, stopped, squinted up at Dorothy. "What's this?" he said.

"A wife," said Dorothy. She was now two strides away, accelerating.

"Jesus Christ."

"Look at me," said Dorothy.

He glanced at her shins.

"Higher," she said. "Pretend I'm a Volvo."

She had braked directly in front of him, seven or eight inches away. Her smile was genuine, even dazzling in the July sunlight, but it was also a foolhardy, belligerent, challenging smile.

"Suck it up," she said. "One look."

"Honey," Ron said.

He rose to his feet, threw an arm around her.

"Come on," he said. "Inside."

"One look. Don't be afraid."

"What is this?" Ron said. "Lady Godiva? Some nude freak show?"

"Freak?"

"I didn't mean freak."

"You did. Very distinct. Freak."

"Dorth, you're drunk."

She spun out of his arms and stepped back to present a vista. Ron's gaze shifted into the summer distance, as though seeking a more easeful angle on the world, and then, with a hiss of dismay, more or less directly, he looked at her.

"Ghastly?" she said.

"No," he said. "It makes me want to cry."

"Touch me."

"We're in a driveway, honey. It's daylight."

"Go on. Touch."

"Don't do this," he said. He spoke quietly, almost in a whisper, as if the essential problem were one of volume. "I'm asking nice, Dorth. Let's please go inside. Fred and Jimmy, they're getting an eyeful."

"Half full," said Dorothy.

"Half full. Touché. Can we go inside?"

"You haven't looked yet."

"What the hell am I doing right now?"

"Pretending," said Dorothy.

"I'm not pretending."

"Oh, you are, you are," she said, and then she went up on her toes, extending her arms like a ballerina, and executed a twirl in the driveway. Again her stomach wobbled. It occurred to her that the radio music was coming from the aqua-blue station wagon. She hadn't realized Ron liked Wagner. She hadn't realized, in fact, that he cared much for music.

"There," Ron said. "I've looked."

"Barely. And you haven't touched."

He frowned and said, "Stop this."

"Not in four months," she said. "It's breast cancer, Ron. It's not the flu, you can't catch it."

"I realize that."

"No lookie, no nookie."

"Lay off," he said. "I know."

Dorothy felt a gust of sickness go through her. Stupidly, she giggled. She cupped her hands and called out across the picket fence: "One sec, Freddie!"

"Jesus," Ron said.

Fred waved a hand. Generously, the man kept his back to them, aiming his hose at a patch of giant sunflowers.

"Nice guy," said Dorothy.

"He sure is. Are we finished here?"

"I guess we are." She wanted to be held and loved, wanted to return these things, but she also wanted to notch up the hurt. She flicked her head at his shiny Volvos. "How're the twins?"

"They're good."

"Praise God. Huge load off my mind."

"You're jealous of cars?"

"Gosh, I don't even know," Dorothy said. "Am I jealous? Am I? Too tough to call. Hot cars, obviously."

Ron took a step toward the house. "I've had it. Gone. Out of here."

"Bye, then."

"Yeah, bye," he said. "I'm not begging."

He didn't move.

Dorothy leaned back against the station wagon, tipped up her head, and let the sunlight strike her straight on. She was forty-nine years old. She was a Reagan Republican, mother of two, chemo chick, loser of a left breast, out of kilter, terrified, stomach-sick, head-sick, co-chair with Fred

Englemann of the Highland Park Neighborhood Watch Committee.

Also, at the moment, she was a woman in need of redefinition.

She looked at her husband. The anger was mostly gone now, replaced by a powerful, much more frightening weariness. "No sweat," she said. "Go watch a ball game. I'm fine right here."

"Dorth, this isn't fair."

"Just go. Give me a minute."

Ron made a frustrated choking sound under his breath. He swung around, stalked up the driveway, crossed the patio, and went into the house.

Sad thing, Dorothy thought.

For an instant she considered chasing after him. Put her shirt on. Blame it on the lemonade. After all, he was a miracle of a husband. Wonderful father, wonderful partner. Reliable as a Volvo. Back in 1969, three months out of college, she'd married him for his looks, which were boyish and lean and almond-eyed, a beautiful man, still drop-dead delicious even in middle age. But over twenty-eight years of marriage, Dorothy had come to appreciate him for what seemed, in theory, more substantial reasons. His good nature. His corny, old-fashioned ethics. The uncomplicated pleasure he took in providing for his family: an elegant home, expensive cars, a gardener named Jimmy, memberships in two ritzy country clubs. True, he came off stiff in the personality department—"Anal Andy," the boys called him—but at heart, in soul and spirit, he was a virtuous, honorable, suitably solid man. Through the whole cancer nightmare, he'd breathed courage and confidence into her, citing survival statistics, clipping articles, calling her attention to recent advances in drug therapy. His relentless, can-do solicitude, in fact, had almost killed her. Always the cheerleader. Rah-rahing the oncologists, rooting for the cure, clapping his hands and purring, "Atta girl," as she puked out the chemo poisons.

Couldn't blame him, Dorothy thought. Funny thing about breasts: husbands expect two of them. "Freak" was the word. And in truth Dorothy herself wasn't all that crazy about mirrors or negligees. Still, it seemed a pity that she'd been robbed of a husband and a decent sex life along with the killer breast.

Dorothy gave the station wagon a slap, switched off the radio, and joined Fred in his sunflower patch. "Freddie, Freddie," she said, and kissed the man's leathery cheek. "I've had a drink or two, maybe seven, probably eight, so cut me some slack." She put her hands on her hips. She hid nothing. "Amazing flowers, lovely day. How's Alice? I haven't got a shirt on."

Fred chuckled and said, "Guess you don't."

"I actually don't," said Dorothy. "Apologies."

"No need," Fred said. "Case closed. Over 'n' out."

"I'll go put a shirt on."

"No need for that either."

Fred turned off his hose, took her by the elbow, and in his firm, courtly way escorted her into the shade of an ornate iron rose trellis. They sat on the lawn. For ten years, almost eleven, she and Fred Engelmann had been the closest of friends, trading gossip, trading Clinton jokes, co-purveyors of Nuke the Liberals bumper stickers. Together they had joyfully maligned the modern age. They agreed on certain bedrock principles—less is more in affairs of state, prayer in the schools, the indisputable un-Americanism of so-called affirmative action. With mutual good humor, mutual horror, they had grieved over what seemed a vast ice age of turpitude and moral amnesia. They laughed a good deal. They enjoyed each other. More than that, Fred seemed to understand her exactly as Dorothy most wanted to be understood. On occasion, especially after a few backyard cocktails, it was as if the man had unlocked the code of her personal history, developed a dossier on her dreams: certain regrets and longings. Forks in the road. Missed opportunities. Years ago as a Marine in Vietnam, Fred had been affiliated in some cryptic way with the Phoenix program, which, as he sketchily described it, had to do with terminal solutions. "Find 'em, fry 'em," he'd say, then his eyes would twinkle and he'd gaze at her—gaze through her—and wink and say, "Ghost work. Simple as pie once you get the hang of it."

She'd never pressed him. But it was sometimes spooky. Nothing obvious, nothing conclusive, just that wink of his. The way he'd stare whenever she exaggerated or fibbed or put a little self-advertising spin on the world.

Now, for instance.

As she lay back on his lawn. As she kicked off her sandals and said, "No big deal, Freddie. Woman problems."

Dorothy felt the man studying her.

"The midlife follies," she said, too quickly. "My topless phase."

Fred smiled, cleared his throat, waited, stayed silent, kept smiling, gave her time to consider corrections and modifiers.

"I'm leaving him," she said.

"Gotcha. Ron trouble?"

Dorothy squinted at him. "Don't act like you didn't know."

"Okay, I'm pinned down." The smile didn't change. His eyes were like clean, fresh water. "Maybe I noticed a couple things. One plus one. Did the math, figured out a wee bit."

"Not wee and not maybe," said Dorothy. "You notice everything. But even if I wanted to, which for the record I definitely do not want—and forgive me, Freddie, I'm stinko, totally lemonaded, just psycho-sicko shitfaced. Anyway, even if I actually decided to stick around, let's face it, how the heck *could* I? After this." She gestured at her chest. "God help the one-boobed nymphs. Down with the queen. This Highland Park crowd—me included, you included—they don't go in for risqué. Right

256

now, I'll bet a couple hundred phones are ringing. Bet I'm on their naked-lady watch list."

"You're on mine," Fred said.

"Yeah, thanks. What about Alice?"

Fred grinned. "Put it this way, she had a peek out the window. Probably took to bed."

The man studied her chest, not coldly, not indifferently, but as if concentrating on some intricate endgame. Then he sighed and said, "Lock 'n' load. Old Fred's dyin' to hear this."

"I should really go put something on."

"Negative, let 'er rip," he said.

Dorothy could think of little to say. Words came to her—grotesque, rather be dead, how could this happen?—but it all sounded so banal, so routinely and ridiculously human. After a few garbled sentences, she stopped and stared up at the brilliant July sky. "It's not all Ron's fault. I don't like touching me either. Hate showers. Hate bedtime."

"Oh, yes?" Fred said.

"Very true. Hate. And I don't mean this chopped-liver mess up here. Not just the breast."

"Right," he said. "You don't mean that."

Dorothy nodded. "It's worse. Like my whole life's got cancer."

"Exactly," he said.

"And I'm not—" She exhaled. "What the heck was *that*, Fred?"

"What was what, darlin'?"

"That word. 'Exactly,' you said."

"Did I?"

"You did. It's *my* screwed-up life—how could you know?"

Fred gave her a pained, persecuted look, as though the question were unneighborly. "Not born yesterday," he said. He grunted, satisfied. "Mind if I take off my trousers? I'm an old bastard. Nothing to worry about."

"You're not old, Freddie."

"Yeah, well, older than you think. Ex-leatherneck, ex-widow maker. Hell, we're all old."

He peeled off his pants, tossed them aside, looked across the picket fence, then waved and saluted. Ron stood watching from the patio. He seemed lost and angry. He did not salute back. After a few moments he turned and went inside.

"Upset husband," Fred said mildly.

"Who isn't?"

"Good point. But if I was in your naked-lady shoes, I'd probably trot back to the drawin' board, start to rethink my tactics. Not too late. Except, of course, this problem we've got here, it's not just Ron, right?" He winked at her. "Can I ask something?"

"You may."

"Yeah. May. Ever vote Democrat?"

Dorothy glanced up. It was not the question she'd expected, but still it unnerved her. "Vote Democrat?" she said. "Maybe once. Maybe."

"May I guess?"

"You may, sure," Dorothy said, "and I've got this strange feeling that you can."

"Sixty-eight primary. Gene McCarthy."

"Freddie, how do you know all this?"

"Sources. My ex-specialty."

"Fred!"

"Deal is, you're my best pal, my neighbor," he said, "so it's good to figure out what's what. One more question. Ever tell Ron? About—you know—the fall from grace? The pinko leftwing lapse?"

"You tell me, Freddie. Did I?"

His eyes brightened, impish. "No, sweetheart, I reckon you probably didn't. Not a bad place to start, though. Might clear the air about a whole bucketful of trouble. Second thoughts. Life cancer." Fred lay back in the grass, shading his eyes against the sun. He wore black boxer shorts, black socks, black tennis shoes. The skin on his shins and thighs looked mummified. "If it helps any . . . Me, I was a Kennedy man. RFK. End the war, save the intestines."

Dorothy hunched forward, rocking, arms across her chest. She now felt the pressure of her nakedness. "I surrender," she said. "What's the point?"

"Points," Fred said lightly, "are mucho overrated. By the way, Ron's back. Patio. Binoculars."

"I can't look."

"Up to you. Anyhow, this harebrained Clean Gene business, I'm not gonna pry. Had your reasons. Maybe that college boy you almost ran off with. The one before Ron. What's his name?"

"Billy."

"Yeah, yeah. Billy. Left him in the lurch, I'd say. Cold, cold Winnipeg. Draft dodger, sure, and I don't truck with that, but even so it's gotta be tough gettin' dumped for your best friend. Good pals, weren't they? Ron and Billy? No fun. Figure it had to eat at you, too, the way you changed horses in midstream. Missed that flight to Canada. Went for handsome. Went for conservative. No-risk marriage, so to speak. And then all these years down the road, yikes, along comes cancer, eight nodes, enough to give a gal the middle-age willies. Certain what-ifs pop up. Roads not taken. Grass-might've-been-greener poppycock."

"That was decades ago," Dorothy said.

"You bet," he said. "Yesterday, huh?"

Dorothy tightened her lips, straightened up. "I need to put something on," she said. "This instant."

"Oh, boy."

"Hand me those pants, Fred. And I don't appreciate the snooping." She covered herself with his stained chinos, tied the pant legs behind her neck. "Not funny, not a joke. It's like you've been checking up on me. Had me followed or tracked or . . . What's the word?"

"Tailed," he said.

"That's it. And we were friends."

Fred clenched his jaw. "We are, darlin'. Can't get friendlier. Fact-finding, that's probably more like it. Research, you could say."

"Whatever," Dorothy said. "Shame on you."

She began to rise, pushing hard, but it was as if her muscles had come loose from the bone. Too much lemonade, she reasoned, or too much stress, but either way she had the sensation of being fastened to the lawn by Fred Engelmann's water-clear gaze.

It was now 2:43 P.M., Saturday, July 19, 1997. Still hot, still sunny. A light breeze had come up. The two Volvos glistened in the driveway. Her left breast was gone. Her boys were at camp. Her gardener had vanished. Her husband was back on the patio, pacing, a very nice man. Dorothy Stier could not move and was not sure she wanted to.

"Yeah, shame on me," Fred Engelmann said. "Old habits."

"I'm shocked and I'm hurt," said Dorothy. She felt paralyzed. Speech was an effort. "You voted for a Kennedy?"

Fred nodded unhappily. "Don't tell Alice."

"Well, I won't, but you have to explain."

"RFK? The fella had this—"

"No," she said. "The spying. I mean, God, I tell you everything anyway."

"Not quite everything," he said, and his eyes crinkled. He seemed gleeful, plainly enjoying himself, but there was also a patient, expectant quality in the way he regarded her. After a second he motioned at his swimming pool. "What say we invite Ron over? Take a dip, pry Alice out of bed, grill up some burgers? Might file off the tension."

"I'm leaving him," said Dorothy. "Maybe you

didn't stumble across that little fact in your research."

"Oh, I did, I did," Fred said.

"Then you know. He won't come near me. Hideous, repulsive, freaky wife." She paused. "Is he watching?"

"Appears so, unless he's asleep behind those binoculars." Fred pulled off his shirt and tennis shoes and socks. "Come on now, let's you and me hop in the pool. If I got this doped out right, Ron'll be showing up pronto."

"I can't move."

"Sure you can."

Fred did his winking thing and took her by the wrist and helped her stand. She seemed to glide the ten or fifteen yards over to his pool.

"My pants," he said, and removed the chinos from her chest. "Expensive fuckers, no need to ruin 'em."

"Who *are* you?"

He chuckled and said, "Name's Freddie. USMC, retired."

The water was warm and lovely. Highland Park was a new place. Fred swam a few laps, Dorothy floated, and then the man paddled up beside her and said, "Eight nodes, that's a killer. Some gals make it. Not you, I'm afraid. I'll give it five years. Five years, two months, handful of days. Can't nail it down any tighter."

"Five?" Dorothy said.

"And two months."

"You seem sure."

"I am. Awful darn sure."

"One more time. Who are you?"

He grinned and said, "Neighbor."

Dorothy looked at the bright suburban sky. She was on her back in the middle of the pool, pleased to be wet, pleased to be floating. Her wig floated beside her.

"We're talkin' five real good years," Fred said. "Way I see it, you won't be heading for Hong Kong. Not Duluth. Not Winnipeg, either. Two super kids, one fairly rock-ribbed husband. What I'd recommend, though, I'd recommend you take what you took. Went the comfy route. Nice house, nice cars. Not so terrible." The man started to swim away, but then turned and treaded water. "No need to feel guilty, either. That old boyfriend you're dreamin' about. Billy. He's fine. He made it too."

"Sources?" said Dorothy.

"Roger that. Here comes Ron."

Dorothy Stier took a breath, went under, came up again. It was July 19, 1997, but no longer seemed to be. Dorothy hit the water with the heel of her hand. "Five years, what a pile of bull," she said. "Stick around, Freddie. I'll make it. Wait and see."

"Will do," he said.

CHAPTER 16

CLASS OF '69

A few minutes before 3 P.M. on Saturday, July 8, 2000, more than two hundred members of the class of '69 gathered in the Darton Hall chapel to celebrate the abridged lives of Harmon Osterberg and Karen Burns. The service was scheduled to begin at any moment, but the PA system had gone faulty, and now repairs were under way. The crowd of mourners had turned garrulous and lighthearted. A gallon of home-brewed spirits made its bumpy passage from pew to pew. At the rear of the chapel someone was blowing into a tuba, unmusically but with vigor, and others clapped and kept time, and up on the altar three dozen flower arrangements surrendered to the scent of dope. Marv Bertel, who sat next to Spook Spinelli, lunched on a Devil Dog and a thermos of martinis. One more bite, Marv told himself. Maybe polish off the martinis, maybe prime rib this evening, and then nothing but saltines and water. Drop ninety pounds. Get his ass divorced. Sell the mop factory and see what Spook was up to for the next twenty years or so.

★　　★　　★

Spook was on her cell phone. She leaned against Marv, waiting, sucking her thumb. The two husbands exhausted her. She exhausted herself. A few minutes ago, feeling blue and underappreciated, she'd put in a call to her ex-keyboardist out in L.A. At the moment she was on hold.

The tuba player, who had gotten into the spirit of things, notched up the volume and pumped out "Personality."

Directly behind Marv and Spook, Dorothy Stier had exchanged sharp words with Billy McMann, whose grudge was apparently lifelong and who had just muttered a creative obsenity and marched off to join David Todd and Marla Dempsey in a front pew.

Billy was ready to head home. He was ashamed of himself.

He'd come here to get revenge, to inject grief into Dorothy Stier's iron heart, but as it turned out, he'd only hurt himself and Spook Spinelli. He felt like an idiot. A manipulator, too. All that rage, all those wasted years. "Look, if you want to screw Spook, that's fine," Dorothy had said. "Have a ball, join the crowd, but why brag about it? Especially to me. I'm a married woman, Billy. I don't get jealous."

Paulette Haslo waited in a doorway for Ellie Abbott; Ellie was in the ladies' room, applying mascara, composing herself. Harmon was drowned. And

Ellie, too, felt the lake in her lungs. She'd had no idea secrecy could be such a killer.

In a middle pew, sitting by themselves, Amy Robinson and Jan Huebner took turns nipping from a depleted flask of vodka. Amy was studying the service program. "'Abridged lives,'" she said, "is not exactly how I'd phrase it. I might go for the word 'dead.' Maybe 'slain.' Maybe 'drowned.' Dead's *dead*, isn't it?"

Jan Huebner nodded. "Believe so, babe. Except the word's right there in black and white. 'Abridged,' it says. It also says 'celebrate.'"

"It does indeed."

"There you are," Jan said. "We're here to celebrate an abridgment, no more, no less. Done deal."

"You're right," said Amy, "and celebrate we shall. Remind me this evening. Light on the vodka, heavy on the romance." She looked at Billy McMann. "Which leads us to one other crucial subject. Have you ever gone the group route?"

"Threesome, we're talking?"

"Threesome. Foursome. Yes or no?"

"Sadly, I have not," said Jan. "Cheers."

"Bad idea, probably."

"Impeccably bad," Jan said. She bent down, took a bracer from the flask, wiped her mouth, sat up again. "Anyway, have some respect. Karen's blushing in her grave. Let's face it, she *was* shy."

"Shy and sly," Amy said. "Never gave up. Always a crush on somebody."

"Also getting crushed," said Jan. "That sociology professor—what was his name? Some color."

"Brown," said Amy.

"Brown, that's it. And hurt-me-till-I-scream Karen, she kept writing the guy these long, elaborate love letters. Stapled them to essays, turned them in like homework."

"I don't recall that," Amy said.

"Factual."

Amy sighed. "What happened?"

"What you think happened? Karen gets an A in the guy's course, decides he's in love with her. All those Karen fantasies. Next thing you know she's an orangutan. Back to the psycho ward."

"She was sweet, though," Amy said.

"Sweet as can be."

"Too heavy, of course."

"Way too heavy," said Jan. She yawned and looked around the chapel. "This group thing. Have *you?*"

Spook was still on hold. A brusque, ill-mannered male secretary had seemed dubious when she'd asked to speak to a famous keyboardist for an even more famous rock band. "We'll see," the secretary had said, after which there was a click, and now Spook sat swaying to one of the keyboardist's best-known tunes. Years ago, in a smoky studio off Wilshire, she'd been present at the song's creation: sexy, stoned, impossibly young, lime-eyed and tanned, rich with joys just around the corner, as upbeat and mindless as the song itself. Presently it struck her that she had nothing to say to her aging keyboardist. All she wanted was to fly off somewhere, or drink from a fire extinguisher, or find one crummy thing to love about herself.

Paulette Haslo led Ellie Abbott into the chapel, saying, "You can do it."

Minnesota's lieutenant governor introduced his new wife to Darton Hall's dean of students. The three of them clasped hands as a school photographer snapped their picture. A few feet away, the lieutenant governor's ex-fiancée laughed hard—almost shrieked—at a Harmon Osterberg story someone had just told.

The inspired tuba player segued into the sixties, and people got up to dance, among them a physician and a former basketball star, now a mother of three. Outside, the temperature hit ninety-eight degrees, closing in on triple digits. Ellie Abbott feared she might pass out: the sadness and the loons and the awful secrecy combined to make heat waves in her head. Harmon Osterberg had gone to the bottom. Karen Burns had been murdered. America was at peace. Still, this was an abridgment, so the class of '69 sang about the rising sun—all of them, even Spook, even Dorothy

Stier and Marv Bertel and Billy McMann—and at the rear of the chapel the exuberant tuba player disgorged adrenaline. A distinguished physician, who three decades ago had been voted Most Arrogant Bastard on campus, made Tom Jones moves and crooned to a former basketball star.

The temperature rose a full degree. Heavy rain fell over the far Dakotas. There were high winds in northeastern Colorado, tornados in Nebraska.

"I must ask about something,' Jan Huebner said.

"Shoot," said Amy.

"This heat, girl. Why in God's name—pardon me, we're in church—but what's up with this hell-hot reunion? Why July?"

"You haven't heard?" Amy said.

"Heard what?"

"I shouldn't say."

"You sure shouldn't. Talk till I say stop."

Amy scanned the chapel. "Marla. You know about her problem, right?"

"I do not know."

"Oh, my. I feel catty."

"You *are* catty. What problem?"

"Depression," Amy said. "Spiritual crisis. Lost marbles, basically. Class secretary, she's supposed to arrange the whole deal. Banquets, reservations, all that. Ends up in the Mayo."

"Marla?"

"Six weeks."

"Jeez," Jan said.

They glanced over at Marla Dempsey.

"Love problems," Amy said.

"Sorry?"

"You know."

"Do I?"

"Sure you do. She adores David—crazy about him—but the girl won't let herself believe it. Thinks she can't love anybody."

"Oh, *that*," said Jan.

"Nothing changes," said Amy.

"Zilch," said Jan.

Billy McMann sat chatting with David Todd and Marla Dempsey, whose calm, easy company he enjoyed. But Billy's thoughts were on Spook Spinelli. In a minute, he told himself, he would excuse himself and go over to Spook and apologize. He'd been drunk and stupid. His brains had come down with his zipper. If Dorothy happened to overhear, so what?

Almost an hour late, the sound system issued a fearsome squeal, succeeded by a hum, and Paulette Haslo rose and moved to the pulpit and asked people to settle down. There was applause, some whistling. Thirty-one years ago Paulette had been a long-legged, busty, powerfully attractive college student, a hurdler, a swimmer, and the years had been merciful to her. Now, even in a plain white blouse and gray skirt, Paulette elicited whoops from a row of gone-to-fat jocks. No one in the chapel, including Paulette herself, understood why she'd never married.

She adjusted the microphone, smiled once in the direction of Ellie Abbott.

"Harmon Osterberg," Paulette said, "loved every one of you. Karen Burns, too. They loved like crazy. Way too much, it turns out. Let's all settle down and spend a lousy half hour loving them back."

Marv Bertel moved his fingers along Spook's thigh. He ignored the uneven thump in his chest.

Now or never, he thought.

"Thirty-one years ago," Paulette said, "Harmon and Karen believed in miracles. Didn't you?"

Spook looked up at Marv, stroked his cheek, punched the off button on her cell phone, and allowed herself the thought that Paulette might soon be saying sweet and beautiful things about Spook Spinelli. Almost a certainty. Yes, loving things. Spectacular, glamorous, memorial things.

"I'm talking about real miracles," Paulette said. "Every one of us. We were young. It was 1969. Man on the moon, those amazing Mets. We *had* to believe."

Marla took David's hand and gripped it in her lap. She understood the consequences. His love frightened her—its durability, its ferocity—but at the same time he was the most decent human being Marla had ever known. She couldn't promise much, only that she was ready to be forgiven.

Dorothy Stier had no tolerance for nostalgia. She tuned out after the word "miracle." Her left breast was gone, which sometimes made her feel asymmetric and unwomanly, other times proud. A hard decision, but in the end she'd done the intelligent thing. She always had. For a moment or two, Dorothy wondered how the world might've been different in Winnipeg, but again, now, she did the smart thing and locked away the past and congratulated herself on a good life, a good husband, and her own willingness to undergo radical surgery.

"It's tough to remember," Paulette said, "but back in those golden-oldie days we had faith. No more funerals, no more toothaches. Undo the wrongs, erase the pain, grow younger every day, fall in love forever. So dumb, so quixotic. But we did believe. And then we became America. Peddlers, cynics, nesters, practical as the Puritans, cold as the North Pole." Paulette ran a hand across her eyes, looked again at Ellie Abbott. "I don't exclude myself. I'm lost right now, I'll admit that. Having my own trouble with this belief business. Truth is, if there's a God, only God knows. But I will suggest this: Harmon Osterberg and Karen Burns were among the pitiful few who never abandoned themselves.

Harmon and his Project Smile, hauling those drills and braces off to Africa. Karen watching after the elderly. Maybe they never had time to drop the dream. Maybe in a few years they would've turned into you and me. But right now, if we close our eyes, Harmon and Karen are here with us. They're alive. They're twenty-one. They're kicking a soccer ball and rushing off to class and falling in love and falling out, and I guess that's miracle enough. Just to remember."

Amy Robinson passed the flask to Jan Huebner. "One thing in Karen's favor," Amy whispered. "Lucky girl doesn't have to listen to eulogies."

"Or have to pee," said Jan.

"Or cry," said Amy.

"Exactly," Jan said. "And no more reunions."

CHAPTER 17

NOGALES

K aren Burns is fifty-one, single, sturdy, a graying redhead, bashful with men, undistinguished of face and figure. She directs a retirement community in Tucson, and today, full of hope, she leads several of her charges on a walking tour of a desert park just outside the city. They have arrived by van: Karen, five residents of Homewood Estates, and a driver named Darrell Jettie. Single file, they plod down a marked cinder trail, past wildflowers and dwarf piñons and twisted old saguaros. The day is a scorcher, but the group moves along dutifully, the men chatting about golf, the women dabbing at their foreheads as Karen reads aloud from a park brochure.

Karen is not dressed for a desert outing. She is dressed for Darrell Jettie—in black slacks, gold sandals, a black cotton blouse. Black slims her down.

For six weeks, since hiring Darrell as a part-time driver, Karen has entertained robust, minutely detailed romantic fantasies. She cannot help herself. Even now, under the desert sun, her head is cluttered with voices not quite familiar. She imagines Darrell Jettie's tongue in her mouth. She

279

imagines preparing his breakfast, honeymooning on an exotic island.

Maybe love, someone, or something, whispers to her. *He wants you. He's watching.*

Karen blushes.

Still reading aloud from the brochure, she tells herself to take ten more steps, then stop, then look back at him and smile. Instantly, however, she revises this thought. Twenty-five steps, she decides. Fifty for sure.

And then she counts to herself.

At fifty, she stops and turns, bravely, but can manage only a weak stare.

Darrell frowns. He takes a half step.

"Problem?" he says.

Karen's heart clenches up. She shakes her head, spins around, and strides down the cinder trail.

At noon, when the group returns to the air-conditioned van, Karen sits in front next to Darrell, who is thirty-six, blond, excessively polite, a chain smoker. Karen has been dreaming love dreams all morning.

"Back to the ranch?" says Darrell.

"Oh, naturally, the ranch," Karen says, and tells herself not to hope.

Darrell pulls onto the highway.

He drives fast, smoking, two slender fingers hooked over the wheel. Though she does not smoke, and hates the smell, Karen has a sudden craving to put his cigarette to her lips. She almost reaches out. *Do it*, a voice urges, but she folds her hands and stares at the road.

They return to Homewood Estates in time for lunch. Karen checks in at her office and then hurries to the dining room, where she takes a seat at Darrell's table. It is no surprise to find him testing his charms on Bess Hollander, a balding, partly deaf eighty-year-old. Darrell flirts with a luxurious, practiced, night-club voice, and with a boyish slant to his lips, but mostly with his eyes, which are pale blue and untroubled.

"Go down through Nogales," he's telling Bess. He speaks loudly, each syllable seductive. "Cross over there, head for the good times. A day trip. Kick up our heels."

Bess is enchanted. "We'll just see about that," she says. "Don't count chickens, buster. It's not like I'm a two-bit floozy."

"You are so," says Darrell. "You're a harlot."

Bess laughs at this. Her husband—Ed Hollander, age seventy-six—grunts and says, "Count me in. You chase Bess, I'll chase señoritas."

"Fair enough," says Darrell. He turns to Karen. "Ready for an adventure?"

"Adventure?"

"We're taking the van to Mexico."

A roller-coaster feel comes into Karen's stomach. "Are we?" she says.

"Yes, ma'am."

"Well, then," Karen says.

It crosses her mind that Darrell has been hired as a driver, not as a tour leader, and that he ought to have cleared this with her. But she has already nodded. And Darrell has already reached across the table and gripped her wrist and said, "Tomorrow morning, first thing. Wear something sexy."

A silly crush: Karen understands that. Even so, in her apartment that evening she tries on a number of outfits in preparation for Mexico, posing before a hallway mirror, settling on a navy-blue skirt and a simple gray blouse. It may be true, Karen realizes, that she is pursuing a pipe dream. But it is certainly true, beyond question, that since childhood she has had trouble separating the world of fantasy from the world of human experience. Voices, for example. They come and go, most often male voices: a life-guard at summer camp, a sociology professor, a gynecologist who paid nightly visits to her dreams. In each case she had dropped hints, then later worked up the courage to make overtures. The rejections had been curt and crushing. Twice she had ended up in hospitals.

But it's different this time. "Wear something sexy," Darrell had said. The words were real, no delusion, and Karen chooses her underclothing carefully, with an eye for what might appeal to Darrell's taste.

She puts on a black bra and black panties. She frowns at herself in the mirror.

Maybe love, she thinks.

Later, she slips into bed with the thought that Nogales has a reputation for excess, and that excess is something she has been craving since she was a girl.

They head south on U.S. 19, Darrell Jettie at the wheel, Karen beside him, four elderly residents of Homewood Estates conversing in the rear seats. The discussion is loud and lurching. Elaine Wirtz, age seventy-nine, defends the claim that she was a jaguar in an earlier life. She knows this, Elaine says, the way she knows she ate a bagel for breakfast that morning. Bess Hollander squints and cups an ear. "She was what?"

"A bagel," Norma Ickles says.

"A what?"

Two rows back, Ed Hollander yells, "A goddamn Jaguar! One of them rich-man cars."

"She ate a car?" says Bess.

"She *was* a car," says Norma.

"Not a car," says Elaine Wirtz. "I was a jaguar. A cat. Like a puma."

"Well, for chrissake!" Ed yells.

"What's a puma?" says Bess.

Darrell's eyes sweep sideways. He grins at Karen. They cross the border at Nogales.

Darrell bypasses the center of town, cruises down a series of streets lined with chollas and barbed wire and forlorn adobe shacks. After ten minutes he turns onto a two-lane highway that winds back into the Sonoran Desert.

Karen asks where he is taking them.

"The real Mexico," says Darrell.

"Well, that's fine. But what about . . . What happened to Nogales?"

He laughs. "Cheap booze, cheap women. Who needs it? I promised an adventure, didn't I?"

"I think you did."

"All right, then," he says, and flashes her a polished grin. "Take it easy. Let that pretty hair down."

Twenty minutes later Darrell pulls in at a truck stop. The day is desert-hot and dry. They troop inside, order coffee, sit around a table discussing the day. No one seems perplexed by the absence of any clear destination, or by the fact that they are well beyond the world of turquoise bracelets and straw sombreros. Bess and Elaine and Norma review their shopping plans. Ed talks about finding a bullfight. "Bloody beef," he says slyly, knowing this will cause controversy. Elaine glares and says, "No bullfights. Molesting animals, that's all it amounts to."

"Because she used to *be* one," Norma says.

"A puma," says Bess.

"I was not, not, not!" Elaine says.

Karen threatens to turn back to Tucson. But as she speaks, as she says "Turn," she detects movement against her knee. Darrell smiles at her. His hand has slipped beneath her navy-blue skirt; it glides upward a few inches, stops at midthigh. Karen freezes. By reflex, she repeats herself. "Turn back," she says, but without conviction, and Darrell laughs and says, "Hey, we're having a ball, aren't we?"

His hand remains on her thigh, confident. His smile, too, is confident, very mild and well mannered. "Let's finish our coffee, folks, then hit the road. Don't forget that big adventure we were talking about."

His hand goes to her black panties, goes inside.

Karen cannot wholly comprehend what is happening. She's giddy. She's terrified. She has not been touched this way since the night of her sixteenth birthday.

For almost an hour Darrell drives straight south, through rugged, repetitive desert, then he turns onto a gravel road that wanders past abandoned houses and vast tracts of sagebrush. Off to the left, both close and far away, is a range of purply black mountains. There are no towns. There are no road signs or people. They have not passed another vehicle in many miles, nor a single living creature, but Karen isn't thinking about this. She's thinking about the truck stop and the feel of Darrell's hand beneath her skirt. The terror is gone now. She wishes he'd do it again.

She fusses with her hair, listening to the hum of the air conditioner, trying to dredge up something worth saying to him: a hint that under the right circumstances she would be prepared to accept his touch again. If it were possible, if she were another woman, she'd find a way to let him know how savage she is, how female, how she would claw and wrap herself around him and keep him prisoner forever, make him feel everything she felt, make him crazy with desire and hurt.

In the back seats, Norma Ickles and Ed Hollander argue about the meaning of the word "mesa." Neither has trouble saying the most idiotic things, which gives Karen the courage to clear her throat. She will count to seven, she decides, and then speak.

She counts to fifty, starts over, then says, "Darrell, you're an excellent driver."

His forehead wrinkles. He seems bewildered, or apprehensive, but he nods and says, "Well, sure, I've had experience. Six, seven times I drove clean across country." He grins at this. "Guess I like to watch the miles go by. Like to roam."

"Roam?" she says.

"Anywhere. Everywhere."

"Well, you drive perfectly," says Karen, "and I mean that."

She can think of nothing else to say, her head as empty as the desert, but Darrell seems not to notice. He is deep in thought. Maybe he's forgotten that not an hour ago his hand had slipped beneath her skirt, inside her black panties.

"Driving's a tricky thing," he tells her. "Especially the cross-country hauls. Like Zen, sort of. Main thing to remember, you don't fight the road, you don't worry about every dip and curve, you just keep your eyes pointed way up ahead. Go with the flow." He flicks a cool smile in her direction. "Like sex, I guess. Enjoy the ride, kick back, let the road drive *you*."

"Interesting," Karen says. She has no idea what he means. "So where does the road take us?"

"Ma'am?"

"Where does it go? This road."

Darrell tosses his shoulders. Slowly, as if his tongue has gone heavy, he says, "Exactly where it wants."

"I meant—"

"A shortcut," he says. "Ten or fifteen more miles, we're there."

Then again, for no obvious reason, he shrugs. With one hand he opens a fresh pack of cigarettes. He glances into the rearview mirror, frowns, taps out a smoke, lights it, and says, "I don't plan to hurt anybody."

Karen isn't sure she heard correctly. "I don't understand."

"Nothing to understand."

"You said hurt."

He turns up the air conditioning. "Real nice of you to hire me, ma'am. Hell or high water, I'm grateful for that."

In the back seats, Bess and Elaine and Norma are commenting on the desert scenery unfolding before them, how untamed it is, how unspoiled.

For a few moments Karen listens to their chit-chat.

"Hurt how?" she says.

Darrell pats her forearm as if she were a child. "Men, I mean. From what I can tell, you don't have a whole lot of experience."

Karen nods. She is conscious of her black underwear.

"I suppose that's right."

"Can't mess with virgins. Wouldn't be civil."

"But what if . . ." She loses her breath, begins again. An angry snarl goes through her thoughts. "What if it doesn't matter to me?"

"Doesn't matter?"

"Experience with men. I can imagine, can't I?"

Darrell laughs.

"Apparently so," he says.

The road becomes dirt. After twenty minutes it ends entirely. In all directions there is wilderness.

They bump along for another two hundred yards before Darrell pulls up alongside an old red pickup truck. For a few seconds it appears the truck is empty, then the passenger-side door swings open and a young man in coveralls and a white baseball cap emerges. His face is sunburnt, his left cheek discolored by a birthmark. He strolls to the van, leans forward to speak with Darrell. The young man looks to be in his mid-twenties. He is slim and blue-eyed, and except for the birthmark he could pass for Darrell's twin brother.

Darrell opens his door, gets out, follows the young man over to the red pickup.

In the back seat, Bess says, "What's this?"

"Not good," says Ed.

They sit now in the bed of the truck: Karen, Bess, Ed, Norma, and Elaine. It's early afternoon. Darrell and the young man have removed portions of the van's floor carpeting, and Darrell bends down with a screwdriver, muttering, his expression intent. Karen is baffled by this. Now and then the birthmarked young man seems to offer suggestions, which Darrell ignores. Plainly, both of them are agitated. At one point Darrell's screwdriver slips, and he jerks back and utters a pair of shocking mismatched nouns.

Elaine Wirtz lets out a noise from her lungs. She glares at Karen. "You hired this monster."

"Very polite, though," says Norma Ickles.

"Baloney," Elaine snaps. "Don't you get it? They intend to murder us."

Bess leans forward and says, "They what?"

"Murder!" Elaine yells.

"Jesus Christ," Ed says.

Karen is perplexed, barely listening. She watches Darrell go back to work with his screwdriver. He's on the floor of the van, directly behind the driver's seat, and Karen cannot help noticing that his shirt has slipped up to expose a flat, tanned belly. She is afraid, but she is also spellbound. He reminds her of a boy she'd adored back in high school—a boy who used to smile at her in the cafeteria, who once drew graphic, exhilarating pictures in a book she'd dropped, but who in the end was too shy to respond to the many, many love letters she had placed in his locker. That early affair of the heart had gone nowhere. It was sterile and one-sided; the boy had almost suffocated her in the back seat of a car on the night of her sixteenth birthday, almost broken her in half, and then dropped her off at a Dairy Queen and stared at the steering wheel and asked if she'd mind walking home. But now, for a moment, Karen finds herself contemplating a happy ending. Darrell will soon say there's nothing to worry about, that he wishes to marry her and peel off her underwear and do all the bestial things she has read about in magazines, back-seat things, those things she so desperately wants, but also doesn't want, or only on her wedding night, only on a remote island with soft winds and flower smells.

Karen knows better, yet the knowledge doesn't puncture hope.

Despite herself, she feels an expectant tremor when Darrell slides out of the van. He tucks in his shirt, speaks briefly with his friend, and then the two of them stroll toward the pickup.

Elaine Wirtz stiffens. She nudges Bess and says, "Murder time."

"Do something," says Norma.

"Me?" Elaine says. "I'm seventy-nine."

They glance over at Ed, who makes a hapless

movement with his head. He tells them to quiet down.

"You're the *man*," says Norma.

"Old man," he says. "And not stupid."

"Well, personally," says Bess, "I'm thirsty. Not to mention you know what." She pauses dramatically, lifts her eyebrows. "I'm a lady. I need conveniences."

Even now Karen cannot purge herself of hope. She looks for a sign from Darrell. A smile, maybe, or a bashful bit of eye contact. But instead he leans down and removes six green shoe boxes from a compartment in the floor of the pickup. He passes the boxes to his friend, who carries them to the van.

Elaine Wirtz gets to her feet and says, "Don't kill me."

Darrell grins. "Easy now."

"No, I just want . . . What's happening here?"

"Smuggling, I'd guess," Ed says.

"Smuggling?" says Bess. "Smuggling shoes?"

"Drugs," Ed says. "Ten to one—drugs."

Darrell stands in the desert sunlight, the corners of his lips seeming to teeter on the edge of a smile. When he looks at Karen, there is an apology in his eyes. Something else, too. A kind of longing: she's sure of it.

As if to confirm this, Darrell shifts from foot to foot. He can't hold her gaze.

"Twenty more minutes," he says graciously, "then we'll pile in the van and have ourselves a nice happy ride back to the border. Cross over, home free."

Elaine snaps out a mocking laugh. "Except you've forgotten the murder part."

"Sorry, ma'am. No murders."

"What a liar."

"No," Ed says. "Bastard needs us, don't you see? Bunch of old codgers. Makes it easy at customs." He peers at Darrell. "Am I right? Right I'm right."

"Yes, sir. Just so everybody behaves."

Once again Darrell's chivalrous eyes brush across the surface of Karen's face.

She straightens up.

Inappropriate, of course, but she's struck by an urge to tell him about the aftertaste of a Dairy Queen cone on the night of her sixteenth birthday.

Darrell is at the wheel again, Karen beside him, Darrell's friend sitting in back with the others.

As they approach Nogales, Darrell turns off the radio.

"Attention, all hands," he says. He slows down, smiles at Karen. "Listen up good. When we hit the border, I want this whole crew to act super-duper normal. No nonsense, no funny faces." He chuckles. His voice is courteous and uninflected. "Hands in your laps, pretend it's church. Anybody asks questions, we're a gang of tourists."

"Or else what?" says Elaine.

Darrell thinks about it.

He stares straight up the road and says, "Or else I shoot you in the face."

The crossing is a thrill. Darrell has taken Karen by the hand. He holds it comfortably, whistling under his breath while a border guard studies their passports. The guard peers into the van, waves them through. It's like pausing at a stoplight.

A quarter mile up the road Darrell takes his hand away.

"Easy as can be," he says to her. "Exactly like I promised. Adventure of a lifetime—I bet you'll be talking about it for years. You and your pals, over cups of Geritol."

"I imagine so," Karen says.

She is thinking about his hand, how his fingers had interlocked with hers, how he'd volunteered an encouraging squeeze when the guard leaned down to ask for the passports. She craves more. She wants him to take her hand on a beach somewhere, and at breakfast, and wherever and anywhere else.

For a few moments she floats in fantasy. Then something happens in her head: a tiny explosion.

She reaches out toward Darrell.

Without volition, without even counting to herself, she pries his right hand from the wheel and takes it to her lap and holds it tight. Darrell mutters something. He tries to pull away, but Karen hangs on. She has appropriated a luckier woman's life.

293

She's a fashion model. She's on her honeymoon. She's aware of the hum of the tires against the road, the heat of a man's flesh.

Darrell releases the wheel. He strikes her on the forehead with his free fist.

"Holy shit," he says.

Forty minutes out of Tucson, Darrell pulls off onto a side road. He drives west into the desert for several miles, through barren alkali flats, then halts at the edge of a dry creek bed. He steps out. He invites the others to join him.

"Last stop," he says.

He helps Bess from the van, escorts her down into the gully. Single file, Karen and Norma and Elaine and Ed follow along. It's late afternoon. A wind has come up. To the east a stain of dusk darkens the sky.

Darrell's friend gives Elaine a nudge and motions toward a large, flat boulder. "Sit," he says, "and don't flap them bitch lips of yours."

Elaine sniffs and sits.

Bess, Norma, and Ed settle down beside her.

A few feet away, Karen waits for dispensation. The wind nips at her navy-blue skirt. She looks at Darrell, whose eyes have no focus. "Come on, now," he says quietly. "Take a load off."

His friend chuckles. "Big load. Shoulda holed her, man. Reamed off some lard."

Darrell shakes his head and says, "Cut it out. Karen's my princess. My sweetie pie."

The two men climb out of the gully.

They talk in low tones, put on identical nylon jackets, get into the van, drive away.

Already the day is cooling. In twenty minutes it will be dark. As she watches the van disappear into its own rising dust, it occurs to Karen that she has been here before, or in a place much like it. She sits down. At the roof of her mouth she feels a bud of thirst. Soon it will be all she knows. But for the present Karen slides into the fantasy that Darrell Jettie will return to take her away. She has waited a long while. She can wait a bit longer.

"I'll tell you this much," says Bess Hollander. "I'm totally pooped. Boy oh boy."

"At least they didn't murder us," Norma says.

"Oh, they did," says Elaine.

CHAPTER 18

CLASS OF '69

At 4:45 P.M., Saturday, July 8, 2000, immediately after the memorial service, there was a gathering in the ballroom of the Darton Hall student union. The college's president delivered cheery remarks, plugging for donations, then a number of important-looking plaques were presented in recognition of alumni achievements. A Lutheran missionary, a chemist, a physician, and Minnesota's lieutenant governor were among the recipients.

Afterward, with two hours to kill before the evening banquet, Amy Robinson and Jan Huebner rounded up their friends for a late-afternoon assault on the Red Carpet, a hangout during their college days. Jan and Amy led the march up Grand Avenue. It was a tiring expedition for all of them: humidity like bubble gum, middle age, little sleep. A swirl of low, ugly clouds was moving in over the Twin Cities, and rain seemed a certainty, but for now the thermometers still burned in the high nineties.

Behind Jan and Amy, strung out in a ragged column along Grand Avenue, Paulette Haslo trudged side by side with Ellie Abbott, followed by Marla Dempsey, then Billy McMann, then David Todd, then Spook Spinelli in crocheted hot pants and spike heels, then Marv Bertel sweating his heart out a block or so behind. Dorothy Stier had also been enlisted, mostly for Billy's sake, but at the last minute she'd gone AWOL, begging off for domestic reasons. Dorothy had a husband, after all, and two terrific kids; she might or might not make it to the banquet.

It was a few minutes past 6 P.M. when nine weary friends straggled into the Red Carpet. The place had changed with the times. Once psychedelic-seedy, the bar had taken a sharp right turn toward collegiate-chic, lots of chrome and exposed brick and stained glass and fake ferns. Only a jukebox and two pool tables remained from the old days.

"Well," Jan said. "Want to plan a merger?"

They took seats around a large, circular table, ordered pitchers of designer beer, and launched their offensive. Time was short. The concluding banquet, they knew, would be a sentimental nightmare, false promises rolled up inside platitudes, and now, with various shadings of motive and intensity, each of them was aware of a growing pressure to fill these last hours with significance. Spook Spinelli had made up her mind to be jolly. She would leave her friends some exemplary pictures to remember: foxy, flamboyant Spook. She would say nothing about drinking from fire extinguishers. If anyone suggested it, or even if not, she would climb up on the table and reprise a striptease from three decades ago. Flick her tongue at David Todd. Put a slither to her hips and giggle like a schoolgirl and let Marv slip a few bucks into the waistband of her crocheted hot pants and pretend she was young and ready to be ravaged, by whomever or by whatever, Queen of Sluts, happiest hussy in the house.

At the moment, under the table, she was unbuckling Marv's belt. "Sandra, Sandra," she was saying to him. "Now, correct me, but that's the wife, right? Or is it Sandy?"

"Sandra," said Marv.

"Exactly. Sandra it is. Sandra we'll definitely call her." Spook looked down at his lap. "Comfortable?"

"Very, thanks," Marv said.

"We don't want to be cramped, do we?"

"No, that we don't want," he said. He smiled at her. Moron love, he thought. "One question. I was under the impression—here's the dumb impression I was under—I was pretty much impressed by the idea that you and I were just swell friends."

"Oh, we are. Except you're so wonderful and true blue. Hot pants come to those who wait."

"Really?"

"Of course, really. Old saying. Chairman Mao."

"Bless my fat soul," said Marv. "Last of the Mohicans, am I? Batting cleanup?"

"Pretty much. So sorry." She pulled off the belt,

wound it around her neck, buckled it up, handed him the flap. "Is chronology an issue?"

"Guess not," Marv said.

Across the table, Amy Robinson said, "Careful, Marvy. Don't you dare break her heart."

"He knows better," said Jan Huebner.

Marv rose to his feet. He secured the flap of his belt with one hand, his trousers with the other. "To the price of mops," he said, "may they never tumble. And to what mops can buy: fame, power, pretty women. Spook and I—she doesn't know this yet—we're soon off on a booze cruise to the Tropics. Never underestimate a fat guy."

"Or patience," said Spook, and Jan Huebner yelled, "Mops!"

Paulette Haslo went to the jukebox and helped Marla Dempsey feed in quarters. Paulette wasn't sure why, but she was feeling a little lighter about the world. The memorial service, possibly. The knowledge that she was still a minister, job or no job. She loved helping people; she loved the idea of faith, if not its elusiveness. After a time she returned to the table and sat in Billy McMann's lap and said, "Forget Dorothy, make me pregnant."

Billy chuckled. "You had us worried," he said.

"I'm good now."

"You look good. Shipshape."

"Sweet of you, sir. Needed to go to church."

"That'll do it," said Billy.

"Yes, it will," said Paulette.

She tilted her head back, looked at him closely for several seconds.

"Confession," she said. "Truth time. It's June '69, graduation day, I'm a God Squadder, you're with Dorothy, and the whole time I sit there staring at that ponytail of yours. Can't stop. Poor unponytailed Paulette. I've got this crush on you, just like Amy and Jan and Spook and everybody else. Ruined it for me, my own graduation. Surprised? Shocked?"

"I am," Billy said.

"A little or a lot?"

"A very little little."

Paulette pretended to smack him. She liked being on Billy's lap. It was the liquor at work, and sentiment. But there was also that new buoyancy inside her. Fifty-three years old, and her sell-by date had long since expired, but now, when she did a bounce on Billy's lap, when she laughed, it was as if she weighed less than nothing.

"What does surprise me," Billy said, "is that you're sitting where you're sitting. Feels terrific, don't budge, but I never thought this particular lap was up there in your league."

"Oh, it is," said Paulette. "First-rate lap."

"You think so?"

"Yes, I do."

"In that case," Billy said, "may I look at your chest?" He looked at her chest. "Now, this might be too bold, but that chest is also enormously first rate. Always thought so. May I be bold?"

"I insist."

"Minister, et cetera. Don't want to offend."

"None taken," said Paulette. "But I hope you don't mean too hugely first rate."

"No. I mean massively adequate." Again Billy looked at her, this time in the eyes, straight on, and then he slipped his arms around her and locked his hands at her spine, lifting slightly, taking her weight. He kissed her nose. "Back in school, you were always . . . Don't hold me to these exact words, but you were always so damned unapproachable."

"The first-rate boobs," Paulette said. "Hard for people to get close."

"Maybe."

"I'm kidding, Billy."

He nodded. He kept looking at her. "So how come you never hooked up with anybody? Man, woman, animal?"

"Marriage, you mean?"

"Yes."

Paulette shook her head.

She had no idea, really. A female minister, sure. Except that was only part of it.

After a second she said, "That ponytail of yours, Billy, maybe I never found one up to snuff," which sounded true, and so she said, "And you were brave, too. Saying no, doing no. Just walking away. People don't use the word 'hero' for it, they don't even think that word—hero, I mean— but I do." She moved on his lap. She felt a rush of self–consciousness. Thirty-one years, she thought. Two boyfriends, six months each. "Anyway, there you are. My hero. Plus the ponytail."

"I'll grow it back," he said.

"Deal," said Paulette. "Glad you're home."

"Thank you."

"One more time. On the lips this time."

"Okay," Billy said.

He kissed her, and Paulette returned it, and then she said, "Well, now. Where's Dorothy?"

"I forget," he said.

"Pity. So about my pregnancy."

"Pretty old, aren't we?"

"Yes, but don't forget my eulogy. Miracles and all that."

"Oh, yeah. Like Viagra."

"Right. Except no quintuplets. Once more—on the lips again."

It was closing in on 6:30 P.M., July 8, 2000, and the bar had begun to swell with a good many thirsty patrons, mostly young people, mostly unborn in 1969, mostly tattooed or pierced or bejeweled, but the jukebox was well stocked with coins that had been slavishly acquired over thirty-one years, by toil, by risk and heartache, and the music was therefore "Lay, Lady, Lay," to which nine dear friends provided choral accompaniment, tipsy, off-key, singing loud, surprising themselves. In the old days they would've sneered, and did sneer, at such flagrant sentiment. Now it felt like love.

305

"The revolution," Amy said later, "wasn't about *that*, it was about us."

"'That'?" Jan Huebner said.

"Everything else."

"Don't follow, dear. One more time."

"Oh, you know. Stopping wars, things outside us. We tried to change the world, but guess what? World changed us. Dumbass cliché, I know, and that's what makes it so sad, so depressing. All those platitudes Mom and Pop used to feed us like baby food. They're true."

"Is this good or bad?"

"No idea," Amy said, "but it looks like I won't be intercoursing Billy McMann."

Not without delight, they watched Paulette dance on Billy's lap.

"Behold, a happy gal," Amy said. "Maybe that's my point. Older you get, more it comes down to not being Harmon Osterberg."

"Or Karen Burns," said Jan.

"Yeah," Amy said. "Lay, lady, lay."

Ellie Abbott, too, was feeling lighter, though not by much. In less than an hour she would be meeting Mark at the farewell banquet, where she would dine on chicken tarragon and listen to speeches and make deft conversation, and then on the drive back to the hotel, in the dark, when Mark's eyes could not be seen, she would say, "Remember Harmon?"

★   ★   ★

David Todd knew pretty much what the future would hold. For three decades now, amid dense morphine dreams along a river called the Song Tra Ky, Master Sergeant Johnny Ever had kept him well informed. The man didn't shut up. Even now he rattled on. "Born to jabber, love the mike," he was saying. "Can't stop myself. But, Davy boy, I warned you at least ten zillion times. Dotted the *i*'s, crossed the *t*'s. No offense, but I got zero tolerance for that poor-me attitude of yours. Let's be honest, you knew the score before the friggin' game got played. Every inning, every pitch. You asked for it, man. You took the ride."

David Todd acknowledged this.

He understood that Marla's hand in his meant only that she craved forgiveness, and that when the question was finally put to him, the forgiveness question, he would nod and say, "Sure," because long ago he already had. He realized, too, that a little later in the evening, if he were to get up to shoot some pool, Marla would find a way to join him, and that after a couple of games she would suggest that they skip the banquet and seek out a place to talk, and he realized that he would then hear considerably more than he wished to hear about Harleys and stock-brokers and how much she regretted hurting him, how it was a horrid, horrid memory that she'd be revisiting forever. But she had no serious interest in trying again. She cared for him, yes, but passion was a problem, and in the morning he would have only the ghost of a hand in his, those Marla fingers, that perfect fit, a phantom ache, the pain of what was lost, just as he sometimes felt the ghost of his missing leg.

He looked over at Marv Bertel.

"Pool?" he said.

"Sure," Marv said. "If my pants stay up."

"Excellent muscle tone," Billy said to Paulette. "You're in shape."

"Bicycling," Paulette said. "Swimming."

"We have bikes in Winnipeg."

"Do you? And water?"

"Water, too. We're famous for water."

"Wet water?"

"Oh, yeah. Every drop."

"Wet," Paulette said. She wiggled on his lap. "I like it that way."

"Jesus Christ," Jan said.

"Cute couple," said Amy Robinson.

Jan wagged her head. "No lie, I'm doing something wrong. This lipstick, you think?"

"Not the lipstick."

"Personality, then? The face?"

"Probably the face," Amy said.

As David and Marv racked up for eight ball, the others drank and lap-danced and reminisced and listened to the jukebox and flirted or pretended to flirt and made secret resolutions and tried not to think about the press of time. Outside, the sky was bruised and tumbling. No rain yet, but it was on the way. There were floods in Colorado, thunderstorms all across the Dakotas. Amy Robinson explained the impoverishing rules of blackjack. Jan Huebner talked about a dwarf she once knew. Spook Spinelli talked about her number coming up, how she could feel it, even hear it. Like this voice inside her, Spook said. Some old woman's voice, mumbly-sounding, always yakking away about Indians and grass and metal fatigue.

"Imagine the funeral," Jan said. "Noah's ark. Two of everything."

Later on, they played a game called Truth that had originated in their college days. Amy Robinson reviewed the rules, which even thirty-one years ago had been fluid and mutable, subject to inspiration. "What I remember for sure," Amy said, "is we have to confess the most terrible thing ever about ourselves, something we did or didn't do. Whatever keeps us awake at night. Something monstrous. Evil."

Jan Huebner raised a hand. "I think you've forgotten the basic point, Amy. I'm pretty sure it was a fun game."

"Back then it was," said Billy. "Terrible things weren't so terrible."

"Goes without saying," Jan said, "but I believe there's a drinking part, I'm almost positive. At some point you get to drink, or you have to, or I don't know. You do in fact drink."

"Probably if you lie," Marla said.

"Or if nobody believes you," said Jan, "then you definitely drink. There's drink involved, I promise you."

"I'm not playing," Ellie said.

"You are so," said Spook, "and I just wish Dorothy were here. Honest to God, I'd give one of my husbands to hear *that* girl's most terrible thing."

"Forgot recycling day," Amy said.

"Burned Ron's supper," said Jan. "Served TV dinners to those two groovy kids."

Paulette Haslo suddenly felt heavier in Billy's lap. She could feel his thoughts congeal. "Let's be fair," she said. "Every morning, every night, maybe the cancer's back. Chemo. Radiation. Tough girl."

"And she lets you know about it," Amy said.

"Every stinking node," Jan Huebner said.

"Seriously, I'm out of here," said Ellie Abbott. She reached down for her purse. "I hate to say it, but in a few minutes I have to—"

"Ellie," Paulette said.

"I can't."

"We're your friends, sweetheart. Practice makes perfect. Let it go."

Ellie blinked as if someone had switched on a floodlight. For a few seconds she seemed disoriented, blinded by the inner glare. "All right," she said, and placed her purse on the table, squaring it with both hands. "One game, that's all. And I go last."

"Last is fine," said Paulette. "Last comes soon enough."

"It's settled," Spook said, and pulled out her cell phone. "Dorothy goes first. This I'm dying to hear."

Spook dialed three times, but Dorothy's phone was busy, so Marla Dempsey volunteered. She was aware of David at the pool table behind her. In a minute or two she would get up to join him. "You all know this anyway," Marla said, "or at least the basics, but I guess it's something else, something healthy, for me to get the actual words out—from my own mouth, I mean—just to say it," and then she talked about Christmas Day, 1979, and how vile it had been, how sinful, to choose that morning of all mornings to walk out on her husband, a good man, a beautiful and loving and devoted man, by name of course David Todd. But back then, she said, it seemed the only thing to do, even the right thing, because to fake a merry Christmas, to ooh and aah at new toasters and Santa-wrapped sweaters, well, that seemed infinitely more evil—deception piled on all the other horror—but now, with the perspective of sanity, she had come to realize otherwise, because it wouldn't have killed her to wait a week or two—she was being deceptive anyway, lying through her teeth—and because in truth another man, a somewhat younger man, was at that instant waiting down the street on a black and red Harley, a fact she'd failed to mention, and because for David there would never again be another Christmas, a real Christmas, a Christmas that truly meant Christmas and did not mean, for example, *Goodbye*, and did not mean *I love you, David, but I'm not in love, and I don't think I ever can be.*

A malnourished young man, really a boy, in baggy jams and with a silver-studded nose, approached the table to request that the jukebox be rescued from "all that soupy sixties bullshit."

"Go kill yourself," Amy said.

Marla rose and went to the ladies' room. No one looked at David Todd, who had just blown a tap-in, and no one but Jan Huebner said anything.

Jan said, "Isn't *this* fun?"

Paulette Haslo got off Billy's lap. He seemed nervous and distracted—Dorothy, no doubt—and with counterfeit gaiety, Paulette moved to the far side of the table and sat beside Ellie Abbott. No harm done, she decided. Nice memories. Besides, the little romance had lasted longer than most, a solid twenty minutes, and she regretted not a word, not a single covert touch. And if it ever came down to it, if for instance she were to start crying, she could always plead the reunion crazies.

"My turn," she said.

"Okay, but lie through your teeth," said Jan Huebner. "Otherwise we don't drink. Am I right or am I totally right?"

"Let the girl talk," said Amy.

"A whopper. Please."

Amy looked at Paulette and said, "Go ahead, hon, I'm listening," and then for the next several minutes Paulette talked about a late-night burglary and a lovable old man named Rudy Ketch.

Billy McMann wished Paulette had stayed put. He liked her in his lap, liked her in general, but it was also true that guilt had become a problem. What bothered him was Spook Spinelli, to whom he owed an apology, and who at the moment was behaving oddly: too manic, too giggly. Marv's belt was still wrapped around her neck. She kept yanking at it, pretending to hang herself, rolling her eyes back. Maybe it was his imagination, Billy thought, or two days on the bottle, but more likely he'd triggered it with his own stupidity, using her the way everyone else used her and the way she so often used herself. At some point, Billy concluded, he would have to say something. And he would also have to take Paulette aside and confess to her about last night. At least be honest. Let her know what happened and that he wished it hadn't, or, more accurately, that he wished it had happened instead with her.

He watched Spook get up and saunter over to a group of young college kids, all male, and lean over their table to suggest, it sounded like, "a good gangbang."

Marv Bertel noticed, too.

He put down his pool cue, took Spook by the arm, led her over to Ellie Abbott.

"Something's wrong," he told Ellie. "I don't know. Just watch her." Marv paused, then shook his head. "And see if you can get my belt back."

When Paulette finished, Amy Robinson and Jan Huebner rose to the defense. The break-in, it was stupid, obviously, but far from evil. Farther still from monstrous. "This Janice woman, she dropped a dime?" Amy said, the lawyer in her. "Cops got involved?"

"Naturally," said Paulette.

"Arrested?"

"Yes."

"Booked? Arraigned?"

"Whole deal."

Amy nodded. "But it never came to trial?"

"No need," said Paulette. "Old lady got her pound of flesh, plus some. Talk of the town, talk of the presbyters. Not good for employment prospects."

"Dropped the charges?"

"Sure. Damage done."

"Well," Amy said. Her voice trailed off. She looked to Ellie Abbott for help, but Ellie had her hands full with Spook Spinelli, whose thick makeup had gone moist and cakey, whose lips were twitching.

"Fun, fun, fun!" Jan Huebner said.

Marla Dempsey had joined David at the pool table, where under the liquid growl of the Saturday-night crowd David had just said to her, "No sweat. What's a Harley between fondest friends?"

"Please," she said.

"Fond, fonder, fondest. All forgiven."

"Doesn't sound that way," said Marla. "Not that I deserve it."

David affected a breezy flounce with his shoulders. What he felt, though, was the inexpressible emptiness of what was soon to come. "Nifty thing about pardons," he told her, "is you don't earn them. They come gratis. *Casus belli* not required. Here, take a shot. Six ball. Lightly."

"I'm not a sports fan, David."

"Correct," he said. "What's a bunt?"

"Sorry?"

"Stupid question. Are you by chance a banquet skipper?"

Marla eyed him with displeasure. "Right there, David. There's *casus belli*. Always telling fortunes."

"My fault, then."

"I didn't say that. But sometimes—maybe this isn't fair either—sometimes it seems you decided everything in advance. Made up your mind, made it happen."

"Imagined a Harley, did I?"

"Good question," Marla said.

She began to turn away, stopped, then turned back as David knew she had to and absolutely would.

"Do we duck out or not? Yes or no?"

David nodded. He loved her too much. "Tell you what, we'll hit the banquet, say our goodbyes, then go find some nice schmaltzy spot to talk our brains out. Forgive, forget. That what you had in mind?"

"More or less," said Marla.

He nodded again. It was no joy, but he knew. "And then?" he said. "Happily ever after?"

"David."

"Didn't think so."

"So smug. You make up my answers."

"Remarry me?"

"Stop it."

"Surprise," David said. "Fortuneteller."

Along the Song Tra Ky, thirty-one years away, Johnny Ever cackled and said, "Hot damn!"

Truth was wearing thin, but Amy Robinson gamely described a filthy Texaco station, an even filthier washroom, and how near the end of her honeymoon she'd locked herself in and wiped off the toilet seat and sat down and decided to get unmarried. "Luckiest time of my life," she said, "and I end up alone. Weird thing, because I used to be so damned spunky. Smart as a whip, right? Freckles, bobbed nose? Cute? I mean, really cute?"

Spook Spinelli talked about two husbands and a lover named Baldy Devlin.

Jan Huebner talked about the trials of Snow White.

David Todd started to talk about a shallow, fast-moving river, a transistor radio tuned to the universe, but then he looked at Marla and decided to stop.

Ellie Abbott had disappeared.

It was just after seven o'clock, and a few blocks away the class of '69 was sitting down to its farewell banquet.

In the bar, though, faces turned toward Marv Bertel, who had yet to play a round of Truth.

"Who's hungry?" he said.

Then he said, "Give me a break."

Then he said, "What?"

A long moment passed before Marv sighed and said, "All right, I'll give it a shot. But it's embarrassing."

CHAPTER 19

TOO SKINNY

In March of 1988, Marv Bertel settled into the first rigorous diet of his life, nothing fancy, mostly water and willpower. By early August of that year, he had shed forty-one pounds of lifelong flab. "Boy, I'm so incredibly, incredibly proud of you," his wife said, which in Marv's moth-eaten memory was the one and only time she had offered him praise of any sort. Two and a half months later, in mid-October, Marv reached his target of two hundred and twenty pounds, the least he'd weighed since twelfth grade. That same morning, after a breakfast of salad greens and sparkling water, he celebrated by filing for divorce.

On the first day of November, Marv moved into a furnished apartment just down the road from his mop and broom factory on the western outskirts of Denver. He purchased a new wardrobe, signed up at a tanning salon, installed an Exercycle in front of his TV, and, in an exploratory sort of way, began spending his evenings in a number of chic bars around town. Women took notice. Marv took heart. He was forty-one years old and ludicrously well off, even factoring in the pending divorce.

To manufacture a high-end industrial mop cost just under a dollar and a half, the perfect broom substantially less. Dirt was forever, demand was steady. It was true that Marv had never found the business challenging, or even mildly interesting, but for a man who had spent a lifetime caught up in the sluggishness of gross obesity, there was always the entrepreneurial virtue of sitting at a big rosewood desk for hour upon profitable hour, more or less motionless, more or less dead.

Now, though, Marv Bertel daydreamed. Infinite new futures appeared.

In bed at night, flexing his abdominal muscles to the uneven beat of his heart, he imagined himself on the cover of *Forbes:* capped teeth, an expensive haircut, maybe decked out in one of those fancy double-breasted suits that not so long ago had made him look like a giant Easter ham. No more blubber jokes. Just cheers and hugs and dietary inquiries.

Such thoughts inspired him.

Impetuously, consulting only his own fantasies, Marv set a daunting new goal for himself, a hundred and ninety-nine pounds. He achieved it in just under three weeks.

A breeze, he decided. No reason to stop.

He cut out his late-afternoon martini, doubled his time on the Exercycle.

In the bathroom mirror, slowly at first, then rapidly, Marv's ribs began to surface like the skeleton of a sunken galleon, ancient-looking, a little frightening. He dropped a full shoe size. Even his new wardrobe fit loosely. Equally dramatic, but at times more alarming, was the transformation in Marv Bertel's personality. From boyhood on, he'd been a reserved, soft-spoken individual, tentative, shy, a loner, but now he found himself passing along scraps of TV dialogue to his gorgeous young executive assistant, or telling jokes in elevators, or exchanging life stories with the women he chatted up in local bars.

Often on these occasions Marv invented anecdotes befitting his slim new body: a robust detail here, a charming fib there.

At various times, in various night spots, he became a third-base coach for the White Sox, a plastic surgeon, a priest, a former priest, a scuba instructor, an ex-convict, a contortionist for Cirque du Soleil. To one young lady, an effervescent redhead of twenty-four, he claimed to be a retired rodeo cowboy. The following evening, in the same establishment but to a transfixed brunette, he omitted the word "retired," which worked wonders, and which he helped along with a little limp as he made his way to the men's room.

Remarkable, Marv observed, what hogwash women will swallow from the physically fit.

Almost anything.

He did not mention his mop and broom business. He avoided the inconvenient detail that his divorce wasn't final.

All this left him with an aftertaste of fraudulence, but still, given Marv's unhappy history, the tall tales appealed to his sense of humor, and even more to his sense of revenge. For as long as he could remember, he'd been teased and ridiculed and ignored, always the chubby sidekick, always the comic relief, and it gave him intense pleasure to behold the respect, even the awe, that spilled out like paint in the fetching eyes of women half his age. He feigned boredom. He went out of his way never to make advances. Even with the prettiest young lady, Marv was polite to the point of indifference. And this, too, had the feel of revenge: payback to those legions of blind-eyed, fat-biased women from his past.

Marv felt no guilt at all. And no remorse. On the contrary, there was nothing more satisfying than to hoist up his eyebrows as some buxom porker dipped into a bowl of guacamole or mixed nuts. Sometimes, depending on his mood, he would deliver an earnest discourse about the elements of responsible nutrition. More often, he would issue a disgusted sigh, excuse himself, and wander off to another table.

On the morning of December 4, 1988, Marv Bertel's bathroom scale registered just a hair under a hundred and ninety. He wept in the shower. He wept again as he toweled off. For the first time in more than three decades, Marv felt firmly human, a blessed buoyancy of body and soul.

That afternoon, on impulse, Marv hosted a bois-terous office party, loud music and early bonuses, after which he invited his sleek and very lovely executive assistant to join him for dinner at one of Denver's upscale restaurants. She accepted, as the trim new Marv knew she would, and at seven o'clock they were led to a coveted corner table. The menu was northern Italian, tempting in the extreme. So, too, was Marv's executive assistant, a dazzling twenty-six-year-old by the name of Sandra DiLeona.

Wisely, Marv seated himself out of harm's way, across the table from Sandra. He did, however, order his first martini in nearly two weeks, minus the olives, and within ten minutes called for another. It was the alcohol, without question, that soon inspired him to modify the seating plan. Marv moved to Sandra's immediate right, loosened his tie, and leaned toward the young woman with mischief in mind. In a low, already slurred voice, he confided that there was a matter he wished to discuss with her. "A personal item," he said. "It's ticklish."

Sandra's eyes narrowed. She was a business-school graduate, chilly by disposition, nothing if not canny. "Personal?" she said. "What would that be?"

Marv had no idea. He was playing this by ear, adjusting to the harmonics of the moment.

"Ticklish," he repeated. He flexed his biceps, sucked in his stomach. "The fact is, I'm not sure where to start. A confession, I suppose. You've worked for me—what?—almost a year?"

"Ten months," said Sandra.

"Right, ten months," Marv said. "And you know me strictly as a boss. A mentor." He hesitated. "I've made a favorable impression, I hope?"

"Just fine," she said.

"And you're happy?"

"Happy?"

"With me. Your job."

"Well, I guess," Sandra said. "It's not like I dream about mops at night."

Marv gave her an appreciative smile. "But you're satisfied with the salary, working conditions, all that? It's your overall welfare I'm concerned about."

Sandra's wily brown eyes conveyed a mix of puzzlement and suspicion. She was a tall, masterfully assembled blonde. Five-ten, Marv estimated. Not an ounce over a hundred and twenty-five pounds. Cover-girl complexion. Pouty lips. A few months back, in his fat days, he'd paid almost no attention to the girl. No point: she'd seemed beyond reach, as icy and unobtainable as Neptune. Now things were different. Bravely, with the inflated confidence that accompanies a shrunken belly, Marv took her hand and said, "Anyway, a confession. Here goes. I'm not just a mop man, I've also tried my hand at . . . I'm really not sure how to say this."

In truth, he was equally unsure about what to say. He thought fast, reviewing options, but in the end he did not think nearly fast enough. For the remainder of Marv's life, he would regret his next utterance. It came to him exactly as all the other barroom lies had come, out of the old fatness, the new thinness, those deferred dreams and a job he hated and a stale marriage and a lifetime of mockery and humiliation and a craving for something better. Even as he spoke, Marv realized it was a mistake. He tried to stop. He put a hand to his throat, squeezed his eyes shut. *Don't*, he thought. His tongue kept moving. Four syllables. Three words—"I'm an author"—that would cost him dearly: panic attacks, sleepless nights, heart trouble, endless shame, endless rationalizations, another miserable marriage. Vaguely, at least, he apprehended all this. Not the details, just the general appalling drift. And yet still he could not stop. In the years ahead, Marv would reflect upon this instant with the same self-loathing and self-pity that a lung cancer victim must feel at the memory of his first cigarette.

"Author?" said Sandra. "An amateur, you mean?"

"Well, no."

"Like a hobby? Dabbling?"

A door swung open.

Right then, for a miraculous split second, Marv had a last opportunity to rescue himself. He could've nodded and said, "Sure, a hobby," or he could've smiled and said nothing. He could've been enigmatic. He could've feigned modesty. To the end of his days he would be haunted by these options. But the disbelief on Sandra's face—the contemptuous slur of the word "dabbling"—made him stiffen and take his hand from his throat.

"No," he said coldly. "A real writer. Fiction."

Sandra studied him. What was happening behind her crafty eyes Marv could only estimate. A number of minute calculations, obviously. Various prospects and possibilities tempered by a healthy dose of MBA skepticism.

"So you've published?" the young woman said.

"Certainly. That's what we're discussing here."

"But I've never even heard of you. Authorwise."

"No, dear, of course you haven't," he said. "Which is why I bring it up." Marv finished his drink, studied the glass. He was committed now. "You've heard of pseudonyms? Common practice, actually."

"Yes, I'm sure," Sandra said. "What is it?"

"What's what?"

"The pseudonym," she said.

Swiftly, Marv flipped through an internal card catalogue. Only the most ridiculous possibilities occurred to him, brand-name writers whose faces she would surely recognize from magazines or television. He began to shrug, to laugh it off as a bit of predinner fun, when he heard himself utter the name of an accomplished, highly regarded, largely unread, obsessively reclusive literary figure. Here, he knew, was the point of no return.

"Thomas Pierce?" Sandra said. "That's you?"

A muscle at Marv's eye twitched. "Impressive," he said. "I'll be honest, I'm surprised you're familiar with him. With me. Very pleasantly surprised."

"Well, why not?" she said. "I mean, God, he's one of . . . *You're* one of our great, great, great writers."

"You've read the books?"

Sandra wagged her head. "Of course not. Nobody does. That's not the point. You're famous. Everybody knows *about* you."

"Not everybody," Marv said modestly.

"Well, no, not compared to—you know—not like a movie star. Even so." She stopped and chewed on her lower lip. The skepticism began flooding back into her sharp brown eyes. "Okay, so you're Thomas Pierce, that's amazing. But I don't see how it's a confession."

Marv did not, either.

He took out a handkerchief, wiped his forehead, and called for another martini. His thoughts were divided. He wanted nothing more than to slither through some convenient loophole in the lie. Yet he also felt a savage need to press the issue. To make her believe. Even to make himself believe. The years of fat-boy mediocrity had somehow warped his common sense. Clearly, he told himself, there was no way he could get away with this, yet something pathological egged him on. Morbid curiosity. Certain secret longings. He *could* have been a writer. He should have been. He loved words, the sounds and syllables. Back in college, Marv had majored in journalism; he'd edited both the yearbook and the Darton Hall newspaper. Even after graduating, over the next several years, he'd often envisioned himself heading for New York, hanging out in coffee shops with a notebook and some pencils and a ravishing editor or two.

Mops and brooms had put an end to it. Inertia, too, plus a cumbrous marriage and the burdens of obesity.

Now, staring into his empty glass, Marv took a few moments to gather himself. "I'm sorry," he said, "you were asking—?"

"The confession thing," said Sandra.

"Right. Misleading, I'm afraid. What I meant was . . . It's embarrassing, actually, but now that I'm unattached, nearly divorced . . . Well, I needed to share the secret. A friendly ear. Someone to listen."

Sandra thought about it. "But why me? I'm an executive assistant."

Marv smiled, reached out, and took her hand.

"Very true," he said adroitly. "And therein lies my confession."

"You mean—?"

"For ten infatuated months."

Marv broke his own rule that evening. Not only did he make unambiguous advances toward the starstruck young lady, but he also went home with her, and to bed, under what even he recognized as false pretenses. Worse yet, Marv fell in love, or imagined he did. True, it was not the dry-mouthed, head-over-heels love of his youth. At best, he decided, it was the sort of love that visits a man who has recently shed a third of his body weight, whose divorce is six weeks from final, and whose self-esteem has long been crushed by mops and brooms.

He slept with Sandra again the following night, and then every night for the next two months. In most respects, the affair was thrilling: the way she looked at him with deference and delight, sometimes outright veneration. He liked the girl's intelligence, her bedroom professionalism, even her calculating, what's-in-it-for-me posture toward the world. She had the body of a fashion model, the central nervous system of a Pentagon mainframe. For Marv, all this was new and exhilarating, but at day's end his thoughts were drenched in the purest terror. He couldn't sleep, couldn't think. As a literary alter ego, Thomas Pierce had been an unfortunate choice. The man was a hermit, true—aversion to cameras, aversion to people—but he was also a master of the written word, a linguistic wonder boy destined for Stockholm, and the enormity and gross stupidity of the fabrication made Marv's spine go cold. At random moments, he was paralyzed by shame, by the pending horror of discovery. And there was no escape. All day, Sandra sat at an operations desk just outside his office. At night, she lay beside him in bed, scanning one of Pierce's most abstruse novels, now and then looking up to inquire about a metaphor or an obscure scrap of language. Marv did what he could to deflect such questions. He would sigh, or shake his head, and explain that literature was meant to be experienced, not explicated. Other times he would roll over and feign sleep. Eyes closed, frozen stiff by his own foolishness, he'd listen to the whispery sound of pages being turned, of Sandra's breathing, and in those miserable moments he would count himself lucky for even the smallest blessings. Thomas Pierce, praise God, did not permit photographs on his books. Nor had Sandra yet inquired about such sticky matters as royalty statements or work in progress.

The strain on Marv's constitution began to tell. By the end of December, he'd dropped another twelve pounds, tightened his belt a notch. In the office, behind a locked door, he spent his workdays trying to come up with some honorable solution. He considered firing the girl. He considered selling the factory, removing himself to another continent. But Marv's heart was now engaged. Despite Sandra's flaws—especially that hard-edged, profit-and-loss shrewdness in her eyes—she was a living emblem of all those lovely young women who eight or nine months ago would not have given him the time of day. He didn't want to lose her, or the idea of her.

In the end, therefore, Marv did nothing.

He waited.

He envisioned miracles. Nuclear holocaust. Epidemic amnesia.

At the turn of the year, on January 1, 1989, Marv Bertel weighed in at a hundred and seventy-eight pounds, which for a man standing six-two, with a heart condition and chronic insomnia, bordered on the unwholesome. Eighteen days later he was down to a hundred and seventy even. The diet, he knew, had little to do with it; fear alone was sucking the muscle from his bones. He had no appetite, no energy.

There were times now, numerous times, when Marv found himself looking back on his obesity as if recollecting a dear departed friend, a steadfast comrade who was always on hand with good cheer and a quart or two of premium potato salad. Not that Marv had been a happy man back then. Far from it. All the same, for better or worse, he'd managed to waddle through the world with at least the appearance of contentment and portly self-respect. He had gotten by. For forty-one years he had slept the sleep of the nearly innocent. Now, odd as it seemed, he could not help mourning the jolly old Marv.

These changes were nerve-racking. And there was also the deceit: it was eating him up. With each miserable day, he turned a little jumpier, a little more irritable, his stomach fluttering whenever Sandra entered a room or started to speak.

Exposure was a certainty. A matter of when and where, never if. And yet Marv was surprised, even shocked, when the inevitabilities tracked him down in early February. For several days, Sandra had become uncommonly quiet, stealing glances at him, and at dinner one evening she put down her fork, wiped her mouth, and said, "Something's bothering me."

Marv closed his eyes. He knew what was in store.

"I don't mean to pry," she said, "but I really, really have to ask this. You and me. We're a team. And we need to be open about everything."

"Open," Marv said.

"Right. And I feel . . . I get suspicious sometimes. I can't help it."

Marv looked away, then looked back at her with hurt in his heart.

He was struck by the indignation of a man not trusted.

"Look, I know it's not healthy," Sandra said, "but I'm not used to putting faith in people. Especially men. Older men. And that's important, isn't it? That's what makes a relationship tick." She averted her eyes. "So I've been thinking—and I don't mean this in a bad way—but the thing is, you're a writer, a famous writer, except you don't ever *write*."

Marv stared at her. "Don't I?"

"Well, no. Do you?"

"Ceaselessly. Endless struggle."

"Yes, but *when?*"

He glared, folded his napkin, leaned back, and lied. He informed her with vehemence, voice quavering, that literature was not some seedy public sideshow, that it was pursued in absolute artistic solitude, paragraph by paragraph, syllable by syllable, and that in point of fact he slaved over his work every day, every hour, every minute, every instant of every minute. "What else," he said, "do you imagine I might be doing behind that locked office door? Computer games? Solitaire?"

"I didn't think—"

"Moreover," he said, "this isn't something a real writer talks about. We don't chat our books into oblivion, we don't broadcast creative news bulletins." His voice had sailed up an octave. Even as Marv spoke, elaborating on the theme of privacy, it struck him that he meant every ardent word. As if under hypnosis, transfixed by a besieged, self-righteous passion, he talked about the incessant turmoil of any worthy writer, the uncertainties, the subjectivity, the failures of nerve and language, the strain of wrestling with Satan for a line or two of decent prose. He cited Conrad on the subject. He cited Baudelaire. "You of all people," Marv said, "should understand that literature bubbles through my blood. It's my oxygen, my heartbeat."

Sandra surveyed his face. She backed off. "Fair enough," she said. "If you're actually writing . . . Fine. I'm glad."

"Swell of you," Marv said, though his tone was

begrudging and whiny. In part this was genuine. But in much larger part it was a mask for his amazement at how easy it had been, how swiftly she'd surrendered. Then again, he thought, who would not? The audacity of the lie, its scope and grandeur, its breathtaking magnitude, suddenly unnerved him. It was not, after all, as if he were claiming to be some backwater hack, some scribbling midlist nobody. He had appropriated genius. He had taken for his own an entire life's work, a couple of masterpieces, a way of thinking, a way of being, another man's energies and chemistry and fame and labor and God-given virtuosity.

The realization sickened him.

Something sour and deadly rose into his throat, like the taste of cancer, and at that instant Marv came within a breath of disclosing everything. But also at that instant, across the table, Sandra gave her hair a toss and said, "Problem is, I still don't get it."

"Get?" said Marv.

"I'm an executive assistant," she said. "I see your mail, I take your calls, and there's never anything literary. It's all mops and brooms."

"Oh, really?"

"Yes. Really."

"My God," said Marv. "What galling cynicism."

The impulse to confess evaporated. He launched into an angry soliloquy about the role of literary agents, about the importance of anonymity and creative deck-swabbing. There were people, he told her, to whom he paid a pretty penny to handle fan mail and contracts and all the other petty distractions. "I'm a language man," he said, too ferociously, "not a garbage man."

Sandra nodded, pushed to her feet, and without a word began clearing the table.

She was silent for the remainder of the evening. Several times he caught her looking at him, biting her lip, and at one point he had the sensation of being studied as if at a police lineup.

Marv mistook it for adulation. It was not.

In bed that night, lights out, Sandra said, "I went to a library today. Found a photograph."

"Did you?" said Marv.

"I did. An old one. It was pretty fuzzy, and I guess it was taken twenty-five, thirty years ago. But no resemblance. It wasn't you."

Marv heard himself chuckle. Not a single exculpatory thought came to him.

A trillion years ago, it seemed, all this had started as a way to get noticed, a way to be somebody, a sort of game, and now the convolutions had him tumbling in the dark.

"If you think this is funny," Sandra said quietly, "you're a pitiful human being."

"Right," he said. "It's not funny."

"So explain."

Marv sat up in bed. He was very, very hungry. "Yes, why on earth not?" he murmured, and pinched the bridge of his nose. He swallowed hard. He yearned for a T-bone. After a moment he took a breath and spoke slowly, painfully, but with immense valor. "The fact is," Marv said, "two of us write those books. I'm shy, he's not. What you saw was the other guy's picture."

"Other guy?"

"Precisely. My co-author."

Over the next twenty seconds, which had the half-life of plutonium, Marv unearthed several nuggets of wisdom. Most alarmingly this: There is no outer limit to mankind's credulity. Anything goes. The Easter bunny. The indelibility of love. A god with white whiskers and a hearty laugh. Almost always, the human creature prefers an elusive miracle to an everyday lie.

Moreover, at the last minute, Marv blurted out a piece of dialogue worthy of Thomas Pierce himself, a stroke of genius that instantaneously bought him both trust and time.

"Will you marry me?" he said.

The victory was short-lived. There was a three-day erotica-fest, with all its illusory distractions, after which Marv awoke to a headache and the knowledge that he'd managed little more than to deepen his grave and dump in the worms.

It was true that Sandra's will to believe had short-circuited her common sense. But it was also true that for Marv the consequences had multiplied beyond measure. There was nothing droll about it. Each tick of the clock pumped poison through his veins. At night, his dreams were blistered by cartoons of Judgment Day: truth cops with halos, heavenly polygraphs. His misery was absolute. By daylight, in the mop factory, Marv's heart would snap at the sound of Sandra's approaching footsteps. His breathing would go shallow, his future would go void. There were times, many times, when he had trouble accepting the reality of his own fraud. It didn't seem possible. Always the merry fat boy. A mop man. A pitiful, puffed-up yo-yo with a couple of secret chips on his shoulder. Nothing more.

In a sense, Marv thought, it was as if the diet had stripped away two hundred pounds of spiritual camouflage. What remained was a ghoulish, unrecognizable bag of bones, a stranger who terrified and disgusted him.

Over the next several days, he dropped another three pounds. Tufts of hair fell from his scalp. A pair of teeth loosened in his jaw. His appetite had returned—he was starving—but he couldn't make himself swallow. Each hour of his life, it now seemed, had the nap and weave of one of Thomas Pierce's most grotesque fictions, freakish and scary, ruled by entropy, a madhouse of make-believe looping back on itself in infinite ellipses.

In the first week of March, on the day Marv's divorce came through, Sandra mailed out a stack of engagement announcements. "I have friends, I have a family," she said. "Why keep it a secret? Unless there's something to hide."

She squinted up at him, holding his gaze until he looked away.

For Marv, it was a hard moment.

"Nothing hidden in the least," he said. "But I do hope you're not letting on about the Pierce business. That's sacred. That's holy."

"Understood," Sandra said. "Holy."

"A promise, then?"

"Not a peep."

Nonetheless, that evening, Marv overheard fragments of a whispered, disturbingly boastful phone conversation in which Sandra violated the spirit, if not the letter, of her pledge. Plain as day, he caught the phrase "literary bigwig"; also the words "stupid recluse."

When the girl hung up, Marv confronted her. "That," he said crossly, "was a peep. A complete squawk."

"Look, I'm proud of you," she said. "I want people—"

Marv waved a hand. "What happened to holy? You flat-out lied to me. A blatant, point-blank lie, and don't you ever, ever forget it."

"All I said was 'bigwig.' I didn't name names, did I?"

"Hairsplitting rubbish," Marv said. "What about 'recluse'? '*Stupid* recluse'? One thing I can't tolerate, not ever, is duplicity."

"And what does that mean?" said Sandra.

"It means," he said gamely, "squawk, squawk."

He said nothing else.

The end of the road, he realized. No more.

He grunted, spun on his heels, moved briskly to the refrigerator, and wolfed down his first full pint of ice cream in nearly a year. His appetite was huge. He could eat again. It was a kind of quittance, to be sure, but it was also a joy. Already, ounce by ounce, he could feel the ice cream converting itself into the old Marv, maybe bigger, maybe better. Before retiring that night, he consumed a can of unheated baked beans, a Key-lime pie, a lamb chop, a pear, a jar of chutney, and two or three fistfuls of chopped walnuts.

In bed, after he'd lost a portion of his snack to the toilet, Sandra said, "You're not Thomas Pierce, are you?"

"I am not."

"Not a writer at all?"

"No," he said. "But I'm skinny."

They married anyway. But there were terms: a cash stipend, separate bedrooms, a half-interest in the factory, an ironclad will. "If you ever cross me, ever so much as irritate me," Sandra announced on the eve of their wedding, "the whole world finds out what a creepy, contemptible liar you are."

"We could call it off," Marv suggested. "The wedding, the honeymoon."

"Now that," Sandra told him with a glare, "is what I mean by 'irritate.'"

Her MBA training had been brought to bear. She

341

was already in possession of the family checkbooks and an altogether rigorous prenuptial agreement.

By and large, Marv had no quarrel with any of this. He deserved his punishment. He'd been expecting it, even craving it, although perhaps not the life sentence that had been handed down. Still, as in anything, the pluses and minuses balanced out. All said and done, he had secured the glossy veneer of the wife he'd always wanted. He had visiting privileges. He had off-and-on conjugal rights. There were times, in fact, as he lunched on brisket or supped on a soufflé, when Marv found himself swollen with admiration for his bride-to-be; more important, there was never a time when he did not unequivocally respect her. In the end, Marv noted, he'd had the amazing good fortune to bump into a woman who could appreciate a straightforward lie or two, who could give credit where credit was due, and who could without compunction return tit for tat. Under this woman's hard-headed leadership, the mop and broom enterprise would surely flourish.

There were also liabilities. On the debit side of life's forthcoming ledger, Sandra had imposed the condition that he remain forever Thomas Pierce, literary loner, evasive man of letters. "I've told my mom and dad, both my sisters, my masseuse," she said. "There's a price. If I have to live a lie, then so do you." She gave him a warning frown, allowed the coming decades to take traction in his soul, then primly kissed his forehead.

"And by the way," she said. "Stop eating."

The ceremony, like the bride, was expensive and lovely and thoroughly businesslike. A sunlit day in June. An outdoor wedding. Three hundred guests, all but twelve known only to Sandra.

Blackmail aside, conscience and wisdom long abandoned, Marv Bertel made the best of it. The champagne helped, as did four slices of a superb rum-and-chocolate wedding cake, and after some bleak moments Marv offered up a congratulatory nod to fate and began to bask in the bright side, especially the chance to reprise his much-rehearsed literary role of Thomas Pierce. He took pleasure in the autograph requests, the hushed greetings from longtime fans. One of Sandra's teenage nieces, who came equipped with a suggestive smile and largely bared breasts, represented the day's high-water mark: all the signs of a groupie in the making. She gawked. She fed him oysters. At one point, when the girl's zealous tongue slipped into his ear, it occurred to Marv that to every dutiful husband came the annual responsibilities of the family reunion. And it also struck him, as the admiring niece's breasts opened up to take the curve of his belly, that this unlikely marriage, conceived in Hell, might well prove enduring.

As for Sandra, she was radiant.

During the toasts, Marv's new bride tapped his nose with five carats of compressed carbon. "If you put the scam on that bitch niece of mine ever again," she said gently, almost with compassion, "you're just a dirt-poor ex."

They honeymooned in the Alps. Resolutely, with exhaustive self-discipline, Marv worked his way through the sauces of Switzerland, France, and northern Italy. Sandra shopped. In early July, when they landed back in Denver, Marv stepped on a baggage scale, waited for the needle to settle, and sighed with the satisfaction of a man who, after a long, fugitive absence, had finally found his way home. Or almost home. The sober truth, he perceived, was that his fling with fantasy had put a seal on his life. Except for mere flesh, which might well compound itself even in the grave, he had come to the bitter end of things. Which was partly sad, partly happy. For all those ravenous decades Marv had been governed by gluttony, not solely of the stomach, but even more of hope, a hunger for all that he was not, all that he would never be, a hunger of dream and vision, a rapacious, bottomless, ultimately fatal appetite for an ever-elusive otherness. He had squired fantasy to the dance. He had left alone.

With that ended, and with Sandra now calling the mop and broom shots, Marv settled into what remained. He took solitary lunches. He feasted on anything that presented itself. As before, he waddled through. He had made his own bed. He slept in it. And at the first impossible whisper of reverie, even the most banal little aspiration for himself, he would switch it off as if it were some rigged TV game show that had never paid a winner.

A languid life, yes. And mostly pointless. But not entirely unsatisfying.

To pass the days, Marv sometimes locked his office door, put the intercom on mute, and jotted down memories of his encounter with skinniness. Not for public print, of course. He'd learned his lesson. Still, he had fun with sentences. He changed a few names, his own included, and chuckled over delicacies of motive and meaning. He invented some things. He enlarged upon others. It became in the end a sort of romance, and he a writer, as if by now doing it he could undo a lie, dissolve the fiction of his own disgusting life.

CHAPTER 20

CLASS OF '69

The farewell banquet had reached its dessert-and-coffee phase when nine exhausted, fast-aging members of the class of '69 straggled in to take their seats. Marv Bertel had been weeping. Spook led him to a back table, waved others away, touched Marv's cheek, straightened his tie, whispered something.

"Poor guy," said Jan Huebner.

"Poor us," said Amy Robinson. "He's got Spook. What do we have?"

"Each other, I guess," said Jan. "Unless something better shows up lickety-split."

"Something meaty," said Amy.

"Châteaubriand," said Jan, "for two."

Amy made a quick pointing gesture with her chin. "Over there. Look, don't stare."

"What?"

"Paulette and Billy. Can't stop ogling each other. Who would've predicted it?"

Jan sighed. "Private dancer. My kind of preacher."

"Amen," said Amy. "But there goes dinner."

★　　★　　★

Paulette Haslo and Billy McMann had fallen in wary, could-be, wait-and-see love. Though they trusted each other, and in particular the integrity of their motives, they did not yet trust love itself. They sat at separate tables. They were discreet with their emotions, polite to their table mates, but now and then, at the same instant, they'd glance across the room at each other and then grin at the embarrassment of having been caught glancing. Love was a surprise to both of them. Billy had come looking for revenge. Paulette had come looking for God. Both of them had suffered disappointment. But in another, less literal sense, which was just beginning to unveil itself, they'd found things neither had known were desirable or even possible. That love could happen at all struck them as extraordinary; that it could happen between old friends, so untouched by betrayal or prior pain, so easy, so comfortable, seemed to both of them either a great miracle or a cheap magician's trick. Life had made them skeptical. Neither Billy nor Paulette was yet prepared to believe in whatever this was, or to believe in each other, but at the same time they were finding it hard to disbelieve.

Across the table from Paulette, Ellie Abbott was in muted conversation with her husband Mark, whose expression was amused and expectant, a little perplexed, as if he were having difficulty following the setup to an elaborate but promising joke. Ellie's eyes did not once move from the crème brûlée on her plate.

What she was seeing on the plate, however, was not crème brûlée, and what she was telling her husband was not a joke.

Two tables away, Minnesota's lieutenant governor and his new wife made political small talk with an assistant provost. Directly behind them, too giggly, too garrulous, the lieutenant governor's ex-fiancée, a Lutheran missionary, reached for a bottle of champagne.

"Whatever you do," Jan Huebner told Amy Robinson, "don't get philosophical on me. I'm in pain. I need . . . You *know* what I need."

"How long's it been?"

"That?"

"What else?"

Jan shrugged. "Put it this way. Right now I'd settle for a Jimmy Dean's."

"Sad sacks, aren't we?" Amy said. She took a flask from her purse, swallowed twice, handed the flask to Jan. "I *will* make one tiny philosophical point. Maybe it's the lawyer in me, maybe the years, but when you look around this room, all these people—and I mean good people, too— nice people, almost all of them, Dorothy not excepted . . . And by the way, where is she? Primping, I'll bet. So what I mean is, you can't help but think . . . Fuck me, I forgot the point."

351

She blinked at the tablecloth. "Maybe that's the point."

"All you need is love," said Jan.

"I guess. Go ahead, girl. Sing."

"Not alone. You have to help."

When the coffee cups had been replenished, Marla Dempsey passed around a cardboard box. "What we'll do," Marla said, "we'll each draw a slip of paper with somebody's name on it. Friend or foe, creep or otherwise, we swallow our pride and get up and give that person a big juicy kiss. Tongues not required. Make sense?"

The game was a dud. It was too late in the reunion, too late in their lives. There were groans, a few halfhearted catcalls.

Ellie Abbott stopped in midsentence, having just mentioned a lakeside resort called Loon Point. "Mark, I'm sorry," she said. "I shouldn't have started this now. I was afraid I couldn't do it if we were alone."

He stared at her.

"I don't get it," he said. "What do loons have to do with anything? Water? All that?"

"Later," said Ellie.

By good fortune she'd drawn the name of Paulette Haslo, and in a rush Ellie pushed her chair back and went off in search of counsel.

Paulette was occupied with Billy McMann. They had pretended to draw each other's names. Elsewhere in the room, a physician and a mother of three had devised the same strategy. So too had Marv Bertel and Spook Spinelli, though they defaulted on the kissing, just held hands at their back table. Marv was feeling better. "Wish you could've seen me," he was telling Spook. "Once in my life I'm a movie star, I'm the Thin Man, I'm Dick Powell or Cary Grant or whoever, no jowls, no belly, didn't need one of those special periscopes to check out my dick. Skinny as all getout. Would've knocked you dead."

"You knock me now," Spook said. "A writer *and* an actual rodeo cowboy."

"Calf roping," Marv said, "in between masterpieces."

Spook gave his belly a pat. "If you're interested," she said, "I've got my own wish. I wish I weren't so inexcusably married. Otherwise, periscope time."

Marv looked at her. He wanted to hit something.

"Love you so much," he said.

"Yes?"

"Just so much."

Spook held his gaze for a second, started to smile, raised a thumb to her mouth.

Marv sighed. "Gonna break my heart, aren't you?"

"Oh, God, I suppose," Spook said.

Dorothy Stier arrived late. She'd had dinner at home with Ron, slipped on her prosthesis, changed into a pretty red cocktail dress, taken her evening tamoxifen, fussed with her hair and eye shadow and fingernails. "I won't be too awfully late," she told Ron, "but I don't suppose there's any reason to wait up for me."

"Well," he said, "I could come along."

"You could." Dorothy smiled radiantly. "No reason for that either."

She grabbed her car keys, blew him a kiss.

It was a fifteen-minute drive. At a couple of traffic lights, and as she turned into the Darton Hall parking lot, Dorothy rehearsed what she would say to Billy McMann, how she would concede certain issues, not concede others, and how she would allow chance and opportunity to govern what remained of the evening.

She felt brave. She had survived cancer, she would survive this.

At 9:15, when Dorothy walked into the banquet room, the name-drawing game had just trickled to its end. Only Paulette and Billy still found it fruitful.

Dorothy halted in the doorway.

Instantly, she began revising her speech, the concessions in particular.

She considered heading home.

Simple jealousy, she realized, and a touch of surprise, but the whole atmosphere stuck her as too collegiate, too saturated with sentiment. It crossed her mind that these people were strangers, complete aliens, like a new life form dredged up from the bottom of the sea. And they'd always been strangers. Except by an accident of birth, this was not Dorothy's generation. She didn't fit. The generation didn't fit her. Not the music or the politics or the fuzzyheaded ethics. Right now, stepping gingerly into the crowd, she detested that all-you-need-is-love drivel that Jan and Amy were half singing, half screaming to the ceiling. Love, Dorothy thought, was plainly not all you needed. Not by half. You needed a roof over your head. You needed a first-rate oncologist, a dexterous surgeon, a medicine cabinet stocked with some very powerful chemicals. You needed tamoxifen. You needed Xanax and Paxil and a fake breast and luck and guts and something to get you through the fires and thirst, the irritability of instant menopause. You needed brains and common sense.

Dorothy worked her way to the bar, ordered a gin and tonic, drank it down, then fell into conversation with a tearful, nearly incoherent Ellie Abbott. Something about water, something about Harmon.

"I wouldn't bother you with this," Ellie said, "but it's just . . . I can't *do* it. Paulette told me to blurt it all out, not even take a breath, but I can't say the right . . . not even . . . God, I'm sorry. I should talk to Paulette, I guess, except she's up to her neck with Billy."

"So I see," said Dorothy, and edged off toward David Todd.

★   ★   ★

355

David had just returned from the men's room, where he'd indulged in a substance that made him luminous. Half a hit was plenty. He was a kid again, light on his feet, winging a baseball against the garage, and his brother Mickey was saying, "Man, you're *it*, you're major league," and David laughed and found himself on the shaded bank of a narrow, fast-moving river called the Song Tra Ky, almost dead, getting deader, and Master Sergeant Johnny Ever wouldn't shut the fuck up, the guy kept babbling about this and that and all things between, the curvature of the earth, the reasoning behind pi, why Marla had left him for a shitball on a Harley, and why, in nasty detail, she would never be coming back.

When Dorothy Stier said hello and hooked his arm, David looked up into the slack, insinuating death's-head of Johnny Ever. It was Dorothy's voice, though, that informed him he was looking pale, a little off-center. After a second Johnny's face became Dorothy's.

"No, I'm fine," David said.

"You're sure?"

"Picture perfect. Talking with an angel."

"David, that's so sweet."

"Yeah, it is." A thought came to him. He took Dorothy's arm. "Want to try something interesting?"

Marla Dempsey watched her former husband, the man she wanted to love, guide Dorothy Stier into the men's room. It was difficult to know what to feel. As always, therefore, Marla found herself feeling almost nothing.

Anyway, it was her own fault. Mostly her own.

She waited until the men's room door had swung shut, and then she turned and wandered over to join Amy Robinson and Jan Huebner in a last, loud chorus.

Billy McMann and Paulette Haslo had moved into the banquet hall kitchen. The lights were out. Paulette's skirt was at her knees, Billy's jeans were coming down.

"Is this sex," Paulette said, "or something else?"

"Tell you in a second," said Billy.

A number of people were already saying their good-byes, hugging and exchanging phone numbers and moving toward the door to catch cabs or buses or late-night planes. Others planned to stay the night. Minnesota's lieutenant governor was undecided. His new wife wished to leave; his ex-fiancée wished to talk. Not twenty feet away, a former basketball star, now a mother of three, had just called home to say she would be returning a day late. A prominent physician had done the same. The two were now at the bar, toasting their reprieve, elated and ashamed, each feeling the press of tomorrow, each speculating as to whether a day would do it.

Some found it easy to go, and to let go. Some talked

357

about their distaste for reunions, how this would certainly be their last.

Some were crying.

Some were bored.

Two ex-football players, maudlin and drunk, huddled up one last time, slapped hands, and broke for the door.

Paulette and Billy emerged from the kitchen. Paulette was laughing, Billy was pulling on his shoes.

At a littered banquet table, cold sober, a silver-haired chemist and a retired librarian made peace with the frugal laws of temporality.

Better this than nothing, they said.

They said, Maybe next time.

Among those scheduled to depart that evening was Marv Bertel. He had a seat on the 11:30 flight to Denver. "I could always change the reservation," he said, although without much hope or enthusiasm, and when Spook Spinelli fell silent, Marv patted her arm and said, "Sandra'd have my nuts, of course. Which, I might add, would be a very definite first."

Spook didn't laugh.

She would ride with him out to the airport, see him off at the gate.

"Good enough," Marv said.

In the men's room, Dorothy Stier and David Todd enjoyed a meeting of minds. For the next eight or nine hours, he warned her, she would be voting Communist. Dorothy nodded gravely and swallowed half a blotter.

David popped the other half.

"How are the kids?" he said.

Ellie Abbott took her husband out to the parking lot and confessed it all. She would later remember a yellow streetlight just beyond Mark's right shoulder, a blurry glare, and how the light made his face vanish.

More than anything, he seemed embarrassed.

"If you don't mind," Mark said, "I'll drive back to the hotel alone."

He wouldn't look at her. He took out his car keys.

"Later, then," he said. "I'm sure you'll catch a ride with someone."

It hit Dorothy fast.

After twenty minutes she had the amateur giggles. Ten minutes more and she was comparing prostheses with David Todd.

"Nam and putrid breast cancer," Dorothy was saying, "who would've thought it?"

"Same difference," said David.

"Well, of *course* same difference. And nobody even gives a hot stinking darn, do they? I mean, it's nutty. They've all got their ouchies, their little dings and boo-boos. Stubbed their toes on love. Bruised souls. Mangled egos. Et cetera, et cetera, and blah blah blah." Dorothy tugged her prosthesis down, studied the wreckage. "Beautiful, I'd say. Medal of Stinking Honor. Ron—he's my husband, worthy man, loads of dignity—Ron doesn't care to look at it. Republican. No complaints. Should've married Billy, I guess, but who ever . . . These scars here. Zigzaggy, wrinkly. See that? Sort of purply? Real purply?"

"Extremely," said David. "We should get out of here."

"Yes, but here's the deal. Nam and cancer, it's like . . . It's not like anything, is it? Once you're there, you're there. You don't come home. Am I right? And what the heck can you even say about it? Not much. I guess you can say wow, or yuck, or hey, or 'Thank you very much but enough of that, I'll take a rain check, I'll take what-the-fuck-*ever*.' Whoops! Excuse my mouth."

"Let's go," David said. "Pull your dress up."

"Not yet."

"Right now. We could use the breathing room."

"No, honestly," Dorothy said, "I'm good, I'm not even half there, not a tickle." She giggled. She peered down at her chest. "Whoa, too purple! Purple Stinking Heart!"

In the banquet hall, in an open doorway, Minnesota's lieutenant governor said a breezy farewell to his ex-fiancée, now a Lutheran missionary. His ex-financée smiled. "Yeah, bye," she said, then turned to the lieutenant governor's pretty new wife. "We haven't been introduced," she said, "but if you ever need to get yourself good and screwed—I mean, screwed so you don't forget—I recommend the trusty old missionary position."

"What's *this?*" said the lieutenant governor's bride.

"Screwed royally," said the missionary.

David Todd helped Dorothy get reconfigured, led her back out to the banquet room, sat her down, found some orange juice to loosen up her chemistry.

It was just after 10:30 P.M. The mood had gone dismal. Fifteen or twenty people still lingered at the bar, a few others near the door. Minnesota's lieutenant governor had just departed. Paulette Haslo and Billy McMann were kneeling down to comfort Ellie Abbott, who sat cross-legged on the floor, her face blank and white.

Ellie hugged herself, shivering a little.

The singing had ended. A few people spoke in murmurs, most not at all.

"It's okay," Paulette was saying, "it'll work out, it's better this way. No more secrets. That's a huge, huge start."

Ellie didn't speak.

She watched Harmon reach out of the water and try to grip the sky and then slip away from her, dead-eyed and bewildered, a lot like Mark.

Marv Bertel and Spook Spinelli made the rounds,

saying their goodbyes. Marv put a hand on Ellie's head, held it there a moment, and then he took Spook by the elbow and guided her toward the doorway, and through it, and back toward their lives.

In the cab, halfway to the airport, Spook leaned against him and said, "How do we tolerate it?"

"Being us, you mean?"

"Us. Anybody."

Marv was quiet for a time. "We were happy once."

"Really?" said Spook.

"Oh, yeah. Or we thought so. Same thing."

Spook brightened.

"Like everything else," she said. "If you don't think you're happy, what good is it?" She moved closer to him. "Let's be married someday."

"Sure," said Marv.

"You and me, happily ever after."

"La-la land," said Marv.

Dorothy Stier and David Todd were already there.

The banquet hall was dark. No lights, no air conditioning, no people, no music, but they were dancing anyway, although not touching, and not to the same beat. Dorothy had removed her pretty red cocktail dress, turned it inside out, and put it on backward. She was proving her courage to Billy McMann, who had departed ten minutes ago with Paulette Haslo.

David danced sitting down.

He'd been here once or twice before.

At one point he heard footsteps and looked up, thinking Marla had come back for him. "Man, I warned you," said Johnny Ever, contemptuous and self-important. "Warnings here, warnings there. Had to be a hero. Had to suck it up and take the heat, thirty years' worth, who knows how much more still to come? Wake up, my man. All you gotta do, you just gotta yell 'Uncle.' I take it from there. I mean, Holy Ghost and shit on a shingle, what the hell's wrong with you people? This ain't Thermopylae, it ain't the movies. You're allowed to quit."

Across town, Paulette Haslo and Billy McMann dropped Ellie at her hotel. "I don't want to go in," Ellie said. "I don't think I *can*."

"You can," said Billy.

"Go on now," Paulette said. "The whole truth, nothing but. I promise he loves you anyway."

Ellie took a breath, hugged her friends, and got out of the car.

"What do you think?" said Billy.

"Give it a minute, let her catch the elevator." Paulette stared straight ahead. "Then I guess we check in."

Silently, in the humid dark, Jan Huebner, Amy Robinson, and Marla Dempsey walked across the deserted campus. It was 11:10 P.M., the temperature still in the mid-nineties. They sat on the steps to their dorm, shared a cigarette, said nothing at all for some time.

Then Marla said, "It was my fault, you know."

"What was?" said Amy. "David?"

"That, too. But I meant the reunion. Class secretary, responsible Marla, but last year I totally forgot to book it. Announcements, reservations, catering, everything. And then this year—you see what happened—this year I almost forgot again. Idiot. Best I could do was set it for July."

"Oh, well," Jan said, and looked at Amy.

Amy looked back.

Neither of them saw any gain in bringing up unpleasant questions.

"Actually," Amy said, "it was nice this way. Band of brothers, all that. Had the place to ourselves." She paused. She couldn't resist. "Forgot how?"

Marla shook her head.

"Electrical overload, blown fuses," she said. "I'm not human."

CHAPTER 21
WHAT WENT WRONG

On the last day of July 1969, David Todd arrived at the Hubert H. Humphrey VA Hospital just outside Minneapolis. His right leg had been amputated in Japan. His left leg was in dispute. Over the next three and a half weeks, off and on, a number of meditative, glutinous-sounding voices discussed the possibility of another amputation, the pros and cons. David himself was too far gone to care. He was back at the Song Tra Ky, conferring with angels, watching a colony of ants consume his feet. Fascinating, he decided. Feet to food. The morphine took him to places he had never visited before, black holes and white dwarfs, ancient cemeteries, the walls of Troy, a ditch outside Tu Cung, the gaudy bedroom of a corrupt, complacent, leg-eating, gone-in-the-teeth Cleopatra. He witnessed his own decorous conception. He played shortstop for the '27 Yankees. He was there in Sugamo Prison, a few minutes past midnight on December 22, 1948, looking on as Hideki Tojo dropped out of time through a squeaky gallows trapdoor. He bossed mules for Wellington. He scrubbed the ovens at Dachau, rode point at

Washita, sat in on LBJ's war briefings, attended a mediocre comedy at Ford's Theatre, listened to the insane blather of Hector Ortiz's transistor radio. At one point, near the end of his first week in the hospital, David took vaporous note of Marla Dempsey leaning over him, her lips poised in concern, her eyes filled with something just short of love. His own imagination, he reasoned. Or maybe not. Either way, when Marla smiled and kissed his forehead, or seemed to, David screamed. He couldn't help it: there was pain in the most delicate touch, in the simplest sound or passing image.

He started to apologize, to sit up, but Marla was no longer present. Nor was David, entirely. He could hear the Song Tra Ky bubbling nearby. He could smell dead friends and mildew and his own rotting feet.

Days later, in a moment of narcotic clarity, Marla Dempsey appeared again. She murmured endearments. She promised to be true. When she vanished, however, someone issued a chuckle from the hospital ethers. "Relax, my friend, it ain't what you think. You're alive, just like I swore, but from here on, that's basically the whole shitty shebang. Gotta be honest. One of the rules, right? This honesty thing, Davy, it drives me nuts. Bureaucracy up the bazoo. Boss lets me exaggerate all I want, wax eloquent, but I don't get to tell no fibs. Real temptation, too. Hate to break hearts." Johnny Ever clicked his tongue in false exasperation. "Anyhow, here's the scoop. What the lady feels right now—Miss Marla, that is—what she feels is real extra sad. Not much else. Maybe some guilt tossed in, which is why she's gonna marry your ass. Pure pity, man. I seen it plenty times before. Eva Braun, Dale Evans." He chuckled again. "Giddyap, cripple."

David was released from the hospital on Christmas Day, 1969. He and Marla were married in the Darton Hall chapel on New Year's Eve, a few friends, nothing elaborate. "I'll try hard," Marla told him during their honeymoon in Miami, on a crowded white beach behind the hotel. "The thing is, you need to know how scared I am. My whole life, David, I never thought I'd end up married, not to anybody, and I have to admit it's a strange feeling." She paused. Her eyes were hidden behind sunglasses. "You know me, David. I'm not a welcome-home-honey housewife. I'll need room. Time to be myself."

"Fine," David said. "I just hope it isn't charity."

Marla turned toward him.

"My leg," said David. "Ex-leg. I'm not looking for pity."

"That's absurd."

"Is it?"

"Yes," Marla said. "It's our honeymoon, isn't it?"

David looked away.

He was tempted to spend the next few minutes discussing morphine and shot feet and a certain cocksure disc jockey wired into the silver-hot center of the universe. Instead, he shrugged. He covered his prosthesis with a towel and stared down the beach at a group of college-age kids playing volleyball. They were drunk. They were happy. They were ignorant. They had their legs. They did not hear voices in their sleep, nor have access to the appalling drift of things to come.

He looked back at Marla.

"Sorry," he said. "But you'd tell me, right? If you just felt pity for me?"

"David, I do feel pity. Losing your leg, all those baseball dreams. It's ghastly. Not to mention stupid. The war, I mean, not you. How it's wrecked things for so many people. Honestly, I'd be a moron *not* to feel angry and sick about it. Even some pity. But that's not why we're married."

"Except you're not sure?"

"I didn't say that. I said I was scared."

"Which sounds unsure."

There was a moment of severe silence. Marla pulled off her sunglasses, rubbed her eyes, sighed, and glanced down at her wedding ring as if it were something she'd picked up off the beach. "David, you're precious to me," she said. "True, I'm not the beaming bride. That's not the person you married. A hard thing to explain. I don't understand what it is or where it came from, but there's something inside me that's just totally alone, totally private. Like a rainy day that goes on and on."

David nodded and said, "Fine, then."

"Not fine," said Marla. "But the truth. I won't lie about it."

Then she rose to her feet, tossed her sunglasses aside, waded into the Atlantic, dove under, and spent thirty seconds of her honeymoon near the bottom, remorseful and frightened, exploring her life, telling herself she should never have gotten married, not in a thousand years, and certainly not to a decent, loving man like David Todd.

In the autumn of her junior year at Darton Hall, while dating David, Marla Dempsey began an affair with a former high school teacher, a married man. The romance lasted just over a month, not long by some measures, a light-year by others. During those four weeks in 1967, Marla seemed to float from spot to spot in a great sparkling bubble. She found herself shopping for sexy clothes—lace panties, see-through negligees—things she'd once despised and ridiculed.

People noticed the change. David, too.

"Query," he said one morning. "Where's Marla these days?"

His tone was cheerful. His eyes showed concern.

For a time Marla said nothing, considering her options, and then she said, "On vacation, I guess. A brain resort."

In mid-October the affair ended in the parking

lot of Marla's dorm. Lovely day. Antique red Cadillac. Engine idling, windows open to the autumn air. The high school teacher, a blond, dark-eyes, poisonously handsome specimen named Jim Anderson, explained the dynamic to her. His voice was slow and condescending, as if he were teaching phonics to a class of dimwits. He talked about guilt and insomnia and issues of honor.

Maybe in another life, he said.

Maybe if x ever intersected with an unlikely y.

"I follow you perfectly," said Marla.

She got out of the car, went up to her room, sat on the floor, filed her nails, dialed David's number, hung up after two rings, screamed an obscenity, changed into shorts and sneakers, and jogged three miles to the teacher's house in a middle-class suburb of St. Paul. The antique Cadillac was parked in the driveway. Nearby, under clear plastic, was what appeared to be a brand-new baby stroller.

Just before dusk Marla rang the doorbell.

Why she was there, or what she expected, was unclear to her, and when Jim Anderson's wife opened the door, Marla found herself unable to think or speak. The woman was an emaciated, brittle-looking creature, thirty-five or so, her reddish brown hair arranged in a pair of pigtails secured by rubber bands. She wore faded blue jeans, a yellow gauze blouse loose at the waist. In her left hand she gripped a plastic spatula. A TV set blared at full volume in the room behind her: the evening news, trouble in Asia. Dense odors of broccoli and frying pork chops swamped the doorway. These details—the spatula, the pigtails, the smells, the evening news—would remain with Marla Dempsey forever.

The woman seemed to nod.

There was an instant of silence, succeeded by a dull explosion on the TV, succeeded by the sound of a flushing toilet.

Jim Anderson's wife stepped back and used her free hand to tug at one of the pigtails. "Aren't we cute?" she said. Her voice was matter-of-fact. "Awful young to be a husband fucker."

Marla had nothing to say. But she now realized that this woman's sad, unsurprised, washed-out face offered exactly what she'd needed, everything she'd run three miles for, which was to know that she would never be forgiven.

After the honeymoon, David and Marla rented a two-bedroom house in St. Paul, walking distance from the college. Money was a problem. David's disability checks helped a little, but still they needed a bed and a sofa and hot water and something to eat. They had student loans to repay. Their parents could contribute almost nothing. After some discussion, Marla postponed graduate school and went to work as a paralegal in downtown Minneapolis, which seemed fine at first, but which in the end amounted to little more than a poorly paid, coffee-fetching gofership.

She was advised to widen her smile, shorten her skirts. It was 1970.

Through their first month of marriage, David continued with his rehab, four hours a day, six days a week, learning to use escalators and climb stairs and navigate slippery surfaces with the aid of a mahogany cane. Progress was slow. Sometimes his stump felt as if it were plugged into an electrical outlet; other times he'd find himself scratching at thin air where his shin or ankle used to be. In a physical sense, David knew he'd make it. His head was something else. At night, often for hours, he lay awake listening to the accusatory chatter of dead friends, Kaz Maples and Buddy Bond and Alvin Campbell and all the others. He watched Doc Paladino get sucked away into the tall, dry grass. "Man, I told you," Johnny Ever whispered. "All them shot-up buddies of yours, they got scads of time on their hands. Eons, you could say. Just harps and halos and virgin-ass angels. Nothin' much to do except talk their guts out." Johnny paused to admire his own gift of gab. "No offense, Davy, but I'll tell you one more thing. Them dudes got long memories. We're talking forever. And I fear they ain't gonna let you forget, neither. Survivor guilt, it's a bitch. Killed Custer's horse. Would've killed Custer."

In late April of 1970 David took a part-time job refinishing furniture. The work brought in some cash, boosted his morale, made him feel a little more whole. He was good at it. After two months he opened his own shop in the garage, building customized cabinets and a few finely made desks and dining tables. The business propsered, and near the end of the summer David expanded his operation into a closed-down gas station off Snelling Avenue. He hung up a handmade sign and hired a helper. "You should be proud," Marla said, and in many ways David was. Carpentry was not baseball, not the majors, but it was something he enjoyed. He liked the feel of tools in his hands. He liked the scent of good wood, the satisfaction of coming up with tidy solutions to problems of geometry. Also, the work helped to push away the voices, kept his mind off the Song Tra Ky.

A week before Christmas he built a delicate black-walnut nightstand as a gift for Marla. While he sanded and stained and oiled, humming to himself, David daydreamed about the big leagues. He had his legs. He was quick on the pivot. He was happily married. He would stay that way. The prophecies were bullshit, nothing but smoke, and Johnny Ever was one more blowhard with a microphone.

From the start, in too many ways, Marla and David were uncomfortable in the marriage. Distracted and wary. Always on edge. Sometimes frightened.

On her part, Marla could never eradicate the high school teacher from her thoughts. The man lounged in her head as if he'd taken up residence inside her, uninvited, sharing her pillow at night, pulling up a chair at meals. Marla missed him. And she missed the happy, wildly infatuated young woman of 1967, bowled-over-Marla, girl-Marla, the Marla Dempsey who for a few incredible weeks had floated around campus in a bubble. Now the black days were back. Not despair exactly, not even unhappiness. Just that familiar old passivity, a cool and listless neutrality of spirit. Nothing moved her. Nothing hurt. She felt sealed off from things: from pain, from joy, from her own emotions. No big ups. No miserable downs. At times, Marla thought, it was as if she'd been pumped full of some powerful drug, Valium or a handful of those new knock-you-dead sleeping pills. She could move through an entire day, sometimes a week, without once laughing. Sex was fine, never more than fine. Life was good, never more than good. Still, as if to balance things out, her daily routine had a sumptuous tranquillity, the sort of peace that attends a solid marriage to a solid man like David Todd. And the last thing Marla wanted was to hurt him. Which meant faking things.

"What a beautiful, beautiful nightstand," she told him on Christmas morning, 1970.

She grinned furiously.

"I'm blown away," she said. "Just so happy."

In 1973 they bought a house in Bloomington, not far from Met Stadium, and on summer nights, after work, they'd often make the nine-minute drive to take in a Twins game. David would keep a meticulous box score, frowning into a pair of binoculars, analyzing plays or situations that caught his attention. Most of it meant nothing to Marla. To pass time, she would offer her own commentary on what she called the "team costumes," evaluating fashion issues, chattering about cut and color. She liked the bright stadium lights, the seventh-inning stretch, the smells of beer and popcorn. The game itself remained a mystery to her. Even after David's lectures, all his charts and diagrams, Marla still had no idea about the function of a bunt, or why anyone in his right mind would want to execute a hit-and-run. "If you ask me," she'd tell him, "the whole thing sounds pretty shady, pretty crooked." In a way she was kidding, in a way she wasn't, but it was nice to see a smile come to David's lips, to watch him laugh and shake his head and explain all over again.

Early on, Marla worried that these nights at the ballpark might undo the whole rehab process, send him over some wartime edge, but the effect on David was clearly the opposite. Almost always, his mood would soften. The tension would drain from his eyes, flushing away the war, and at night he didn't talk so often in his sleep—not with the same rage or violence. More than anything, it was the late-hour babble that alarmed and sometimes terrified Marla.

She dreaded bedtime. She dreaded the end of baseball season.

In mid-February of 1975, Marla carried a tape recorder into the bedroom, put it on her dresser, and hit the record button.

At breakfast the next morning, she played the cassette for David.

"That voice," she said. "Who is it?"

David didn't look at her. He pushed to his feet, went to the sink, rinsed his cereal bowl, and poured himself a cup of coffee. He kept his back turned.

"This scares me," she said. "That voice. It's you, but it's not you. All the swearing. Whoever it is, I feel like he's dangerous."

"Dangerous?"

"Like he could hurt somebody."

David swung around toward her. For a few seconds his expression went thoughtful.

"Right," he said. "I suppose he could."

"Who?"

"I'm not sure who. Nightmares. Let's try to forget it."

"David, did you listen to the tape? How do I forget? Tell me how."

"I don't know how."

"So that's it? Don't talk about it, don't look at me? I mean, God, let's just play the tape again, have a laugh, pretend it's the comedy hour. Chalk it up to dreamland. Rub it out."

"Hey, stop." David jabbed a finger at her. His voice rose from deep in his chest, from the darkness inside him, a ravening, suddenly brutal sound. "You don't understand. Nothing. If I tried to explain, if I started to explain—" He shook his head hard, reached down, pulled up his right pant leg, and rapped his knuckles against the prosthesis. "See that? Chop off a leg, baby. Watch sixteen guys die. Smell the rot. See if you don't cuss in your sleep."

"I wasn't criticizing, David. I was trying—"

"Trying what? To talk?"

"Yes."

He dropped the pant leg, took a jerky half-step toward her. Something changed in his face. "Excellent," he said. "Let's talk about red Cadillacs. Baby strollers. One leg, honey, but I'm all ears."

Marla looked at him. Outside, an ambulance or a police car went by, its siren at high emergency, and in those miserable moments it occurred to Marla that the world was indifferent to all of this, deaf to betrayal and deceit and petty passion.

David's lips curled into a strange, skewed smile she'd never seen before. "Cat got your tongue? Maybe we should rev up that tape recorder. Capture the silence."

"You knew," she said.

"Day one. Lace panties. I'm not an idiot."

"And you never said anything."

He made a contemptuous spitting sound. "What's to say? 'Pretty-please love me'?"

"David."

"Hard to find words, isn't it?"

He took the cassette out of the tape recorder, tossed it in the garbage.

"Ex-teachers, what's a guy to do?" he said. "Thought to myself, Hey, give it time, she'll come around. Leg or no leg. So I wait. Five years, three people. You, me, Mr. Teacher. Eat dinner together. Group sex. Christ, I'd watch you sometimes, sailing away to fantasyland, wherever the fuck you'd go." He laughed. "Robot wife. Makes a guy wonder who the cripple is."

He put his coffee cup in the sink, turned on the water, stared at the faucet. He seemed dazed, unfixed to the world. "Writing on the wall. Knew all along."

"Ridiculous," Marla said. "Nobody knows that."

"Yeah, well. In the stars."

"You're saying we're finished?"

He didn't answer.

Marla waited a moment, then went over to him and put a hand on his arm. "I know it's not enough, but I tried hard. That's the truth. Sometimes, though, it felt like you'd already decided everything. Who I was. What I wanted. Almost like you *needed* to drive me away."

"I'm the villain?"

"No. But people get what they imagine."

David raised his eyebrows, mocking. "Pigtails? Baby strollers?"

"Not that."

"What about the cool Caddy?"

Marla took her hand from his arm. She had the

sensation of talking to a new person, someone who'd put on David's face for a Halloween party. "I love you," she said quietly. "But when you suppose from the start that everything's fake and rotten and doomed . . . Then it *is* doomed. That's how I've felt for years, like you wanted me to hurt you." She stopped. Something struck her as wrong. "Pigtails? Where did that come from?"

David made a casual motion with the palms of his hands.

"Little birdie," he said.

"That's not an answer."

"But good enough."

For several seconds David looked at her, sadly, yet also maliciously, and then he grinned and glanced at the water faucet, where Johnny Ever waited. "What a bitch. Give it time, she's out of here. Ta-ta. Gone as Goebbels. Believe me, partner, we're talkin' history here. Future, too. Cooked goose. Roasted romance."

Marla said, "*What?*"

The marriage lasted four more years. Both Marla and David did what they could to keep it alive, to work toward some condensed version of happiness, and for periods of time they made themselves believe that whatever they had together—the bond, the covenant—might still be salvageable. They didn't quit. Twice a month, David went to see a VA psychiatrist, a woman his own age, also a veteran of the sixties, with whom he'd share a couple of joints and vigorous assurances that Master Sergeant Johnny Ever was no angel, no devil, no ghost, no middleman; that, in fact, the man at the microphone was none other than David himself. This made sense. In a way, somewhere inside him, he'd known all along. He slept better. His dreams went foggy and bland. Only rarely did he hear Ortiz's transistor radio, or yipping sounds, or the murderous drone of the Song Tra Ky.

With Marla, he'd come to an accommodation. Tacitly, as if silence could obliterate pain, they avoided conversations that might wander toward Marla's teacher or David's ordeal at the river. Neither of them asked questions. Neither of them volunteered anything. In 1976, Marla quit her paralegal job and began graduate studies in art history at the University of Minnesota. David's furniture business flourished. On the surface, and sometimes beneath, their lives moved along smoothly enough. They had sex three or four times a month, whenever the pressures accumulated. They ate meals in front of the TV, chatted amiably, laughed sometimes, took vacations, planned an addition to their house, visited with friends, gave up cigarettes, started again, celebrated birthdays and anniversaries, listened to music, bought a Chevrolet, took up yoga, realized none of it was sufficient.

By early 1978 the calm had become excruciating. They never fought, which was like fighting. Acts of kindness had the bite of bribery.

Yet even then they kept trying.

They put *x*'s and *o*'s at the bottom of their grocery lists. They signed up for ballroom dance lessons. In mid-December of 1978, about a year before the end, they began attending services at a Quaker meetinghouse in St. Paul, where silence was the rule, and where they would sit side by side on sturdy oak benches, exhausted skeptics in search of a miracle. "Man, you just plain don't pay attention," Johnny Ever would whisper. "All this wasted effort, it's like watchin' some poor bastard try to breathe underwater. Go ahead, hyperventilate like the dickens, nature just don't work like that. The woman's fadin' fast, Dave. Them gray eyes, that out-of-here stare. Blind man could see it." Sometimes Johnny would sigh, other times he'd chortle. "An' this church crap, Davy. I'll tell you right now, it didn't do jack for ol' Bonhoeffer. Your Nam buddies, either. Should've heard 'em—'Dear God, dear God!'—real impressive, except all they ever got for it was hoarse, then dead. See, there's good news, bad news. Bad news: you're gonna end up munchin' your heart out. Good news: everybody dies. Face it now, face it later. *I'm* church."

In those moments, when the inner dialogue went loopy, David realized he was talking to himself, though it didn't quite seem that way. He'd reach for Marla's hand and grip it hard and wait for something in return, a little pressure, the slightest heat.

"Whoa, Nellie," Johnny would mutter. "You're a scrapper, kid."

★　　★　　★

383

Marla met a man in the spring of 1979. She thought it might be love: a younger man, a trader of stocks, a rider of motorcycles, no rivers bubbling through his dreams.

She confessed to David on Christmas Day.

A despicable thing, Marla knew, but the alternative was worse.

She slipped out of bed before daylight. She went to the kitchen, gazed out the window at a neighbor's Christmas lights, returned to the bedroom, lay down beside David, waited for him to wake up, and then moistened her lips and told him.

David put his face in the pillow, Marla got dressed.

There was no sound.

A light snow was falling.

Marla picked up the phone and called her lover and asked him to wait for her down the street. A moment later, as she was hanging up, the thought arose that for David Todd there would never again be another Christmas.

She had some orange juice, half a muffin.

She packed a small knapsack.

At daybreak, she went out the front door and looked down the street to where a black and red Harley waited in the snow.

"The truth is," said Johnny Ever, "I'm not a bad guy. Not a good guy, either, but give me credit. Big John, he deserves one of them blue ribbons in the tell-it-like-it-is contest. Good or bad, up or down, I calls 'em like I sees 'em: broken heart, side pocket. Not much fun. Everybody blames the messenger. No justice in this world, damn little in the afterworld." Johnny sighed. "Got my condolences, man. Heartfelt, et cetera." He sighed again, deeper. "Now comes the tough part."

They divorced in April of 1980. The house was sold for a good deal of money, which they split down the middle, and after a month Marla moved with her stockbroker to Chicago, where she taught art history to business majors, remarried, got pregnant, miscarried, grew restless, grew bored, went through a difficult second divorce, and then found herself back in the blues, alone, not quite happy, not quite miserable, which seemed to her the only way to be.

David took up with his psychiatrist. It lasted six weeks. "You can do better," Johnny said. "Fact is, I'm surprised you even considered it. Just some New Age, doped-up mind meddler. Total pagan, too. Know-it-all. Claims I'm a figment. I mean, seriously, the broad's in for a shock when she finds out what I got waitin' on *her* down the pike." David didn't speak. He had learned to tune out this chatter, to recognize its origins in his own heart and to let it go at that.

In many ways, he now realized, Marla had been

right. He'd believed in his own vision of things, and in the end, to a greater or lesser degree, the belief had birthed the facts. He would miss her forever. He would never quit hoping. He would drink too much, smoke too much, care too little about the consequences. He would never remarry. To his last day, and perhaps beyond, he would regret his own failure of nerve, which was also a failure of imagination, the inability to divine a happy ending.

In 1987 Marla returned to the Twin Cities. David met her at the airport. He helped her find an apartment, loaned her a sofa bed and some dishes.

"I hope it's not charity," Marla said.

"It's fondness," said David.

They remained friends.

Once or twice a year, they'd meet in one of the bars near Darton Hall, talking over their lives, wishing each other well. At college reunions they were inseparable. They held hands and drank together and sometimes slept together. Absently, as if nothing had ever changed, David would sometimes find himself twirling a strand of Marla's hair around his finger, or stroking the small of her back as he talked baseball with an ex-teammate. And for Marla it was the same. A kind of repose. A perfect fit. They seemed destined for each other. They seemed in love. People who knew them well, even some who didn't, would often wonder what went wrong.

CHAPTER 22

CLASS OF '69

There were late-hour thunderstorms just west of Minneapolis, sheet lightning and heavy rain and hail. Marv Bertel's flight had been delayed by an hour and a half. To fill the time, and to smooth out the farewells, Spook led him over to a do-it-yourself photo booth across from the departure gate. It was a tight squeeze. Spook drew the curtain, snuggled in, told him to smile at the camera. "Say Samoa," she said.

"Samoa," said Marv.

"Say someday."

"Someday," Marv said, and the camera flashed.

Afterward they sat in plastic chairs, locked arms, and watched their reflections in the tinted airport windows. There were no signs of the approaching storm. It was a hot, sultry Saturday night, July 8, 2000, close to midnight, close to Sunday, and the concourse was almost entirely deserted. Six passengers sat waiting for the flight to Denver. To Spook's left, a pair of improbable cowboys in fancy shirts and feathered Stetsons spoke in mellifluous voices about the delay, whether they should bag it and find a hotel and try their luck in the morning. Across from them, a very pale, very elderly woman sat dozing in her plastic chair, lips fluttering, mumbling in her sleep.

Spook sighed and handed Marv one of the new photographs. "Add it to your collection," she said.

"I certainly will," said Marv.

"Our secret, yes?"

He looked at her with curiosity. "Give me a hint. Which secret would that be?"

"Samoa. Someday."

"Oh, someday," Marv said. "One of those deep dark secrets. Even from me."

"You don't believe in it?"

"Afraid not."

"Not even for these few tiny minutes?"

"No. Can't."

"Well, then," Spook said, "that's a problem. You don't believe in *me*."

"I'd like to."

"Then do it. Try."

"I could, couldn't I?" Marv said. "Except you've already told me how it ends. Heartache, I recall."

"Did I say that?"

"You said it. Loud and clear."

"In those words? Direct quote?"

"Pretty close."

Spook worried the subject for a few seconds. "All right, I must've told the truth. But that doesn't rule out someday, somewhere, somehow. Who knows when. After I've changed my whole personality. When I'm eight hundred years old."

"Maybe then," Marv said.

"I just want to hope."

Marv tucked the photograph in his wallet. Streaks of rain were now trickling down the window in front of them. The two cowboys had gone off for a smoke; the pale old woman snoozed on, mumbling in her sleep.

After some time had gone by, Marv looked at his wristwatch and stood up. "I should call Sandra," he said. "Back in a jiff."

"Give the queen my love."

"Sure thing," he said. "Consider it done."

Marv was away only a few minutes. When he returned, the night had gone wild with electricity. A ferocious rain blew horizontally across the tarmac.

"Cancel," Spook said. "Go tomorrow."

"Tonight, tomorrow, what's the difference?"

"I don't mean that. This weird, creepy feeling, Marv. I don't want you on that airplane."

"Feeling how? What?"

"Stay one more night."

For a while Marv said nothing. It struck him that he was not yet an old man, that he could always try another diet, another life, walk away from Sandra and mops and lifelong unhappiness. It also occurred to him that he had been drinking heavily that evening.

"Comes down to this," he said. "If I thought there was the slightest hope, I'd toss you into my suitcase right now. Book a flight to who cares

391

where. But I know better." He looked at her. "Want to know why?"

"I do."

"Because you're Spook. Because I'm Marv."

"You're getting on that plane?"

"If I fit."

"Jesus, did you hear me? Creepy. I'm serious."

"I heard you," Marv said.

Just after midnight, as the storm approached, Jan Huebner and Amy Robinson and Marla Dempsey sat on the steps of their dorm, exhausted and forlorn, a little restless, a little depressed, reluctant to go up to their rooms. "Boy, things've changed," Jan said. "Used to be, we'd order a pizza about now, put slick moves on the delivery guy. Now it's cold cream and Letterman."

"And the Web," said Amy Robinson.

"Am I human?" said Marla.

"You are," said Amy.

"What we need," Jan said, "is a male-type human being. I'd settle for part of one."

"Well, listen," Marla said, "if I'm human, what's wrong with me? Why can't I love anybody?"

"You can, you do," Amy said. "You love David."

"But I'm not *in* love."

Jan snorted. "Tie him down, we'll do a demo."

"Yeah," said Amy, and she laughed, and in the next instant the temperature seemed to plunge by ten degrees. There was a brief, sharp wind, then lightning, then a much more savage wind, and then the night was broken by a gush of rain and hail.

"My God," Jan said, "I'm coming."

Across campus, in a dim, empty banquet room, Dorothy Stier and David Todd foraged for food. They moved from table to table, grazing from an array of leftovers. "I'm a veggie, you know," Dorothy was telling him, "so I have to be careful. This lovely chicken tarragon, for instance. I won't actually swallow, except for an itsy-bitsy bite."

"Teenie-weenie," said David Todd.

"Disgusting, aren't I? Wow. Why am I so hungry?"

"Protein deficiency," David said. "Acids, they're the building blocks."

"Ah," said Dorothy.

"It's a historical fact."

"Of course it's a fact. And is *that* crème brûlée? Just a taste. Stop me if I pig out."

"Pig away," David said.

Dorothy ate a drumstick, half a breast. "Our own personal banquet," she said. "We should wear bibs. Formal wear. Lord in heaven, it *is* crème brûlée . . . You know, David, I was wondering. What ever happened to the Cold War? Khrushchev? Where the heck is *he* now? I mean, you were in Vietnam, right?"

"I was," David said. "Didn't spot Khrushchev."

"Well, naturally you didn't. Ducked out, I'll bet." She looked at him. "Very sorry about your leg."

"Yes. Thanks."

"I lost a tit."

David nodded. "I know you did, honey, and I'm sorry for that."

"Totally, totally gone. One minute you're well breasted, next minute you're this lopsided Republican. Kaput."

"I saw. You showed me earlier."

Dorothy frowned. "Did I say tit? Don't tell Ron I said tit, tit, tit."

"Sure won't. Privileged information, Dorothy."

"Not that I'm ashamed. He's rich, you know. Ron is. Tennis freak, control freak, loves his garden. I swear—this is no fib, no exaggeration—he picks up stray leaves by hand. One at a time, you know? Anal Andy. Great father. Flat tummy, quite clean. Doesn't care to dwell on my gone tit. Turns out the lights, pretends I'm twenty-one, perfect C cups. Boy, I *am* hungry." She wiped a spoon on her red cocktail dress, scooped crème brûlée onto a plate, sat down on the floor to eat. "Is it hot in here or am I tripping?"

"It's hot," said David.

"And that noise? Is that thunder?"

"I think it is."

"Thunder! Well, good!" She dabbed at her mouth and looked at him. "Sit down, for crying out loud. Help me out with this luscious, luscious brûlée. Bring some butter."

David squatted down beside her and they took turns with the spoon. The rain was beating down hard now. Lightning made the banquet room blink bluish white.

"Now let's get serious," Dorothy said. "Once upon a time—say, roughly ages and ages ago, almost forever—way back then I was pretty attractive, wasn't I? In college?"

"Attractive doesn't cover it," said David. "You were dynamite."

"Thank you, sir. And I was just wondering. Give me an honest opinion on this, don't hold back. Do you think I should've let Billy . . . How do I say this? I'll whisper. Ready?"

"Ready."

Dorothy swallowed, licked her lips, and leaned toward him. "Don't be Ron, no quibbling," she said. "Should I have let Billy sweep me off to Canada? Make me into Mrs. Benedict Arnold? Don't you dare lie."

"That one's tough," said David.

"Of course it's tough, that's why I'm asking. But, God, I couldn't do it. End of the earth, it seemed. The whole comfort factor. And I was young. Just embarrassing, you know? My family. The way I was brought up. You don't *do* that. I know what everybody thinks about me, Jan and Amy and everybody, they think I'm this country-club moron, this no-blow-job type. But I'm not. I'm wild. And I'm smart. I can read French, I used to have this excellent-to-perfect body, and I don't see why . . . So did I goof up? I mean, you didn't run away."

"I probably should've," said David.

"Untrue. Don't even say that."

"Okay, forget the 'probably.' I definitely and positively should've run. No doubt at all."

"David, you're a hero, you're one of—"

"What I am," David said, "is a divorced, miserable, drugged-up monster."

Dorothy shook her head unhappily. "I'm very, very, very sure you don't mean that. God, this brûlée!"

"I do mean it."

"No way," she said. "And what about me? Did I make a huge mistake?"

"You did."

"Did?"

"Your shoes, not mine. Seems that way."

Dorothy sighed. "Mistake. Billy loved me, right?"

"No question."

"And now he loves Paulette. Looks at her exactly the way he used to look at me. Gaga."

"I don't know. Does he?"

"Don't let me bawl."

"Right, I won't," David said.

She went blank for a second. "David, did you just say 'blow job'?"

"That was you, Dorothy."

"Me?"

"Pretty sure."

"I said that?"

"Almost positive."

"Holy, holy cow." Dorothy shook her head and

looked up at the windows. The pupils of her eyes had vanished. "And is that hail I'm hearing?"

"Acid hail," said David.

"Loud, isn't it?"

"Yeah, it is."

They listened to the hail and rain and thunder, watched the windows flash. After a while Dorothy said, "I'm happy, you know. I have a Volvo. Two, in fact."

In a downtown hotel room, Ellie Abbott lay alone in the sticky July dark. Her TV set was tuned to CNN, but she was watching something else: a dead dentist, a flock of loons. It was 12:12 A.M. Mark had checked out a couple of hours earlier. His suitcase was gone. The note he'd left behind was curt and unpromising. What hurt Ellie now, among many other things, was the fact that she truly loved her husband, and always had, and also the fact that she could not comprehend why she had so systematically ruined her own life. The stupidity stunned her. The self-betrayal, too. In the end, she realized, the affair with Harmon had been an experiment of sorts, a means of testing the proposition that she was more or less happily married, more or less content, more or less a lucky woman. She couldn't cry, couldn't sleep. The rain and thunder weren't helping any, and after a few moments Ellie picked up the remote and began channel surfing: a home decorating show, a weather warning, a Firestone commercial, the Lisbon earthquake, the

Hindenburg in flames, Mark eating a white corsage off her blouse, Harmon drowning, an evangelist with colorless eyes and a hearty laugh and a sly Texas drawl.

In the same hotel, two floors down, Billy McMann and Paulette Haslo ordered champagne and lobster salads from room service. They were on the bed, sitting cross-legged, naked and unembarrassed. They had made love twice in the last forty minutes, and now, as they waited for their food, they discussed the issue of turning points. They agreed that a human life mostly erased itself at the instant it was lived. They agreed, too, that out of their own combined time on earth, which amounted to more than a century, only a scant few hours survived in memory. "It's what we decide that sticks," Paulette said. "When we say yes, when we say no. Those over-the-cliff choices we make. Getting married. Getting unmarried. Like when I broke into that poor woman's house, all the consequences, how I'm not even a minister anymore. And like when you headed off for Canada. That's what makes a life a life, because you lose everything else—peeing, soap operas, scabs, vacations, almost every phone conversation you ever had. Huge chunks of time. Like you never used your own life."

"Tonight," Billy said. "We won't lose this."

"No. Not the storm, either. Just listen to it."

"Should I turn off the light?"

"Not yet."

Billy reached out with both hands, lifted her hair from her face. "I'm not sure how to say this. Maybe I shouldn't. But if you really want it, you're still a minister. Small congregation. Low pay."

"Billy and daughter?"

"Right, just the two of us. Three."

"How's the parsonage?"

"Parsonage?"

"Your house, Billy. I gather you're looking for a female live-in minister?"

"Yes, I am," he said, and laughed.

"And what about Dorothy?"

Billy took his hands away. "You know the story?"

"Most of it. Not all."

"I'll need the light out to tell this."

"Turn it out," said Paulette.

At 1:20 A.M., fifteen minutes after the storm passed, Marv Bertel took Spook in his arms, held her for a long moment, and then grinned and slapped her butt and boarded United flight 878 for Denver. The plane was almost empty. He dropped into a window seat, loosened his tie, and sat looking out on the dark, wet tarmac. Flying had never frightened him, but now, like Spook, he had a wicked feeling about this: a rhythmic code in the pit of his stomach. Marv pulled a pint of bourbon from his coat pocket, took a long hit, took another for the road, and then buckled his seat belt and put his head back. No more reunions, he decided. All tease, no payoff. Replay of the old days, except a whole lot worse, because he was no longer a college kid, and because hope came hard, and because the complications finally wore a man down. Spook was Spook. Fadeout.

And what was the point?

Faulty ticker. Clogged arteries. A few more years, he reasoned, and he'd be a spook himself.

The bourbon ironed out the wrinkles in his head, and for some time Marv watched familiar faces drift by—Billy and Jan and David and Ellie and Marla and all the others—each shopworn by what time will do. Hard to believe, he thought. Thirty-plus years. Even harder to believe that it hadn't been a hundred years, or a thousand. Mops and brooms, two rugged marriages, little to show for it beyond a fifty-two-inch waist and pump problems and a paid-off mortgage. His own doing, of course, but it seemed impossible that he could've squandered his life this way, dumping it into a pit of lies and laziness and gluttony and fantasy and midnight solitaire. He had always intended to reform himself, next week, next year, but somehow his chromosomes conspired against it. Get trapped in a life you despise, a guy starts to take it personally. Starts to believe he deserves it.

Which was how he felt right now.

Like giving up.

To hell with Weight Watchers. To hell with the heart.

He took another pull off the bottle and listened to a flight attendant provide cheerful emergency instructions. The two plastic cowboys had reappeared, settling in at the rear of the plane. The very pale, ancient-looking woman sat dozing across the aisle from him, back in dreamland, older than the world.

Marv switched off his reading light and closed his eyes.

Well, he thought, and then Spook Spinelli slipped into the seat beside him.

"Fancy this," she said.

Amy and Jan and Marla took shelter in their dorm. They cleaned up, changed into pajamas, and gathered in Amy's room.

Minutes later, the storm ended as abruptly as it started—thunder, then dripping sounds. Amy turned out the lights. The three of them lay crosswise on her bed, sharing a blanket, facing the flame of a small green candle. "Now here's an interesting thought," Amy said. "Right here, in this one bed, we've got three card-carrying sexpots. Zero men. What's up with that?"

"Pitiful," said Marla.

"Correction," said Jan Huebner. "Two sexpots, one slob." She lit a cigarette, exhaled with a cough. "Not that I'll stop hoping."

"No children, either," said Amy. "None of us."

"Sad," Marla said.

"Maybe sad, maybe not," Amy said. "But here's the stumper. Thirty years ago, who would've guessed that three incredible women like us, totally hot, fertile as farmland, who would've thought we'd end up alone? No kids, no guys?"

"I did," Marla said. "I thought so."

"Right," said Jan, "but you're not human."

"I didn't completely mean that," said Marla. "A figure of speech." She took a drag from Jan's cigarette. "Tell the truth. Am I?"

"Human?" said Jan.

"Yes," Marla said.

"Almost," Amy said. "Except for the aluminum."

"I'd forgotten," Jan said. "That aluminum heart of hers, drives people up the wall." She swatted Marla's arm. "Cut the hogwash. You're human. But here's a piece of advice. I don't mean to get pushy, but if I were you, I'd hit the road and go find David. Give him something to remember you by. Ugly girls like me, we don't get second chances. Attack. Make the boy squeal."

"Kinky stuff," said Amy. "Send us a video."

Marla watched the candle. "Where is he right now?"

"Not a problem," Jan said. "Frying up brains with Dorothy. Just go. See you in five years."

"I don't know," Marla said. "I'm afraid. What if it doesn't work out?"

"What if it does?" said Amy.

Marla waited a second, hugged Jan, hugged Amy, and went out the door.

Things were quiet.

"Well, girl," Amy said. "It's down to you and me."

Two miles away, in a downtown hotel room, Ellie Abbott was shepherded through her sorrows by a TV evangelist, a man with a pot belly and doughy skin and colorless eyes and a large, jowly, almost featureless face. "C'mon people," he was saying. "I want all you folks in deep trouble to pry yourselves off the couch, off the bed, wherever you're parked right now. All the insomniacs. All you cuckolds and psychos and second-guessers and lovesick sin freaks, I want you to mosey right up close to your TV. Just reach out. Wrap your arms around me, hold on tight."

The man's water-clear eyes had an amused, charming, weirdly familiar twinkle. He seemed to wink into the camera.

"That means you, darlin'," he said. "Upsy-daisy."

Two floors down, Billy McMann had just finished sketching out the story of his years in Winnipeg. "You nailed it earlier," he told Paulette Haslo. "What we choose is what we are. Everything else gets sucked away. All the boring, junk-food nonsense." He chuckled. "I guess that sounds pretentious."

"A tad," said Paulette.

"I'll shut up."

"No, you're allowed to be smart. What you mean is, like when I sat in your lap tonight. That was a choice, obviously, and a very good one."

"Yes," he said. "Like that."

Paulette lay with her head to Billy's heart. She took a breath. She had never wholly loved before. "And right now," she said. "This might be one of those times."

"It might be."

"I'm pretty fried out, Billy. You don't mind if I'm confused? Just a few days ago, I thought my life was over. I honestly thought that." She sat up in the dark. "What if we ruin this?"

"We won't."

"Should we get married?"

"Okay," he said.

Paulette laughed and said, "Just okay?"

"Terrifically okay," Billy said.

"What'll Dorothy say?"

Billy shrugged. "She'll say, 'Oh.'"

Eight and a half blocks from the Darton Hall campus, in an old brick house on Summit Avenue, Minnesota's lieutenant governor was up late, sipping milk, reevaluating his political future. The storm had awakened him forty minutes earlier. He had gone down to the kitchen, poured himself a glass of skim milk, and then, for almost an hour, he'd stood watching the heavy rain and hail and lightning.

404

Now the storm had lumbered off to the east. Stars were out. There was a yellow moon.

Yet even in the freshened nighttime quiet, the lieutenant governor found himself restless and regretful, ill at ease with history. Thirty years ago he had forfeited one dream for another. He had mortgaged love and idealism and a good portion of his youth, choosing politics over romance, breaking off an engagement to a lovely, big-hearted classmate. He had explained to the girl—cogently, he thought—that the missionary life was simply not for him, that he needed to be at the center of things, needed the heat, and that as much as he loved her, as much as it hurt to say this, he could not imagine himself rotting away in some squalid Peruvian backwater.

"How practical," the girl had said, and nothing else.

She went off to become a Lutheran missionary. He became a man of influence. The shame had never left him. Not through four tedious years as a party organizer, then five years as chairman, then eight years in the state senate, then six years—the best years—as attorney general.

Now a two-term lieutenant governor.

Heir apparent, he liked to think, but in fact it was somewhat less than apparent. Fifty-three years old. Longtime hack. Not washed up, not quite yet, but still a political bridesmaid. A catcher of bouquets, a raiser of toasts, a beaming, backslapping, ever hopeful member of the wedding.

Just after 1:45 A.M., the lieutenant governor rinsed his glass, went to a telephone, and began to dial.

Then he laughed at himself.

He said, "Peru," slapped down the phone, and returned to bed. He was a realist. In the morning, he knew, this sentimental slop would be history.

"What I'm thinking right now," said Dorothy Stier, "is that we could do one more of those . . . What do you call them?"

David laughed.

"Blotters, sheets," he said. "I wouldn't press my luck."

"No, really, I'm in sensational shape. Tiptop perfect."

"But easy does it. First-timer, right?"

"Might possibly be, might possibly not."

"Either way. Plenty's adequate."

"Spoilsport," Dorothy said. "If you don't watch your manners, I'll sulk. Believe me, I know how."

David laughed again and handed her a half-smoked cigarette. Forty-five minutes ago the storm had passed, and now they lay transported on the banquet room floor. They had shed their bodies. The walls were moving. It was approaching 2 A.M.

"At this hour," David said, "sulking's uncool. Tell me about your Volvos."

"The twins!" Dorothy cried. "And let's see—oh, my God!—those two boggling boys of mine, and scads of cash, and a couple country clubs, and this huge house I still get lost in. Christ oh Christ, David, I don't want to go home. Not ever, ever, ever."

"You don't?"

"I don't. I have cancer, you know."

"Yes, you showed me."

"Did I?"

"You sure did."

"Eight nodes."

"Eight," David said. "I remember."

"That's thoughtful of you. Eight. What a stinky number." Dorothy made a noise in her throat, as if trying to swallow something foul. She did not cry. Instead, after a moment, she giggled. "This'll sound crazy, I know, but I can tell it's not all gone. The cancer, it's still inside me. These wee specks of . . . Am I stoned? These little hairy specks, millions and millions, all different colors. And I can feel it, David. Like this allergy or something, only it's in my blood, sort of hot and itchy. Cancer for sure. And if I go home . . . I don't want to go home, just don't, and that's final." Dorothy tossed the lighted cigarette at the ceiling and watched it pinwheel through the dark. It seemed to take several hours to come down. "I almost left Ron, you know. A few years ago, like two or three, I came that close. A whisker. Missed it by a whisker—Ron's phrase. Whisker! Boy, I truly *am* stoned, aren't I?"

"You truly are," David said.

"So what happened was, this nosy next-door

neighbor of mine, he talked me out of it. Put the hex on me."

"Maybe you didn't want to leave. Not really."

"Who knows?" She fell into clumsy thought. "Would you mind if I asked something hideously, hideously stupid? Doesn't matter, I just will, but do me a favor first. Put your arm around me. Hold me a minute."

He pulled her close.

"Comfy," Dorothy said, then looked up at him. "I don't mean this to be like sex, you know."

"I do know," David said.

"Good, I'm glad. Pretty glad."

"Me, too," he said.

"Not super glad. Not ecstatic. Now here's my hideous question. At these reunions, David, do you ever look around and sort of wonder who won't make it to the next one? Like with Karen or Harmon? It's ghoulish, I know, but sometimes I can't help myself. I look at the faces, I start to wonder."

David shrugged and said, "No, I don't do that."

"Never?"

"Not like that," he said.

"Well, I do," said Dorothy. "I used to think it would be poor Marv, or maybe Jan, or maybe even you—all those drugs, the cigarettes, that leg thing—but now, God, I'm pretty sure . . . Hope I'm wrong, naturally, but I don't think I'll be showing up here in five years." She shut her eyes. "Sometimes I *see* the cancer. Did I tell you about those specks?"

"You did. Millions."

"Right. Tiny dots. Very alive."

"Alive?"

"I'm not making this up. Right now, I mean. They're in my blood." Dorothy made a low, throaty sound again, as if to cry, but her voice brightened. "My next-door neighbor, he claims I'm a goner. Couple more years, he tells me."

"A doctor?" David said.

"Assassin. Retired, I think, but it's complicated. Point is, he might be right."

David shook his head. "The man's nuts, Dorothy. Don't listen."

"I'm not sure. A strange guy, that's true. But something about him, his voice, the way he looks at me . . . It makes me pay attention, makes me face things. Time, I guess. How to use it. I'm glad we did this tonight." She kissed David's ear. "Back in the old days, I guess I was a tiny bit . . . Help me out."

"Wound tight?" he said.

"I wouldn't say tight."

"Boring?"

"Boring! Boring's more like it. I'm the first to admit—" She stiffened, held a finger to her lips. "What's that noise?"

Dorothy sat up.

"That noise," she said. "You don't hear it?"

"No."

"Behind us, I think. At the door."

"It's nothing."

"Oh, it is," Dorothy said, and laughed. "Marla, I'll bet. I'll bet anything."

A moment later Marla Dempsey walked in. She switched on the lights, surveyed things for several seconds, then looked down at her feet. She was wearing pajamas and flip-flops. "Sorry," she said. "If I'm barging in, I don't want—"

"You aren't barging," said Dorothy.

Marla turned to leave.

"Don't," Dorothy said. She got up and went to the door and took Marla's arm. "Honey, there's no problem, I was heading home this very minute. Husband, you know. Soirees, fundraisers. I'm way, way overdue."

Dorothy found her purse, kissed David's forehead, kissed Marla.

"You're not driving, I hope?" David said.

"No, no. I'll walk. Be home by daylight." She went to the door, then stopped and looked back at Marla. "That's one sweet ex you've got there. Nice-looking. Complete gentleman. Missing a leg, of course."

"I noticed," said Marla.

"Watch after him, will you?"

Marla nodded and said, "We'll see."

High over Nebraska, Marv Bertel and Spook Spinelli levered back their seats, closed their eyes, and sat listening to the hum of the 737's big engines. It had been a stressful two days, at times great fun, at times unbearable, and now a mix of weariness and midlife

410

melancholy had set in. Spook tried to sleep, then gave up and toyed with Marv's wedding band. The cabin lights had been dimmed, the flight attendants were dozing, and the engines made a lullaby sound that seemed to come from another life.

Across the aisle, in darkness, a feeble old woman mumbled in her sleep.

Two cowboys cuddled at the rear of the plane.

After many miles, Spook said, "Baby, I'm fine. Once we get to Denver, I'll give you a big hug, say my bye-byes, catch a flight back to the Cities. Don't worry about me."

"I won't," Marv said, "but what about the husbands? Don't they worry?"

"Yes, no doubt. Guess they've learned to cope."

Marv waited a few seconds. "So what's this all about? Jumping aboard. Your new fly-with-Marv policy."

"I've told you."

"Again."

"Just that feeling I had." Spook cut him a quick, embarrassed look. "I can't explain it. This sad, morbid feeling. Really strange, really scary. Like I knew for sure the plane would crash."

"Then why get on?"

"Oh, please. It's obvious."

"To you it is. Why?"

"Because then it *couldn't* happen," Spook said. "Because nothing can ever hurt me, not unless I do it myself." She stopped and seemed to drift away somewhere. "Maybe that's your answer."

411

"Jesus," Marv said. "Don't talk like that."

"Sorry, my sweet. Can't help it." She looked around the cabin as if to find something else to say. Then she tapped Marv's belt buckle. "We could fool around a little."

"We could," Marv said, "but we've got company."

"Company where?"

"Next door. The old lady."

Spook glanced across the aisle. A pair of fierce, watery eyes peered back at her.

"So much for that," Spook said, "but I still need you to talk about how you'll whisk me away somewhere, carry me off to Samoa or Bangkok, someplace romantic."

"Might be arranged," said Marv.

"I'm waiting. Tempt me."

Across the aisle, the old woman closed her eyes, shook her head, and feigned sleep. The matter was out of her hands. No one ever listened.

Nebraska rose westward into Colorado.

Ahead lay the vast stormy wilds of the Pawnee National Grassland.

"Beautiful to think about," Marv Bertel finally said, "except it won't happen, will it?"

"No," Spook said. "But let's dream."

And then for some time they fantasized, taking turns at inventing a happy ending for themselves. Down below, the great unconscious heart of America glided by, the black earth and pastures and fairgrounds and summer gardens and fields of wheat and baseball diamonds and funeral parlors and lonely farm lights and deserted roadways. It had become the ninth day of July, Sunday, just before three in the morning, a new age, a new century, and for both Marv Bertel and Spook Spinelli, the turbulent world of their youth had receded like some idle threat or long-lapsed promise. Nixon was dead. Westmoreland was in retirement. That war was over. Now there were new wars. But still, as with Spook and Marv and several million other survivors of their times, there would also be the essential renewing fantasy of splendid things to come.

Dorothy Stier trudged happily along Snelling Avenue, night-tripping, carrying her shoes, buoyant and alert and wired to the world. She would live forever. Yes, she would, because in fact she already had, and because no big deal, forever was just a scrap of now, a puddle to be splashed through, a moon, a wet sidewalk, a neighbor watering his yellow sunflowers. The hour was late. There were stars. She wondered if Ron could score some acid. Probably not, she decided, but still . . . Acid golf, acid bridge.

Dorothy yelled, "Nodes!"

Amy Robinson and Jan Huebner lay side by side on Amy's bed, watching wisps of smoke rise from a burnt-out candle. They were planning an August trip out to Vegas. "Your luck, my looks," Jan was saying, "how do we go wrong?"

Amy said, "Break the bank."

★   ★   ★

In her pajamas and flip-flops, Marla Dempsey led David Todd across campus. It was just after three in the morning. "We could sit for a while," Marla said, which for her was brave.

"Sitting would do it," said David.

"I can't promise anything."

"No need. Just sit."

"Are you straight, David? Give or take?"

He smiled and said, "Drop in the bucket." He looked at her. "Want to try some?"

"No," Marla said. "I want you to try not to."

"Where should we sit?"

"I don't know," she said. "The chapel?"

At 3:11 A.M. Dorothy Stier was halfway home.

Minnesota's lieutenant governor was asleep. His ex-fiancée, a Lutheran missionary, had just gotten up to take a sedative.

Billy and Paulette shared a cigarette, making plans, telling each other how lucky they were, how terrified, and how it all seemed like such a sudden and impossible and engulfing miracle. "Like a heart attack," Paulette said, and Billy said, "Almost," and it was still 3:11 A.M.

Not ten seconds had passed.

Marv and Spook were at thirty-two thousand feet over north-eastern Colorado.

A Twin Cities physician and a mother of three, once a basketball star, played make-believe in a ground-floor dorm room.

Three floors up, Jan Huebner explained to Amy

414

Robinson how her ex-husband Richard, an abuser from the start, a tyrant, a manipulator, a curse, an infection, had one day waved and smiled and walked out on her, not a word.

"Please," Amy said, "stop it."

Two miles from campus, Ellie Abbott prepared for the worst, hoped for something better. She had no idea where to find her husband, or if he wished to be found, but with the wise counsel of a TV evangelist, Ellie concluded that nothing could be lost by trying. Her suitcase was packed. In a few hours, when daylight broke, she would check out of the hotel, fly home, walk through the front door, and wait for her life. "You never know," the evangelist said.

It was 3:11 A.M.

Spook said, "What's that?"

Marv said, "What?"

Twenty-six seconds had elapsed.

The pale old woman hissed at the void.

Marla Dempsey and David Todd sat on the damp steps of the Darton Hall chapel. Marla asked why he'd never once tried to talk to her about the war, what he'd seen, what he'd heard, what he'd gone through along that terrible river, and David Todd did his best to explain that most of it was impossible to remember, all scrambled, and that the rest of it could not be believed. "I'd believe," Marla said, and David shook his head and said, "You wouldn't," and Marla said, "Try," but David just laughed and looked at his wristwatch. It was 3:11 A.M. "Maybe someday," he said.

Fred Engelmann's alarm went off. He put on a robe, walked outside, sat on his front steps to see what the night would deliver.

"Someday," a physician said to a mother of three.

"I'm famished," said Jan.

"Someday, that's fine," Marla said. She took a breath. "I love you for sure. I just can't be married."

"Of course not," said David.

Billy said, "Think you can sleep a little?"

"I could," Paulette said. "But why? Let's call your daughter. Right now."

"You'll love her," said Billy.

Dorothy turned off Snelling Avenue, walking briskly, stoned, six blocks from home.

Amy Robinson said, "Me too, I'm starving. I need pancakes."

"Bingo," Jan said.

Dripping sounds came from the trees in front of the Darton Hall chapel.

The lieutenant governor turned in his sleep.

The Pawnee National Grassland lay as it had for centuries, flat and desolate.

There was a shearing noise.

"The thing is," David said, "some of the crap I remember is pretty stupid. Like when I first arrived in-country. I don't know how, don't know where, but for some reason I'd lost my dog tags. You know, just these ridiculous goddamn dog tags. One second they're around my neck, next second they're gone, and I'm scared to death. Out of uniform, you know? There I am, just showed up in Death City, and I'm scared I'll get busted or reamed out or whatever. No kidding, I still dream about it."

"David," Marla said.

"Yes?"

"Tell me about the river."

Ellie Abbott stepped into the shower. Imagination, maybe, but she felt a hopeful breeze sweep through her thoughts.

"Baby," Spook said.

Billy was on the phone with his daughter, who said, "*Really?*"

Amy Robinson and Jan Huebner were getting dressed.

Jan was saying, "There's that all-night diner on Grand. Great pancakes, cute waiters."

Dorothy Stier decided it might be interesting to sit for a few minutes on the sidewalk.

Billy handed the phone to Paulette.

"Maybe we'll score," Jan said.

Johnny Ever twitched and watched the world through water-clear eyes.

"Monkeys," he mumbled.

Marla said, "The river, David, tell me," and David said, "I don't believe it myself."

Dorothy looked up at the opulent summer stars.

"Baby," Spook said, and Harmon Osterberg

kicked a cantaloupe at Ellie Abbott, and Billy burned his draft card, and Karen Burns eyed a newly hired professor of sociology. It was 3:11 A.M., Sunday morning, July 9, 2000, but over the bleak, flaming grasslands it was July now, July always.

"Maybe we *will* score," said Amy.

"Not even maybe," said Jan, and took Amy by the hand. "Follow me, sweetheart. We're golden."